THE EXPERT WITNESS

BOOK ONE OF THE JILL RHODES
MYSTERY/THRILLER SERIES

NINA ATWOOD

The Expert Witness: Book One of the Jill Rhodes Mystery/Thriller Series

Copyright © 2022 by Nina Atwood Enterprises, LLC. All rights reserved, including the right to reproduce this book, or portions thereof, in any form. No part of this text may be reproduced, transmitted, downloaded, decompiled, reverse engineered, or stored in or introduced into any information storage and retrieval system, in any form or by any means, whether electronic or mechanical, without the express written permission of the author. The scanning, uploading, and distribution of this book via the Internet or via any other means without the permission of the publisher and author is illegal and punishable by law. Please purchase only authorized electronic editions and do not participate in or encourage electronic piracy of copyrighted materials.

This book is a work of fiction. Permission has been granted to the author for name use by those with specific references. Other names, characters, places, and incidents are either the product of the author's imagination or are used fictitiously.

[E-book] ISBN-13: 978-1-7363470-4-1

[Print] ISBN-13: 978-1-7363470-5-8

TITLES BY NINA ATWOOD

The Deep End: Jill Rhodes Mystery/Thriller Book Two, is available on Amazon.

About Roxanne: A Psychological Thriller, is available on Amazon.

Free Fall: A Psychological Thriller, is available on Amazon.

Unlikely Return: A Novel, is available on Amazon.

For more of Nina's books, visit Nina's author page on Amazon here.

John Nina's email list for FREE fiction, notification of author inside stories plus upcoming titles in the series, and discounted book deals:

https://www.ninaatwoodauthor.com

Reward Special note: If you introduce me to someone in the moviemaking industry [big screen, streaming content, etc.] that results in a signed contract and paid advance on any of my books, I will pay *you* a reward of $10,000!

– Nina Atwood

Contact: nina@ninaatwoodauthor.com

PROLOGUE

She almost fell over tree roots along the way a couple of times as she made her way to the designated meeting spot. It was late afternoon, and the autumn sun was making its way quickly to the horizon, golden light peeking through the leaves here and there as it drifted downward.

She automatically reached her hand to her back jeans pocket but found nothing. *Crap, no phone.* She flashed to the day before, her mom asking her where she'd been. The denials, the cover story, and her limited acting skills hadn't gotten her off the hook. Now, she was on total screen time-out.

Why was screen time the first thing parents took away? *Her* parents, anyway. Other kids kept theirs no matter what they did for safety reasons.

Safety. A wave of longing and insecurity swept through her. She hated being without her phone. It made her feel incredibly vulnerable.

She pictured the person she was meeting, and the sense of

vulnerability intensified. She might use any number of words to describe how she felt now, but *safe* wasn't one of them.

It didn't help that she was out here all alone, and though she wasn't typically fearful of solitude, today, it seemed different. The wind picked up, and she shivered. She'd forgotten to take a jacket that morning, and though she'd warmed up considerably at practice, the chill in the air had overcome any warmth from the workout.

At the crackle of leaves or branches, she spun around. But nothing was there. She rubbed her hands together, wishing fervently for her phone. At least then, if she needed to, she could call someone for reassurance. And she thought of who she would call—her best friend.

Get it together, Kat. You know what to do. You've got this.

Her self-talk gave her a momentary shot of confidence.

Steely determination had brought her here, to this place, to take back the control she'd so readily given away. Since making that decision, she'd felt a return of her former strength, her fierceness, her confidence. She'd felt like herself again, though not completely. The events of the past few weeks had irrevocably changed her, had opened her eyes to a dark world that she'd never intended to enter.

In retrospect, she'd been so monumentally naïve, completely disregarding her parents' warnings over the years. It had started as a fun adventure to push the boundaries of independence from her over-protective parents, until it wasn't. Maybe they weren't over-protective. Maybe they were just doing their job.

Why hadn't she listened?

You're too trusting. You're just a kid, and there are bad people who will try to take advantage of you. Don't try to grow up so fast.

An uneasiness and trickle of regret made their way into her

chest. It was as if her mom had seen something dark ahead, had predicted the pathway that had led her to this day, to this once familiar place. *You just had to walk right up to danger and poke it in the face, didn't you, Kat? So exciting, right?*

She was early, her intention to be the first to arrive so she could prepare what she wanted to say. But trepidation filled her even though she knew this place well.

She'd explored it for years as a young girl, usually with her best friend in tow. They'd imagined themselves intrepid explorers, armed with sticks picked up along the way, their backpacks loaded with sandwiches and chips. Back then, they'd speculated on the dangerous wildlife, spooking themselves with false alerts. *What was that? A bear? A cougar? A man-eating tiger?*

How their parents must have chuckled when they'd returned home, faces flushed, breathless, stumbling over each other's words with excitement. Their 'adventures' lasted mere minutes, a combination of fear and excitement driving them back to the safety of their quiet cul-de-sac.

Until today, this wooded creek bed hadn't been scary at all. It had been a place she could go when she longed for the quiet, to turn off the noise of her mom's never-ending quest to turn her into the daughter of her dreams.

It had become a meeting ground for her and her best friend, each with their own reasons for escaping the watchful eyes of parents.

But as another crackle had her heart hitching into high gear, what once was a place of refuge now seemed hostile and eerie. Today, the trees reached their tangled branches toward her, snagging her hair and clothing as if to stop her in her quest to regain her life. Low, tangled bushes, some thorny, snatched at her ankles and left small burrs in her socks as she passed. Even the birds seemed inscrutably silent, not the cheery feathered creatures she'd always known.

She turned her attention away from the ominous surroundings and thought about what she'd rehearsed. It had sounded good to her ears. Very direct. Very mature. Words of warning, her flashing eyes, and superhero stance. And the message that she'd no longer be silent, no longer be a willing participant, that she would reveal all of it if necessary. Her problem would be solved after that message was received, for sure. There was far too much to lose to ignore her.

She'd almost given up when she heard someone approaching. She turned, her stern expression setting the stage. But her face fell as she realized she'd made a terrible mistake. The face she saw wasn't the one she'd expected. Her words fell on deaf ears, her stance proved useless, and her pleas went unacknowledged. She'd deluded herself into thinking that everything would all turn out right.

Even her attempt to fight back, to defend herself, and to turn back the tide of events that she'd so desperately wished had never been triggered, ultimately was for nothing.

She closed her eyes, feeling the life draining painfully from her body. The past few weeks flashed through her mind again, heightened with the clarity of each wrong judgment, each stupid decision. In the end, she'd trusted the wrong person, and she'd turned away from those who might have saved her.

Later, still, she thought sadly about the familiar face of her friend, a close best friend. But even his face faded away as the darkness closed in permanently.

CHAPTER ONE

"But I'm not sure what it means," said Michael Fischer. In his early thirties, single, and successful in his chosen profession; nevertheless, he was somewhat clueless about women. His earnest expression and obvious intelligence belied the degree of his befuddlement.

He stared at the small screen he'd shown to her, shaking his head, touching it tenuously. As if he could bring back the lost affections of the woman he'd been yearning for, simply through the fairytale magic of a tiny screen that offered so much promise of true love. If you only just swiped this direction or that.

As if the human heart worked that way.

This wasn't a difficult case for psychologist Dr. Jill Rhodes, although it certainly must feel hard from her client's point of view. But this wasn't emotional resuscitation. He hadn't suffered a heartbreaking loss. Not one tear had fallen in the two sessions they'd had so far, and at no point had he expressed despair or even grief. Instead, he was deeply puzzled. That was understandable.

With little emotional repair required, the best course was a mini course on dating. Rhodes provided such things regularly. She could almost do it in her sleep. Certainly, for others, for her clients.

Maybe for herself.

The frequency of these kinds of issues in her client base signaled once again that it was time to finish that book on dating, the one she'd been formulating late at night for months.

It would be great, at times like this, to simply lean forward, look into the current hapless single person's eyes, and hand over a book. *Her* book—filled with advice crafted to save the legions of tortured singles out there from shooting themselves in the foot so often.

The title, though, was a puzzler. *Swipe Right for Love* initially sounded good, but it turned out there were at least a dozen published dating books with the word 'swipe' in the title. Plus, it would be misleading for readers to think it was all about how to use a dating app effectively. *Nope, definitely not about that.*

Instead, it was about all the stuff that happened so often *after* the swipe. Or without bothering to swipe. Or after the multiple vodka shots at the bar on a Saturday night.

Things Jill Rhodes had done herself in the past, and other things that had happened to her. She touched the bare spot of her third finger on her left hand. A void. One that might never be filled but the filling of which remained a hope.

Outside the window of her ground floor office, which looked onto an outdoor atrium filled with live oaks, a squirrel dug frantically through the Asian jasmine, desperate to find what he'd hidden from himself weeks or months ago. Sunlight struggled to penetrate the leaves and branches of the trees, lending the area a soft, dappled, calming atmosphere. Azaleas bloomed sparsely in the spare amount of sun that made it through the dense shade.

"Dr. Rhodes?"

She'd broken the cardinal rule of psychotherapy: *listen*. Intently. At all times. She was a great listener, prided herself on her ability to hear what people said and, more importantly, what they *didn't* say.

"I'm sorry. My mind wandered for a moment." A terrible thing to admit, but how could you help people without being real with them? At his surprised look, she rushed to add, "Not because your story wasn't interesting or that I didn't care. But I wonder—and I'm just feeling curious—why are you so focused on the meaning of Olivia's text?"

His forehead wrinkled in puzzlement. "Because I don't understand. She sent me this text message telling me she's *not ready for a relationship*, and that's after she went to a hell of a lot of trouble getting my name from a buddy so she could track me down after seeing me on Instagram. We went out for three months, almost every night. We were inseparable. We were planning the whole summer together—trips, her friend's wedding—actually two weddings—everything. How do you go from that much... *intensity* to a freaking breakup text?"

Time for a little education. "It does seem confusing. Let's try to untangle it, but first, I have just a couple more questions about Olivia. Actually, comments, guesses, if you will. When I get something right, give me a thumbs-up. If I get something wrong, do a thumbs-down."

Sometimes you have to switch out of the usual therapist/client role and play a non-verbal game. To switch the brain off one track and onto another. "First, she goes out to bars with her girlfriends at least three nights a week."

He gave a thumbs up.

"Second," she continued, "she has a job but not really a career. Maybe she's college educated, but she doesn't seem to be doing much with it."

Another thumbs up.

"She talks about her siblings, or her friends, who are married and have at least one child already, maybe two. She talks about the kids a lot and takes care of them from time to time."

Thumbs up again, frowning. The train was getting ready to switch tracks.

"She wears really nice clothes, maybe too nice for her level of income. She's invited you over at least once while taking care of an adorable child—a niece, or a nephew, or a friend's little one."

Thumbs up, more slowly, frown increasing. The train was almost on the other track.

"She's sweet but not especially deep. Most of your conversations revolve around other people in her life. Gossip, if you will. A favorite topic is who's getting engaged, and whose wedding is coming up."

Instead of a thumbs up, he held up his hand. "Okay, I get it. She's marriage and baby-minded, and maybe that's her biggest goal in life. And yes... maybe she's husband shopping, but *what's wrong with that?* She's beautiful, she's sweet, and I want marriage and kids, too. *We were on the same page.*" The train was idling on the new track, still unsure.

"And you're right. There's nothing wrong with being on the same page about what you want. In fact, that's the whole point of dating—finding someone who wants what you want. But isn't there more that you want? What about a connection at a deeper level?"

"What do you mean?" He twisted a bit in the chair.

"Come on, Michael. You're a smart guy."

He shook his head and looked away. "I know what you're getting at." He sighed. "But I'm so tired of this cycle. Every time I meet someone new and think it's going somewhere, it just fizzles. Like this."

"Right. And that is the real issue. It fizzled because you weren't really on the same page. Yes, marriage and family. But no, you didn't really click in all the important ways. Yet you pushed for the relationship, wanting it more than she did. It's a pattern," Rhodes added.

Her words sat in the room, and slowly, he seemed to absorb them. "I know. But what do I do about that?"

"I'm not sure. It's hard to get yourself to *not* feel something you feel, to *not* do something you yearn to do. Sometimes, it's more about finding the substitute feeling, or action, something else that lights you up, something else to dive into. Focus on that, whatever it is, and learn to trust that the rest will follow. Be yourself, be real, and *let go of the outcomes*. No one can predict or control the right time to meet the right person." And as the words left her mouth, she knew they were as much for herself as they were for her client.

He swiped his hand over his head slowly. "I have no clue what you're saying to me, what you're suggesting I do. But I do see the pattern you're talking about."

"Try this, Michael. Reflect on where this pattern is taking you. If you keep pushing in the wrong relationships, what happens to the right one? While you're busy pursuing Ms. Wrong, Ms. Right may be observing. And if she's smart, what will she do with that information?"

"You're right. I know it." He sat back thoughtfully, then gave her a look of grudging respect. "You know, I wasn't expecting this at all."

"What were you expecting?"

"You know. A lot of silence. Asking me how it makes me feel." His face reddened a bit. "No offense to the profession, but I find that kind of thing rather useless."

If she had a dollar for every time she'd heard that. "It's okay. I get that a lot. Not to overly defend the profession, but there is a time and place for delving into feelings."

They sat quietly after that. People needed time to absorb new ideas, especially when it came to relationships. It was so simple, yet so complex, finding the right person and finding your way to something that could bind you together for years, decades, of life.

Jill Rhodes saw Michael Fisher at a crossroads. He was young enough to course-correct and find someone good for him. But if he didn't do that soon, she could see him wasting years of his life on nowhere relationships, bypassing his opportunity to have a family. The vision of each pathway hovered clearly in her mind.

But it was his job to see that, hers to merely point the way. He just needed time to see it for himself. She knew she'd continue to see those two pathways until he chose one, for as long as he was her patient. Insight into the future consequences of people's decisions today was one of her special skills. She wasn't a psychic and had disdain for those who professed such abilities.

But at times, though rare, she could see—almost in a visionary way—what lay ahead for people. When she did, it was hard to shake off at the end of her workday.

Time was up, and she moved to send him on his way, but he stayed planted in his seat, something else clearly on his mind. "Dr. Rhodes, there's one more thing, and I'm afraid it's not about me. It's about someone who is in serious trouble. There's a boy, and he killed someone, his best friend."

CHAPTER TWO

Michael Fisher was a criminal defense attorney just a few years out of law school. In their short time together, he'd never really spoken about work, but she was aware of the name of his law firm and a bit about the nature of his work.

"There's this kid," he began to explain. "He's fifteen, and he's emotionally immature, and maybe some other things. He's been accused of murder."

Rhodes immediately recognized the case—it was all over the local news. A teenage boy had murdered a classmate—a girl his age. Both kids were from middle-income families and attended a large suburban high school. It was gruesome and horrifying. He'd apparently lured her into the woods near their homes, stabbed her to death, left her there, gone home, and was found later by his mother covered in blood.

"Anyway, you have a way of getting to the bottom of things quickly. You seem to see things that are not...readily apparent. I wondered if you might help me with the case. I'm involved in it, although I'm not the lead counsel."

"I've heard about that case. A tragedy for both families."

"It is, and I think you can help. I need a psychological evaluation of the kid and maybe some additional interviews—you know, talk with some of the people in his life to understand him better. The state has appointed their expert, and I need one. I can pay you, of course."

She shook her head. "I'm sorry, but you're asking the wrong person. I've never done a psych eval on someone as part of a criminal case. There are lots of people who do that kind of work on a regular basis. You can find people who are really good at it. I'll get a referral for—"

"Wait." He held up both hands this time. "You've got insight, and that's what I need. I just want you to meet him, interview him, or whatever it is you shrinks do, and tell me what you think. It doesn't have to be anything official, and you don't have to show up in court."

"I don't think you understand. I'm not a forensic psychologist, and I have no training. It's a specialty, one that requires a lot of study and training, mainly because there is so much at stake for clients. I couldn't possibly—"

"Dr. Rhodes," he quickly cut in. "Can I tell you a little bit about this kid? Maybe you can just help me figure out what to do to help him."

She waved him back to his seat. *So much for break time.* "Okay, I can do that much. Fire away."

"Appreciate it," he thanked her as he sat back down. "This kid, his name is Shaun, and he's been accused of murdering his teenage friend, a girl. His parents hired our firm to defend him and protect his rights. Actually, his father hired us. But that's not really relevant." He waved his hands dismissively. "Thing is... there are things about the case that don't make sense to me. One, he supposedly killed her violently, then went home and did nothing to conceal the crime. He had blood on his clothes and some on his hands, and he still had the murder weapon in his possession. But that's not the strangest part."

She leaned forward, intrigued now.

"Second...Shaun wouldn't answer any questions posed by law enforcement, which isn't that unusual for a suspect, but the kid wouldn't talk to my law partner, Peter, either. He's not in a stupor or catatonic or anything like that. He simply won't talk. Not about the blood or where it came from, or about his friend, nothing."

He looked strained. "I want to help this kid. I have a bad feeling about where this case is going, and I'm not supposed to care one way or the other if he's innocent, but I am afraid he really is innocent. And he's about to go away and spend the rest of his life in prison if we don't do something about it. It's possible he will be tried as an *adult*, for God's sake," he finished vehemently.

This was more than a legal case to Michael; that much was clear. He was personally caught up in it, emotionally tangled in some way. He was young, not a totally green attorney, but still somewhat new at it.

Maybe he needed to learn how to manage himself, be a little bit detached, no matter how tragic the case. He would have to learn that sooner rather than later, and this case might be the one to teach him.

The job she did every day required that kind of emotional distance. Learning how to do it was not for the faint at heart. You had to be deliberate, almost cold at times. It was one of the toughest lessons learned post-graduation, which was the only way to learn it.

One professor had summed it up nicely. *You're studying hard in your classes, and yes, you're practicing with each other, but the real learning is after graduation, on the job. The good news is you'll have your degree and licenses. The bad news is you won't know shit until you are actually in practice.*

But even with on-the-job training, peeling back the layers of human distress day after day wasn't enough to protect the practitioner, whether psychologist or legal counselor. Empathy—the main tool—was a dual-edged sword.

On the one hand, empathy, coupled with compassion, not pity, was required to do the work, and without it, the deep work couldn't be done. On the other hand, it led to restless nights and the dull ache of exposure to the haunting remnants of personal tragedy.

How much harder would that be in a criminal case, one that involved a teenager? Actually, two teenagers, one dead, the other about to lose his life to the criminal justice system.

"From what you've told me so far, it is possible that this boy killed his friend, maybe in the heat of the moment for some reason—jealousy or some teenage drama. He could have flown into a rage, lashed out, then went into shock of some kind, which would explain his silence. It doesn't mean he didn't do it. Doesn't mean he did, either. Plus, if he's not talking, he may not talk to me, either. I'm not sure I can really add anything to your case, Michael. I'm sorry. I see how important it is to you."

She glanced at her antique clock over his shoulder. She'd have to save the discussion of professional distance for another time. She'd already gone over too long.

"Please, Dr. Rhodes. I *know* you can help, even if we don't know exactly how yet," he pleaded. "And, in case you're wondering, this isn't about me not having professional detachment. I really think this kid may be innocent, and I'm not confident we can convince the police of that, let alone a jury without something more, something I believe you can give us."

This time, as he spoke, she saw something more clearly. His passion, for sure. He was emotional, yes, and the intensity of his conviction fairly radiated. But it was the clarity that got her attention.

Too much sentimentality in professional matters led to a weakness of sorts, a fogginess that obscured insight. But he was clear, certain. She saw it and felt it. "Let me think about it. I will consider what you've shared so far and the gravity of the case…"

"Tomorrow. We have to get started tomorrow. An indictment is imminent, and after that, a hearing to determine if he will be tried as an adult or as a child. We need to go to the hearing with some answers."

"I can't give you an answer right now, Michael. I have to think it over tonight, but I promise, I'll call you first thing tomorrow morning."

He nodded, trying to hide his disappointment. "Thanks. I appreciate it."

"One more thing," Rhodes said as he turned to go. You're my client, so you can't hire me. It has to be someone at your firm. And you and I can't be involved in this case together. And I have to have freedom to do my work the way I see fit, within the boundaries of my license."

"Of course. I'll work it out with my partner. And I'll sign any disclaimers you want." She stood to usher him out. "Oh—" his eyes twinkled with understanding as he stood. "You're officially fired as my therapist. I think I've got it."

CHAPTER THREE

Dr. Jill Rhodes sat in a conference room along with three attorneys, a 35th-floor view of downtown Dallas spreading outside the glass wall. The lighted array of high-rise buildings provided a sparkling foreground. She'd read that it consistently ranked in the top ten most beautiful downtown skylines in the country.

Peter McClure had a commanding presence and wore a dark, well-tailored suit, his jacket tight across a barrel chest. His chocolate eyes sparked with intelligence and confidence under bushy eyebrows that danced in various directions. He was polished and professional times two, perhaps an artifact of having to show up stronger and more refined than most as a man of color in the courtrooms of Dallas, often awash with good-old-boy types—judges, opposing counsel, and law enforcement.

His second attorney, Nancy Barrett, was much younger, dressed sharply for the courtroom as well, but something about the way her eyes darted to McClure's before speaking gave her the appearance of subservience toward her older colleague.

Sitting on Rhodes's side of the table was her former client, Michael Fischer.

"Thank you for coming down here, Mrs. Rhodes," began McClure.

"It's Doctor," she corrected politely, though she knew the slight had been intentional. She'd seen his type before, the need to immediately put her in a demoted position, establish his dominance.

"My apologies." Though he looked anything but apologetic. "As I was saying, *Dr.* Rhodes, we appreciate you coming down here, but I'm afraid Mr. Fischer may have rushed into this a little." He stopped and eyed the papers in front of him. "We often utilize expert witnesses in a trial, but we choose them carefully, based on years of experience, which I see you don't have. Plus, this case may or may not be headed for trial."

Fischer interrupted. "There's a good reason I invited Dr. Rhodes into this case, Peter. She has unusual insight into people, more so than most, and I think she can help us get the case adjudicated. Or, if it goes to trial, help in other ways."

"I know you had good reasons, but no offense," he said, glancing at Jill, "she's never done criminal forensic work before."

"None taken," she said calmly. "This case does involve people, though, does it not?" At their surprised looks, she smiled. "My job is people, and if my years of experience in that regard will help, I'm here to do it." She paused for a moment. "If I may," she continued, giving McClure a compassionate look. "You strike me as someone with a very high standard of excellence. So high, in fact, that at times, you're hesitant to try something new, to take a risk on an unknown variable. What if it doesn't work out? What if it erodes the standards that you have set for yourself and for this firm?"

"That's not difficult to deduce," he returned quickly.

"Maybe not," she said. "But I see the concern you have about me, the unknown variable in this case. And the defensiveness." Here, she stopped. *Had she pushed him too far? And for what?* She was almost as hesitant as McClure about her taking on the case.

"I'm not on the couch here, Dr. Rhodes, and I'm not afraid to try something new." He turned to Michael. "If you think this is a good idea, I'll go along. But there'd better be no negative consequences. It's on you if this damages our case."

"I think you'll be glad you did, Peter," said Michael.

"Maybe," McClure said, still looking skeptical. "We'll see how it goes; give it a shot. But I'm afraid you have a short leash. We'll have to pivot quickly if it's not working out. Understood?"

She nodded, refusing to avert her eyes from Peter McClure's piercing stare. *A short leash meaning what?* Results, with human beings, were unpredictable, often messy, and usually took far longer than anyone imagined.

This might be the shortest professional… what was that word? *Pivot*, of her career. At the very least, she'd get exposure to the legal and law enforcement world, and it could help with a future client. This work promised to be a puzzle of sorts, and few things were better than that, regardless of how much time she'd have or the results she might or might not achieve.

"I appreciate that," she said, "and I should tell you I'm giving this a shot as well. If it turns out I can't do anything to help the case, I'll chalk it up as an interesting experience and fire myself."

"That works for us," said Barrett, smiling sympathetically at Jill.

"Agreed," added McClure authoritatively. "Now, about the case. The client's son is fifteen years old, and as a juvenile, we have options, although ultimately, it's up to the court to decide the pathway. The case can be adjudicated due to his age, which means there won't be a public proceeding, and the records will be sealed. That would be the best scenario because, in that proceeding, multiple factors can be introduced, which would potentially mean leniency for Shaun.

"However, since this is a murder case, he may be tried as an adult. There will likely be a certification procedure in which the court will decide whether or not to try him as an adult. If that's a yes, it turns into the worst-case scenario, so it's one we're trying to avoid. Now, let me tell you about Shaun."

But Dr. Rhodes interrupted. "First rule for me. Don't prejudice me with your own personal judgments about him. I need the facts of the case only. I'll make my own assessment of him when we meet. Also, I thought about it, and I've decided to meet with Shaun a bit later after talking with friends and family."

McClure and Barrett glanced at each other while Michael Fischer tried to hide his smile.

McClure spoke first. "I thought you were here to do a psychiatric evaluation of Shaun. Isn't that your true area of expertise?"

"That comes later. I need context first, and often the best insights come from family. And friends," Rhodes added.

McClure raised his hands from the tabletop in a 'whatever' gesture.

Barrett cleared her throat. "Here's the status of the case so far," she continued.

"Shaun Thayer's mother, Karen Thayer, called 9-1-1 after her son showed up at their home with blood on his clothing, not talking, and appearing distressed. Around the same time, Shaun's close friend, Katie Ramsay, was found in the wooded area near their homes, stabbed to death.

"Officers who showed up in response to the 9-1-1 call

connected the dots and began questioning Shaun. He wouldn't talk. Officers described him as appearing to be in some kind of daze, unresponsive to his mother or to them. A quick search of his room turned up what appeared to be the murder weapon.

"Karen Thayer was directed to take her son to a juvenile processing center the next day. She did, and by then, officers had identified Shaun's knife as the murder weapon. It was a unique combination of a switchblade and other tools designed for outdoor activities. It was also engraved. *To Shaun, love Dad.* Karen Thayer immediately recognized the gift her ex-husband had given their son for his last birthday.

"It is currently being tested to determine the DNA of the blood with which it was covered. Shaun's tee shirt is being tested as well. Both matched Katie Ramsay's blood type and is presumed to be hers.

"With his mother's permission, again because of his juvenile status, they obtained Shaun's fingerprints, which were a match to those on the knife. That was to be expected since it was his knife. However, there is other damning evidence.

"Unfortunately, with no attorney or advocate present to guide them, the interview became an even bigger liability for Shaun. His mother told officers the knife was Shaun's. She pushed him to talk, and he blurted out something about it being his fault, which officers took as an admission of guilt. Then he went back into his former daze and has been unresponsive since then."

Jill Rhodes wrote furiously, trying to keep up. "What happened then? Was he charged with murder?"

"No, not right away. The next stop was juvenile court, where the magistrate read him his rights, including the right to an attorney. He was sent home in the custody of his mother.

Apparently, that's when it kicked in for her to get her son legal counsel. We got the call that day."

"What about his father?"

Michael Fischer spoke up. "We've contacted him, but so far, he hasn't been very responsive other than to give us the retainer. The mother, Karen Thayer, says she has no idea why he isn't responding. She's tried to reach him as well, asking him to come in to talk with us."

"What happens next?"

McClure spoke. "The next steps are determined by the District Attorney's office. They will likely try to get him certified as an adult. That proceeding usually takes place with a juvenile court judge, during which the ADA, Assistant District Attorney, will have to explain why Shaun shouldn't stay in juvenile court. Why he should be tried as an adult. If the A.D.A. wins that point, the road ahead for Shaun will be exponentially more difficult. We need something to persuade the judge to leave him in juvenile court. Maybe a diagnosis that makes him appear less culpable."

Jill paused, thinking. "What if I find out something that points to Shaun's guilt? It seems like, as his defense team, you wouldn't want that outcome. So, why am I here? What is the purpose, if not to exonerate him in some way? Which I may not be able to do. I won't lie for either side of this."

"We would never ask you to lie, Dr. Rhodes," Michael Fischer reassured her. "If you find out things that point to Shaun's guilt, we won't call you as a witness. The burden is on the prosecution, if this turns into a jury trial, to prove his guilt."

"I think we should also tell you that we're not that invested in his guilt or innocence," said McClure. "Our job is to make sure he is treated fairly, that his rights are ensured, and that if there is a trial, he gets a fair one. Ideally, to steer the case toward juvenile court and, hopefully, an outcome that doesn't involve detention of any kind, to keep him at home, get him treatment."

"So, you think he's guilty."

"That's not what this is about," McClure said evenly. "Our job is to represent him, not to ascertain his guilt or innocence. In our representation, we will do whatever it takes to mitigate the wrath of the court."

Not easily provoked, she surmised.

"We would, of course, love to find evidence that Shaun didn't do this," Barrett inserted, "it's just that it's not looking that way, and unlike television court, we don't typically put resources to work on the old SODDI defense," she finished with a smile, clearly placating and humoring Jill. *A rescuer.*

"SODDI?"

"Some Other Dude Did It," Barrett told her with a flourish.

But none of the men at the table smiled. Michael looked slightly embarrassed. An awkward silence hung in the air.

Rhodes gave Nancy Barrett an empathetic smile. She was well aware of her own tendency to rescue and sometimes chose to do it anyway. But she made a mental note to meet later with Barrett. She might have insights that she didn't want to declare in this setting or at this time. Sometimes the person who seemed a bit out of sync was, in fact, picking up on nuances that others missed.

It didn't sound as if anyone at the table believed in Shaun's innocence. Perhaps that was because the case was already decided, the evidence so strongly stacked against him that there wasn't much use in trying to prove anything to the contrary. She pushed on. "What can you tell me about the victim?"

"Katie Ramsay was fifteen, a popular high school cheerleader," Michael told her.

"A beautiful girl from a good family, as far as we can tell," added McClure. "Her parents are understandably devastated." He paused, resigned. "It's only a matter of time before they start talking to the media. They're circling like vultures, which always happens when the victim is young and photogenic. Apparently, they've already obtained a video of her at a cheerleading competition, and they're playing it in endless loops."

They gave Rhodes a list of people to talk to. She gave them her terms, which they accepted.

As she left their offices, she thought about what she knew so far. A bloody knife and tee shirt, both Shaun's. An absent father and a clueless mother who'd reported her own son rather than calling for help, perhaps getting legal support before calling the police.

A teenage girl who would never graduate, never get married, never have her own children. Devastated parents. Lots of media attention.

She was definitely intrigued. And something more. A tingle of excitement about the puzzle, pieces now scattered, waiting to be spread carefully on the table, thoughtfully arranged, and pushed gently into place, one by one.

Like the ones she and her sister, Jade, had helped their grandmother assemble so many years ago at her kitchen table. Her mouth curved upward at the memory of those rare moments of safety and fun.

Now that she'd decided to take the case, she'd have to cancel other clients over the next few days. She knew this case would consume both her time and her attention. She thought about her clients, who she could defer, who she might have to refer to someone else due to the urgency of their case, working through the list mentally, one by one.

Her eyes drifted to the dashboard and registered the time in surprise. *She was late.*

CHAPTER FOUR

Jill rushed into the restaurant and slid into the chair across from Ethan Palmer, apologizing profusely. He held up a dismissive hand, his smile not altogether pleasant. "No worries, Dr. Rhodes. We all know how important *your* day is. We, the little people, must wait for the pleasure of your company. Just how it is."

The slow hum of conversation and soft jazz enveloped her as she watched him take a long pull from his bourbon, most likely not his first, judging by his tone. *Was he being deliberately caustic, or was this his sometimes-sharp humor?* A way of deflating his annoyance, that was certain. A way of pushing her a bit off guard as well. And it usually worked.

The initial flutter of joy in anticipation of seeing him flattened into something less agreeable. "Well, I am sorry. I had to do a bit of research for an unusual case I'm thinking about taking on. I figured you'd rather I finished that first so we can relax. And..." She shamelessly attempted a bit of manipulative charm, "later, *maybe* I won't have to take my laptop to bed."

Irritation quickly morphed into warmth. "Sorry, I guess I did have a bit of an edge. I am glad to see you," he finished, and this time, it felt genuine. He stood, pulled her up, and wrapped his arms around her for a hug. Ethan knew how to hug, full-bodied, so close she could feel his hips press against hers. And he hugged her frequently, for no reason or for any reason. She'd dated men who only hugged to go in for a kiss or as foreplay.

His chin rested lightly on top of her head, his height making her feel small, not an easy accomplishment as she wasn't exactly a tiny person.

When Ethan was happy, his positive mood was infectious and engaging. At those times, they shared laughter and affection. One of the many reasons she loved him, loved being with him.

It almost made up for the chill of his initial greeting. And her ongoing puzzlement over their relationship. Because his happiness was becoming rarer, their joyful connection more elusive. And she had no idea why.

After ordering appetizers, a glass of wine for her, and another bourbon for himself, Ethan asked, "So, what is this unusual case you think you're going to take?"

"You know I can't talk about my clients, even though this isn't exactly a client case. It's a former client," she said, fudging a bit since technically once a client, always a client, "who wants to hire me for a psych eval on a legal case."

She speared a piece of calamari and popped it into her mouth, chewing thoughtfully. It was okay to share tiny bits of her work with Ethan, but not much. They lived in the great metroplex of DFW, so the likelihood of ever running into one of her clients was slim, but still, it could happen. If anything shared with him led to identifying one of them, it put them and her license at risk.

Workdays were often long and stressful. It would be lovely to share about it with a partner, both in and out of the office. Maybe someone in the field, another psychologist in practice together, giving them complete freedom of disclosure about their cases. *What a luxury that would be.*

"Hello? Calling Dr. Rhodes," said Ethan, waving a hand in front of her face.

Working in her field required a leaning toward introversion, not in the social sense, but in the sense of the tendency to let the mind wander in ways that sometimes didn't connect to the conversation at hand. It was difficult not to reflect on the clients of the day, continue the unfurling of their issues, and consider alternative ways to address them in future sessions. Unfair, of course, to Ethan.

"Sorry. I was thinking about the case, which I can't discuss, and besides, it would be rather boring for you anyway." A lie because who wouldn't be fascinated by a teenage girl's murder, most likely at the hands of her friend? Already ideas flowed. *Was he a murderer? Or was it a tragic accident, the police and parents overreacting? Was the boy capable of killing his classmate? Or was he in the wrong place at the wrong time?*

"Are you talking about your typical worried-well, neurotic, needs-a-reality-slap type of client?" She detested it when he made fun of her work, which he tended to do when he drank too much. "For a slight side fee, I'll be glad to tell 'em to get over it."

She cringed inside. "It's actually a criminal case. I've been asked by the defense team to do forensic work."

"*What?* A criminal case," his curiosity piqued. "What's it about? Who is the criminal? Same confidentiality rules don't apply, do they? Hey, is it that case in the news? About the teenage boy who killed his friend—popular, beautiful girl, as I recall."

She steeled herself to address the boundaries of her work

yet again, but not before noticing the couple at a nearby table. They looked in their late twenties. She—flowing hair over one shoulder, plunging neckline, body language relaxed, low laughter as she chattered away. He—dressed for a special occasion, eyes darting downward nervously, with shifting body language, taking hasty gulps of wine a bit too frequently. Something was up with them, their mismatched moods glaringly obvious.

Jill frowned, then a slow smile spread over her face. "See that couple over there? No—don't look at them in an obvious way." It was the perfect distraction, and it was unfolding.

"How can I look at them without looking?" Ethan said, irritated. But he shifted his gaze surreptitiously. "What exactly am I looking at?"

"He's going to propose to her. This is their big night."

"What?" Ethan shifted uncomfortably. "No way."

"Just wait," she said as the waiter uncorked a bottle and whipped out two champagne glasses, setting them down carefully with a pointed look at the guy, who looked even more nervous than before. He took his date's hand at that point, distracting her. The waiter poured champagne carefully, then winked at the guy before leaving the table.

"Wait for it," Jill said, smiling, watching the couple.

She sipped her champagne while seeming to ask a question. He shrugged and waited. She sipped again, set down her glass. He clinked glasses, and she emptied hers, then covered her mouth in shock as she upended it, a ring tumbling out. He slid out of his seat, then dropped to one knee. He took her hand and spoke rapidly, an expression of adoration lighting his features.

The restaurant around them fell to a hush, and people smiled. Before he could finish, she squealed, "Yes, of course, I will!" He slid the ring on her finger to much tear-wiping and further squeals of joy. The people at nearby tables applauded, including Jill and Ethan. Someone let out an ear-piercing whistle, and laughter rippled through the room.

Eventually, the din died down, and everyone returned to their previous activities, as Jill wondered. How many were now focused on their own dates, their own love stories, or lack thereof? How many now smiled in recollection of their special moments, while others distracted themselves from their memories by digging into their food. Which diners now laughed too loudly to cover up the twist of emptiness, purposely yielding to the comfort of sarcasm and irony that seemed to dominate in an increasingly loveless world.

Ethan looked as uncomfortable on the outside as she felt on the inside. "You nailed that one, Dr. Rhodes. As usual. Is anything people do ever a surprise to you?" The last bit was sort of muttered under his breath.

"What?"

"Nothing." He tapped his foot on the floor and spent an inordinate amount of time re-arranging his silverware before taking a long sip of water. He set the glass down gently, keeping his fingers around it for a moment while he stared at the tabletop. His lips moved a tiny bit as though speaking to himself. Finally, he looked directly at her. "Listen, we need to talk."

We need to talk. Four little words that instantly produce anxiety for most people. Needing to talk was shorthand for having not talked or shared in real-time, as the most important thoughts and feelings had occurred. Instead, the need had been to *not* talk. To withhold while considering one's options or while planning one's exit.

Eventually, though, the unspoken made its way into the air, usually to the surprise and dismay of the recipient, and typically at the wrong time and in the wrong place. Caught off guard, the other person couldn't possibly be prepared, would likely be pushed off-balance, and would have no good way to absorb the verbal bullets.

But she knew what he was going to say. And this wasn't the time to re-hash their issues, their recycled problems, after three years of dating. Ethan's issues remained... his issues, not hers. That tiny ache in her chest remained solidly in place, maybe just a bit achier after witnessing the unbridled joy of the nearby couple. She took her bag and stood. "It's okay, Ethan. We don't need to talk. I have a long day ahead, and I'm not really hungry, so let's just go."

He swore softly but stood and followed her out. "I'm sorry," he whispered as if to himself, but she heard it loud and clear.

He was sorry. For what? Was he sorry he'd spent three years with her and realized something he couldn't bring himself to tell her? That he wasn't interested in marriage at all? That she wasn't his person? She wasn't sure because what he usually gave her were vague and incomplete statements such as 'be patient' and 'I just need more time to figure things out.'

But he looked despondent. She slowed and took his hand, once again offering him solace, leaving her own heart to comfort itself. Perhaps she was sorry as well, sorry for having willingly led herself down a path with only painful exits.

Later, as Ethan's breathing settled into a slow rhythm, she slid out of bed and made hot tea. She settled on the sofa in her living room with her tablet. She drew diagrams and made notes as she thought about the two attorneys with whom she'd met and the little she'd learned. Finally felt somewhat prepared for the next day. Sleep found her on the sofa as Ethan slept alone.

CHAPTER FIVE

"Thank you for meeting with me," Dr. Jill Rhodes said to the woman seated across from her. "I know this is a difficult time. I'm here to see if I can add insights to the case your son's lawyers are building to defend him. I was hired by the defense, but my job is to be as objective as possible. Anything you can tell me will either be used to help your son, or it will not be used. Is that clear so far?"

Their setting was the break room at Karen Thayer's place of work. It was early morning, and the place was quiet. Thayer was early middle-aged, wore a button-down shirt with jeans, and her frazzled, graying hair hung limply. Dark circles around her eyes, lines of fatigue around her mouth, the slump of her shoulders, and the posture of defeat told the story of life with a son who was the main suspect in a murder investigation. LED lighting offered low visibility and a lifeless atmosphere for their discussion of things that no one, no mother, should ever have to discuss.

The pull to go into therapist mode, to try to help her shoulder the impossible burden, was overpowering. That wasn't her job now, but it didn't mean the absence of compassion. "Tell me about your son, Shaun," Rhodes prodded gently.

Tears slid down Karen Thayer's face, and her mouth trembled. "He's wonderful. He's smart and kind. He's…dear God, what am I going to do?" She pulled tissues out of her handbag and sobbed. After a moment, she pulled herself together. "What do you want to know?"

"I know this is difficult. What can you tell me about his friends?"

Karen's face paled. "He only had one friend…Katie, the girl who…" Fresh tears coursed down her face, and she wiped them while talking. "They were friends since grade school. They had play dates, sat by each other in class. Katie was sweet to him. You have to understand. Shaun was the most beautiful little boy, so full of life. Here, let me show you." She took out her phone, scrolled, then shoved it into Jill's hands.

Jill stared at the images of a curly-haired little boy with eyes full of joy and mischief, a huge smile, and expressive hands. In one shot, he stood by an adorable little girl with big blue eyes and full, rosy lips who stared up at him, her smile spread wide. She could almost hear the instructions. *Stand together, kids. No, look here at the camera, not at Shaun, Katie…oh, for crying out loud, oh, that's cute!*

"But things changed later, after the divorce. Here, look," Karen said, scrolling and showing Jill the next set of shots, of a gangly adolescent boy with pale skin, sad eyes, and lank hair. "He wasn't the same after his dad left. The kids at school were unkind, sometimes cruel. I complained time after time, but nothing was done. I couldn't afford private school, and I had to work, so he had to stay there."

"What about Katie? Did they remain friends as they got older?"

"They did, but it was different, of course. Since we live on the same street, she still came over occasionally. They'd go in his room for hours and play music. I think they played chess together, or maybe they watched shows on the laptop." She looked slightly embarrassed. "I confess, sometimes I stood outside his door and listened. I heard them talking, and it sounded serious. But Katie was different."

"Different, how?"

"Shaun was…shy. He didn't have friends. Katie was beautiful and popular. She didn't seem to care a whole lot about that, but like it or not, she was a magnet for boys and other girls as well. Everyone wanted to be with Katie. She slowly drifted away from Shaun, and I think it hurt him." Her eyes went wide when she realized the implications. "Oh, not that way…he wasn't angry with her at all. Shaun was never angry. He just withdrew, stayed in his room. He was content there."

Angry over his beautiful friend drifting away? His mother might not want to acknowledge it. She pressed on. "Karen, did Shaun keep a journal of any kind?"

"No. The police looked for that as well." Her eyes flashed. "I swear to you, Dr. Rhodes, Shaun isn't one of those kids who keeps a journal full of slash-mark drawings and psychotic ramblings about killing people. He's all about his schoolwork, especially biology. He wants to be a doctor." Tears slid again.

A doctor. Interesting. "What about when Shaun was little. Did he have problems—sleep issues, anxiety, bed-wetting, food issues?"

"Don't most little kids wet the bed? It doesn't mean anything, and it didn't last long. It was a short phase," Karen said defensively.

"Of course, and you're right. Lots of kids wet the bed. What about fire? Was he attracted to fire?"

Karen's eyes narrowed. "What are you saying? Shaun would never hurt anyone, with fire or in any other way." Her shoulders squared, and her jaw set firmly. "I don't think there's any more to say."

The door of the break room swung open, and a woman peered in. "Oh, sorry. I thought this was empty." Reading the room, she quickly backed out and closed the door a bit too firmly, as though she couldn't escape the densely emotional atmosphere quickly enough.

Jill said nothing for a moment. "It's okay, Karen. I'm not implying anything about Shaun. It helps his case if I can understand him and any issues that the prosecution might bring out in court. Anything you can share with me about Shaun now is helpful." She waited.

Karen's shoulders dropped again, and she took a ragged breath. "He did have a thing about fire when he was little, but it was truly curiosity. Once, he lit the gas stovetop and put a piece of paper over the flame. But it wasn't a big deal. He dropped the paper on the floor, and I got there in time to douse it with water. He never did anything like that again, but we let him play with matches outside on the driveway. He got tired of it after a few days, and that was the end of that phase."

Jill made a note, thinking. That was two of the criteria of the famous Macdonald triad, a well-known theory of childhood behaviors that pointed to future violent behavior in adulthood, if not sooner. *Bedwetting and fascination with fire.*

Karen could be downplaying the degree of fascination, denying the pervasiveness of it, or not sharing that it presented a danger to the family. Or, she could be describing it accurately, which would put it in the category of normal childhood behavior.

Almost all children are fascinated with fire to an extent at some point.

Reluctantly, she queried about the third criteria of the triad.

"And how about pets? Did Shaun have any pets, or did he have any interest in animals in the neighborhood?"

"He was allergic to cats, so we couldn't have one, but he liked dogs. When he was twelve, he got a small job walking the neighbor's dog. Rocco, I think, was her name. Shaun loved that dog. But—" Her eyes pleaded as she stopped herself from saying more.

"But what?"

She shook her head. "It's nothing. The dog died while in his care. It wasn't his fault, and it broke Shaun's heart."

That could be strike three—animal abuse. Even if you didn't believe in the infallibility of the Macdonald triad, you had to acknowledge there was something potentially wrong here.

But nothing, no psychological theory, was irrefutable. Human behavior was far too complex for that. Diagnosing mental illness was truly part of the practice of medicine. *Practice* being the operative word. She didn't know enough yet about Shaun to form any conclusions.

Still, the indicators were pointing in the wrong direction. This sad case was getting more tragic by the minute. And there might be nothing more for her to do but file a confirmation of the prosecution's case.

"Tell me about the divorce, Karen, about your family before and after."

"We were happy together—we were a good family."

"How did you meet your husband, your *ex*-husband?"

"Bill and I met in college. After school, we moved in together, got jobs, and had so much fun together. We got married after a couple of years."

"How did you decide to get married?"

Karen looked uncomfortable, then defensive again. "We got pregnant, and it was the next step. We were totally in love. There wasn't any pressure about having a baby if that's what you're wondering."

"Of course not." She studied her notes. "What happened? Who wanted the divorce, Karen?"

"Bill started working late. He started his own business, an architectural firm, and it took a lot of time because he wore all the hats at first. I didn't think anything of it. But I could tell it affected Shaun. He missed his dad. I tried to talk to Bill about it, but he was so defensive. He said it was temporary, that when the business got bigger, he could hire people to take over some of the work. And then..."

"And then, you noticed the changes in your relationship with him," Jill said softly.

Karen nodded. "I thought it was temporary, that the spark would return when we had more time together after he hired a few people. And he did hire more people. But his hours continued at the same pace—evenings, weekends." She looked up sharply at Jill. "What is it about people who cheat? Why don't they have the guts to tell you?"

"I don't know." But she did know. Infidelity took many forms, from craving the intensity of something new to bridging the end of a relationship played out to the point of no return. The affair sometimes turned out to be the relationship they should have held out for before settling for an incompatible partner, only to later leave them. Leaving behind the devastation of never fully understanding what had gone wrong.

"He ended our marriage with an email. An email, for Christ's sake! He crawled away like a snake with no explanation. I did everything I could. I called, I emailed, I showed up at his apartment, but that was a disaster because that's how I met his future second wife. Four years of college, and a child, with someone who thought so little of me he couldn't even talk to me at the end."

"What about Shaun?"

"Bill remarried as soon as the divorce went through, and he has a new family with two new children. He rarely has time for his oldest. Every so often, he FaceTimes Shaun. FaceTime! As if that's all it takes to be a good father." She snorted in disgust. "He hasn't been once to see him in juvenile detention."

How often had she seen this? One partner moves on from the marriage and starts a new family, never realizing how difficult it is to be an effective parent in two families. Hard enough to do it in one intact household. But two? Most people weren't up for the challenge, so the children in the first family were neglected by the departing parent. Leaving them feeling like second best, replaceable.

Did the impact of the divorce and his father's abandonment push Shaun into a downward spiral, making him so emotionally combustible that he would kill his friend?

Jill moved on. "I know this part is hard, but tell me everything you remember about the day Katie died."

"I already told the police everything I remember," she said, glancing at her watch. "I have to get back to work."

"I know you do. But this is important."

She sighed heavily. "I came home from work. Shaun wasn't home yet, but that wasn't unusual. I went into the kitchen and turned on the television to watch the news while I prepared dinner. The top news story was about Katie, how she'd been found murdered. That was shocking. But I heard a sound behind me, and when I turned around—" She covered her mouth with her hand as a sob slipped out.

Rhodes waited while Karen Thayer cried quietly, her eyes registering the shock she must have felt that day all over again. Having to ask a reeling person to re-live the most traumatic moment of her life was unfortunate and not something she relished. But it wouldn't be the last time Karen would be required to do it if her son's case went to court and if she were called to the witness stand.

"Shaun was standing there, with blood on his clothes, staring at the television and making this terrible sound, like an animal in pain. I'll never forget that sound." She wrung her hands as she spoke. "He pointed at the television screen and said Katie's name and something about it being his fault. I could see the blood on his shirt, and that's when I knew something terrible had happened. I had no choice. I called 9-1-1, but I've regretted it ever since." She sobbed again. "The cops, questioning him…his utter silence, his stare. *It's my fault*. I know he didn't kill Katie, and this wouldn't be happening if it wasn't for me. They would be looking for the real killer if I hadn't reported Shaun!"

Rhodes sat quietly, stunned by the revelation. Shaun's mother had seen him in the bloody clothes, the bloody knife discovered in his room, the evidence incontrovertible. Yet she still maintained her son's innocence.

Denial was a powerful force, deeply ingrained, perhaps for the evolutionary purpose of enabling us to face the unthinkable. To fully confront a horror such as this would take most people to their knees, reduce them to a stricken heap. And perhaps, now, having re-lived the terror of seeing her son the murderer, she *had* been taken to her knees.

A vision of Karen Thayer's future appeared, and it wasn't good. Jill sat with Karen for the next ten minutes, talking soothingly. Gradually, the sobs slowed and stopped. She gave Karen the name of a colleague and made her promise to get an appointment. "You can't go through this alone. You need a sounding board, someone to be strong for you, and Shaun needs a mom who can be strong for him." *And*, she thought, *you have to get off the path you're on*.

But what could possibly comfort the mother of a teenager who was suspected of killing his best friend, a beautiful, popular high school cheerleader? How much could one person withstand? Her husband had left her for a younger woman and a new family. Her only child sat awaiting his fate at the hands of the court system.

Bad things happen to good people. It was the mantra of well-meaning therapists in an effort to explain impossible tragedies. But how was that supposed to be comforting? And how did you reconcile that piece of supposed wisdom? *Since something bad happened to me, that means I'm good*. Or, even worse, *I'm a good person that something terrible happened to, so, therefore…* what?

Was the reverse true? Did it mean good things happen to bad people? And if so, was that evidence of God's twisted sense of humor? Or was it evidence of the absence of God?

Unanswerable questions. Added to the endless list of unanswerable questions in life frequently asked by her clients, many of which she'd added to the list due to the puzzle of her own life path.

As she strode to her vehicle, Jill looked at her watch. It was not even midday yet, and she was exhausted, but there was time for the next round of interviews before lunch. So far, the case against Shaun looked solid. It gave her no joy, no satisfaction at doing the job.

Taking this case was a mistake. Her role was the healer, not the bearer of more bad news on top of tragedy. Not the person who might hold the knowledge to put this boy in prison for the rest of his life.

CHAPTER SIX

The door opened slowly, and a petite blonde girl slipped in. She flashed a timid smile at Jill, who indicated a chair. "Sophie? It's nice to meet you. I'm Dr. Jill Rhodes." She gave her a warm smile to put her at ease, and it seemed to work. Sophie relaxed visibly. She was pretty and didn't yet radiate the jaded look of most of her contemporaries.

"The reason we're meeting is because I've been hired to work on the case of Katie's death. I'm sorry these are the circumstances, but anything you can tell me about Katie or Shaun or anyone else who might know something would really help. Okay with you?"

It was questionable for Jill to be here, and she knew she was on thin ice. Michael's partner had called the school and requested permission for these interviews, and apparently, he had some persuasive skills because the school had readily consented without any sign-off from parents.

Outside the empty classroom, the sounds of laughter, some shouting, and slamming locker doors reverberated.

"It's okay," said Sophie. "But I don't really know Shaun that well. Katie was my best friend, though," she said. Her face fell, and her eyes welled. "I still can't believe she's gone. I keep having these dreams about her, and it feels like she's still here." She brushed away a tear.

"I know it must be difficult. What can you tell me about Katie, her friends, her activities?"

"Everyone loved Katie. The whole school is broken up over this. None of us can believe she was murdered."

"Why is that?"

"Katie was so good to Shaun. She defended him when the other kids teased him. Why would he want to kill her, the one person who was nice to him?" She stopped, looking embarrassed. "I don't mean for it to sound like he was bullied or anything like that. He was just weird, you know...different. It was hard for anyone to be friends with him, except for Katie. That's what I meant."

"Weird, how?"

"I don't know. Awkward. He never talked to anyone, and he didn't make eye contact. If anyone tried to talk to him, he didn't seem to know what to say back. He never showed emotions—no smile, no laughing, no anger, nothing. Just, like, a blank face. Maybe he's on the spectrum, you know?"

Kids these days. They knew one another's diagnoses like they knew who liked who, who had allergies and to what, and who was in or out of the cool kid crowd. They knew about Asperger's, they knew about A.D.D., and they knew all about anxiety and depression, including who was taking what medications to treat their maladies.

They knew where their parents kept the meds and how to sneak them out in small quantities. They knew to whom they could sell their parents' pharmaceuticals for extra pocket cash.

"Do you think Shaun liked Katie more than as a friend? More like a crush?"

"Maybe." She shrugged. "Lots of guys crushed on Katie. But I never saw Shaun do anything around her that looked like it. At school, they pretty much stayed away from each other. I know Katie went over to his house sometimes, but they just talked and played chess."

"What do you think they talked about?" Third hand was unreliable, but kids often thrived on gossip, the passing along of any tidbit of information about another kid in their social milieu.

"I don't know." Sophie went silent, gazing down at her hands, and began picking at her cuticles.

Jill made a note, stalling for time, formulating a new question. "What about the other guy, Sophie?" She caught the shocked expression on Sophie's face, who quickly twisted in an attempt to hide it. The shot in the dark had hit its mark.

"What guy?" Sophie asked innocently, but the artifice of her vulnerability didn't pass the sniff test.

Jill put down her tablet and watched Sophie, saying nothing for a moment. "You might as well tell me." She'd spoken gently, and now she watched the guarded expression melt away. Underneath it all, kids wanted trusted adults to give them a safe place to unburden themselves.

"His name is Trevor," she said, looking at her hands, tears forming in the corners of her eyes.

"Which one of you did he hook up with first?"

Sophie's face flushed. *Bullseye with the second shot in the dark.* Another tear leaked as she said shakily, "Me. I thought he loved me. He *said* he did. But then he hooked up with Katie, and it was like I didn't even exist. He totally ghosted me." Her tone gradually shifted from sad to angry. *Jealousy.*

"That must have really hurt."

"I can't believe he would do that to me, especially after we—" she shifted uncomfortably.

Not surprising. Trust is hard won with teenagers. Jill pressed gently. "After you had sex."

"I mean, sex is no big deal, right? It's just sex. But he was my first, and I—"

"You fell in love with him," Dr. Rhodes finished for her.

She nodded sadly. "Who wouldn't? He was gorgeous and so sweet. He made me feel like the only girl in the world."

Jill found tissues in her bag. *Sweet?* Gorgeous guys didn't usually have to be sweet. But girls Sophie's age often interpreted even the slightest gestures of affection as evidence of true love.

Then again, girls of all ages, even very mature women, could be taken in by a few kind gestures. Her case files were full of examples.

After Sophie calmed down, she continued. "Where does he go to school? Is he here today?"

"No, he doesn't go here."

"How did you meet him?"

"Just hanging out. You know." And she gazed at her cuticles again.

It was clear Sophie wasn't saying more, not then, anyway. Jill stared at her notes while watching peripherally. Sophie reached up, pulled her hair to the side. She ran a finger over her brows, looking down. *Definitely hiding something.*

"How angry were you about Trevor seeing Katie?"

Sophie looked up sharply. "Angry? I wasn't angry, at least not at Katie. The truth is, she didn't know I was with him. It came out after he broke up with me and started seeing her. She felt terrible and told me she was going to break up with him. She said he was a...sorry, but she called him a manwhore, and a cheater. In fact, she was going to talk to him that day."

That caught her attention. "The day she was killed?"

She nodded again, sighing. "I don't even know if she ever talked to him. After that day, I tried again to text Trevor, but he never answered. He didn't show up at her funeral, either. *Who does that?* Supposedly, they were hot and heavy, but it wasn't exactly out in the open. She knew her parents wouldn't let her date a guy like that."

"A guy like what?"

Realizing she'd probably said too much, she clammed up at that point. "I don't know. He wasn't exactly a part of our group of friends," she said, looking down.

"How do you mean?"

"I don't know," she said, clearly not wanting to say. Her eyes flashed again as she looked up. "What a jerk. Who doesn't even go to the funeral of his... girlfriend?" She still seemed to struggle over their relationship, unwilling to accept that Katie could also have been Trevor's girlfriend.

Most likely, it had been both of the girls. *Who does that? Who dates two girls at once and fails to attend the funeral of one?* That was easy. A guy who's too good-looking for his own good, who has his pick of girls. A guy who hasn't yet developed, or never will, a heart for love and care.

And he was probably older, a potential fact that Sophie clearly hadn't wanted to reveal. He was a guy whose 'girlfriend' had planned to confront him and break up. A guy who perhaps hadn't taken that well. Hot guys who have choices typically do the leaving. They don't get dumped. Add in a large dose of self-absorption, and you have someone who might not simply walk away after being rejected.

Had Katie and Trevor actually gotten together that day? Had she tried to break up with him, and had he tried to stop her? How ugly might that confrontation have been? Had he gone into a rage because his shallow ego had never been bruised like that before, especially by a high school girl?

It was an interesting angle, but she didn't have sufficient data to back it up. Perhaps the Katie-Trevor-Sophie drama triangle was merely an interesting diversion in this case, with no bearing on Shaun. Perhaps Trevor wasn't older, either, just an immature boy, one who'd freaked out about his girlfriend's murder. Didn't want to confront that reality by going to her funeral.

And the reality was that Shaun was the one who'd shown up with Katie's blood, the murder weapon with his prints. Trevor could have been the trigger that had set Shaun off, sent him into a blind rage.

Or perhaps there was another reason Shaun might have been spurred to murder Katie, something that hadn't yet been uncovered.

"One more question, Sophie. Can you tell me why Shaun might want to kill Katie? Did something bad happen before that day, something she couldn't tell anyone?" A terrible secret between two teenagers could turn badly. Someone might want to stop the other person from telling.

"Katie never had anything but good things to say about Shaun. If anything, she was protective of him. But sometimes, the way he looked at her... Like I said, Katie was the object of lots of crushes."

"Including Shaun?"

Sophie shrugged, looking away.

Jill switched gears abruptly. "What can you tell me about Katie's parents?"

Sophie seemed relieved at the change of subject. "Her mom was really involved with cheer. She helped us out a lot and got the other moms in line. She's pretty fierce. Hovered over Katie a lot. Her dad is okay, I guess, but I didn't see him much. I feel so bad for them."

Jill briefly reviewed her notes, asking a couple of additional minor questions. Then she thanked Sophie and let her leave. After that, she interviewed three other kids, but nothing new came to light. They all had pretty much the same story. Katie was well-liked and admired. She seemed to like Shaun and, at times, was protective of him. Shaun was weird and didn't have friends except for Katie.

No one else volunteered anything about Katie having a boyfriend—not surprising, given the possibility of an age disparity. She'd asked who Katie might have been dating and gotten only puzzled looks. Apparently, she had plenty of guys who fawned over her, but no one she'd allowed to get serious. At least, no one that her peers knew about.

Only Sophie knew about Trevor. Something seemed off about that. Kids are so on top of each other's lives with social media. Someone would almost certainly have seen Trevor with Katie if they had been together.

Then again, the secret lives of teenagers could fill volumes. The average kid could implement incredibly intricate strategies to avoid detection. It was most parents' greatest fear—that their child could be involved secretly with people who might harm them in irreparable ways or with activities that could harm them. All carried on without their knowledge or ability to intervene.

THE EXPERT WITNESS

The secrecy made it very difficult to counsel teenagers. They were so enraptured with the present moment and so foggy about the future consequences of their poor decision-making that it frustrated Jill, so she avoided taking on those clients. Of course, there were plenty of adults locked in similar adolescent patterns as well.

As Jill drove away from the school, her stomach growled. With only a quick yogurt to go that morning, her system was notifying her it was time for lunch. Her cell phone rang, and she punched the button on the steering wheel to answer. "Hello?"

"Jill. Can you meet me for lunch?" Her sister Jade's voice was low and slightly breathless.

"I actually have a full day. I'm working on a special case, and I'm going to be tied up for hours. Sorry."

Silence. Then, "Okay, how about after work?"

"Not sure when I'll be done. This could take the evening as well. What's going on?"

"Nothing. It's okay. We'll catch up later. Bye, Sis." And she was gone, leaving Jill wondering. But she was right. They could catch up later. Maybe she'd make a surprise visit later in the evening. Jade didn't often call her spontaneously in the middle of the week like that. It was clearly important, and that tugged at her sense of responsibility.

It wasn't only her clients and boyfriend she supported emotionally. It was her sister, too, mostly about their mom. While they avoided the subject most of the time, sometimes one or the other of them would need to vent about the latest encounter.

Mom, who insisted they call her by her first name, Crystal, contacted them in one of two states, the first being frantic, rapid speech filled with drama and absolutes like, "he *never* comes home on time or tells me where he's been," and "he *always* treats me like I'm a prisoner in my own home!" or, "he drinks half a bottle of bourbon every night!"

The other, an emotional flip side of the first—slowed speech, rambling, incoherent, and often punctuated with tears, filled with expressions of regret about how she'd treated her husband and fears of his getting tired of her and leaving her.

Whatever the latest was regarding their mother, it could wait. The clock was ticking on Shaun. She had clients to think of as well. While she'd had her assistant postpone meetings for a couple of days, she couldn't postpone their sessions for long without creating issues for them.

Sophie sent another text, hoping against hope for a response. She stared at the tiny screen, the keeper of her heart and her reason for joy, and waited. And waited. She wasn't even rewarded with those tiny dots, the hopeful indicators that he at least tried to formulate a response. It was the same as it had been for days now. Ever since Katie died.

Her mind swirled with possibilities. She'd done everything he'd asked of her. She'd kept all his secrets, including the ones that Katie had shared. *Why wasn't that enough?*

Guilt flooded Sophie's veins as she thought about Katie. Now that she was gone, instead of mourning her lost friend, she'd been obsessed with getting back her lost boyfriend. The emptiness had agonized her, and there seemed only one way to fill the hole. *Trevor.*

Why hadn't he reached out to her again? After all, she'd been true to him, loyal even after Katie had stolen him away. Even an amazing guy like Trevor would be easy prey for Katie, with her flawless, glowing skin, her long, thick hair, and slender athletic build. Guys couldn't resist her. But she could have resisted taking Trevor away.

Sophie felt torn, unsure of the sequence of events. Was it true that Katie hadn't known Trevor was with Sophie? Was it possible she'd hung out with him, maybe even had sex with him, not knowing Trevor was cheating with her?

Or, had she known and didn't care, or worse, set out to break Sophie's heart? Katie dreamed of being an actor. Had she pretended to be Sophie's best friend those last few weeks, all the while planning to steal her guy? Had she acted her way into Trevor's arms?

Her vision clouded momentarily with a flush of intense anger.

It was the same anger that had led her to the terrible confrontation on the last day of Katie's life.

CHAPTER SEVEN

Jill drove while taking bites of a chicken sandwich and thought about guilt and innocence. So far, all guilty fingers pointed at Shaun, the 15-year-old boy who'd apparently killed his only friend, Katie.

Why hadn't the police looked into Katie's boyfriend at the beginning of the investigation? Why hadn't he been considered?

But she knew the answer. Shaun was covered in Katie's blood shortly after her murder, and the weapon was his. *Why would the police do any further investigating?* It appeared they were unaware of Trevor's presence in Katie's life, and why would they bother to dig too deep. They had their perpetrator.

But to Dr. Rhodes, the potentially inappropriate relationship was something worth looking into. That he'd dated both girls, setting up a teenage love triangle, was cause for concern as well.

But the Trevor story could be little more than teenage fiction. Girls Sophie's age were notorious for embellishing the smallest gestures, turning them into full-blown romances. A smile, saying hello, a random text—sometimes that was all it took to ignite fantasies of a relationship. Sophie may have done that with Trevor. Perhaps she'd imagined his affections, the love triangle only in her mind. But now Jill found herself confused with the information she'd gathered so far.

It was hard enough tracking down the people connected to Shaun and interviewing them. Harder still, to sort fact from fiction. Regardless of the truth of the Katie/Trevor/Sophie triangle, it may very well have little or no bearing on what had ultimately happened to Katie. She put it aside for now.

She sighed, thinking again how unlikely it was that anyone other than Shaun had killed Katie. The most likely scenario was an unrequited crush.

Maybe Shaun had secretly yearned for more from Katie, to be her crush, to be her boyfriend. Shaun was socially blunted, beyond shyness, perhaps *on the spectrum*, as Sophie had so glibly pointed out.

If he'd had a crush on Katie, he wouldn't have known how to show it, his emotions hidden behind the flat facial expressions of a typical Asperger's kid. Katie likely did not know he felt that way, and if not, she'd have continued in the friendship, spending time with him, unaware of his deeper feelings.

Meanwhile, the fires of a first crush might have burned with intensity. Too much intensity, with no outlet. Which might have continued indefinitely, except there was a catalyst of some kind, a turning point.

Maybe he'd found out about Katie's boyfriend. Maybe he'd found something online, been confronted with seeing her in love with someone else. He'd found out about Trevor and realized she had a secret life, one she'd kept from him. Perhaps theorized she was having sex with Trevor and considered it as cheating on him.

Teenage boys were filled with intense emotions, feelings that could spin out of control with the infusion of rampant hormones. It could have manifested as wild, uninhibited physical movements that led to violence.

She could envision how it might have gone down. The confrontation, him grabbing her shoulders, shaking her, yelling at her about what she'd done. Katie—trying to pull away, yelling back, calling him names in frustration, maybe slapping him, throwing him into a frenzy of rage. A weapon pulled in the heat of the moment, used to kill his friend, the rage temporarily blinding him.

She knew a little about violent rage, about how perpetrators often described a fugue state of sorts in which they committed terrible acts without being psychologically present or aware. That their focus narrowed to the victim in an intense way that blinded them to the context, destroying their ability to view the person as a victim.

Empathy, if the perpetrator was ever capable of it, disappeared. The body mobilized in a defensive violence as if the victim were a man-eating tiger that must be destroyed before it killed you.

Whether truth or fiction, there was a narrative by those who harmed or killed in the heat of the moment: seeing the color red, a nearby weapon grabbed and used without any thought of restraint. Implausibly, shock after the fact, a sense of having been out-of-body, or that someone else must have done it, and sometimes, intense remorse.

Although no rational person could empathize, the narrative of the violent person often continued with a story about the after-effect of traumatic response, as if the perpetrator had been the one who was harmed. That traumatic response might include mutism and loss of the ability to talk about what happened, such as Shaun seemed to have exhibited.

This could be Shaun's narrative. A jealous rage, an action that ended a friend's life and destroyed his own. And now, the protective defense of emotional shutdown, his voice muted, permanently or temporarily.

Still, though, Shaun deserved advocacy of some kind. A deeper investigation. Or the intervention of a professional who could minimize the damage if he were found guilty. Someone who could throw enough doubt on the case to generate a modicum of sympathy for him.

Then there was Karen, Shaun's mother, to think about. Her life's purpose—caring for, loving, and protecting her challenged son—now deeply threatened, perhaps destroyed. The guilt, irrational though it might be, was insurmountable. She'd called law enforcement on her own son. The only hope she had was for him to be deemed a minor, to possibly suffer nothing worse than years of therapy.

If there were a way to mitigate the damage, Jill could be instrumental in that endeavor. A teenager in federal prison, surrounded by hardened criminals, was an apocalyptic vision in her mind. That shouldn't happen to any child.

She thought of Katie's parents, whose hearts were broken, who only wanted justice for their daughter. Their loss was permanent. It was the worst kind of loss; all others pale in comparison on the psychological scale of stress.

She felt torn. *Should she feel any empathy for Shaun? Was it appropriate, given the far worse outcome of a lost life?*

But for her to withhold empathy would violate her deepest,

most cherished principles. *Never let other people's bad behavior change who you are.* Her mentor's often-repeated advice to address the confusion therapists often felt as they empathized even with clients who harmed others, emotionally or otherwise. *Be careful you don't let other people and their disheartening behavior change you into a cynical, bitter person.*

But this was different than any scenario she'd explored in graduate school, during her internships, or even in all her years of practice. The stakes here were unbelievably high. And she was, after all, a novice at forensics.

Jill parked in front of the headquarters for the Dallas Police Department. Inside, she was shown into a small meeting room. It was spare, with only a Formica-topped table, cheap-looking folding chairs, and lighting that leached all color from the space. After fifteen or so long minutes, two detectives entered the room. She stood and shook both their hands.

Both detectives wore jeans and sport coats. One was older, balding a bit, heavy in the middle, and sported a salt and pepper mustache, more salt than pepper. He looked at Jill with piercing dark eyes that belied his physiological softness.

The other was early forties, if she had to guess. He was tall, with a sinuous physique and nice features. He seemed more open and friendly, gazing at her steadily with eyes that reflected both green and gray. An unusual color, and was that curiosity in his eyes?

"Thanks for meeting with me," she offered. "As you know, I have been hired by the defense team for Shaun Thayer. I know you don't have to do this, so I appreciate it." She pulled out her tablet and turned it on.

The older guy, Detective Rick Stone, sat stoically while the other, Detective Nick Webb, gave her a warm smile. "No problem. But we can only share the facts that have been deemed discoverable at this point."

"I understand." She looked up from her tablet as if she'd been studying notes. It was one of her favorite moves to slow things down, allowing her to discern things that might be missed. "Can you tell me about the evidence against Shaun at this point?"

Detective Stone spoke first. "He had blood on his clothes belonging to the victim, the knife at the home had his prints and the victim's blood, and there are no other suspects." His expression radiated impatience as if daring her to ask any questions. But not as though he was prepared to answer them. Instead, he seemed to be finished before they'd really even started.

Rhodes was far from finished. "What, if any, further investigating did you do to look for another suspect?" She'd tried to soften the question but knew this line of questioning could get her shown the door in a hurry.

Stone bristled. "Why would we continue to investigate? There was a knife, and the medical examiner confirmed it was the weapon used to kill the victim. The knife had his prints. His clothes were covered in the blood of the victim. A *teenage girl*." He recited this as though she were too mentally challenged to keep up with basic information.

But Detective Webb spoke up. "Why did you ask that?"

She answered with another question. "The knife—what kind was it? Did it have any other prints on it?"

Stone answered. "It was some kind of fancy pocketknife. What does it matter?"

"It was a pocketknife with multiple tools, the kind you use for fishing, maybe hunting," Webb clarified further.

That matched what she'd heard. "And any other prints besides his?" she prodded again.

Stone looked apoplectic, but Webb waved him off, asking a question of his own instead. "What do you know so far on your end?"

But she wasn't ready to give up the results of her investigation so far, especially to the two people who were interested in arresting and charging Shaun. There was one thing, though, that she could offer for a couple of purposes. "Were you aware that the victim had a boyfriend? And that her parents probably didn't know, nor, apparently, did anyone else."

The two exchanged a look before Detective Webb took out a small pad of paper. "Where did you learn this, Dr., uh—"

"Rhodes. It's Dr. Jill Rhodes. Detective Webb."

"Dr. Rhodes, then. Who told you the victim had a boyfriend?"

"One of her friends at school."

"And we all know how reliable teenagers are," Stone scoffed. "Regular fonts of misinformation, spouting all the time on social media. Look, doc, unless you have something more substantial, I think we're done." He stood and looked pointedly at his partner.

"Wait. There's more," she said.

Webb intervened. "We've got a few more minutes. Let's hear her out."

Stone's expression remained skeptical, but he sat back down while Jill continued. "My business is listening, and when I hear things from people, I get a strong sense of whether or not it is authentic. No one knows better than I do how teenagers lie. It's what they do—hide things about themselves from their parents and even from their peers while they figure out who they are, who they're going to be. Even with therapists, they don't usually open up, which is why it rarely works at that age."

She could go on and on about the subject of teenagers, but she was losing her audience. "Look," she said, at their impatient expressions, "Katie's friend Sophie was telling the truth. I believe her, and I think there was more going on in Katie's life than previously thought. There's something Sophie wouldn't tell me. I think it's worth checking out."

Stone looked even more skeptical. "So, you have some kind of Spidey-sense about people. None of that constitutes any real evidence. The evidence is conclusive. This kid killed his so-called friend."

Webb shot Stone a look. He turned to Jill. "Okay, let's say the victim's friend was telling the truth. What do you think it has to do with this case?"

"I'm not sure, but it's a loose end, don't you think? What if Katie's secret boyfriend was involved in something bad, maybe drugs? What if she was keeping secrets for him, and it led her into something that put her in danger? Or maybe she found out something about him, and he silenced her." She knew she was stretching this a bit, but she plunged on. "Can you at least look into this guy, find out more about him and his connection to Katie?"

Webb studied her while Stone's frown and crossed arms signaled his lack of interest. "We're done with the investigation, so no dice," he said firmly. "This isn't a loose end. It's grasping at straws. And we don't need a shrink playing amateur detective, either."

At the same time Stone spoke, Webb said, "Maybe." He looked at his partner in surprise, then rolled his eyes. Webb turned to Jill. "We may be able to do something," he said, cutting his eyes to Stone, who sat shaking his head firmly. "What do you know about the boyfriend?"

"His name is Trevor Cade, he doesn't go to their school, and they met him... somewhere else." She chose to leave out her concerns about Trevor's age until she could learn more. But filled them in on everything else she knew about him.

"I'll get back to you with what I find." Webb's expression was warmly skeptical, but Stone just glared. "But you need to realize that it's pretty much an open-and-shut case. If someone else killed Katie, then why was Shaun covered in her blood with the murder weapon in his possession? It makes sense that he did it." He said it a bit apologetically, as if that wasn't the conclusion he wanted, either.

The meeting had gone better than anticipated, though she didn't feel entirely clean on her part. Shaun was looking like the killer, but if she could point the two detectives in a new direction, cast some doubt, it might be enough to help him get a lesser sentence. That was about all she could do, but it was something, and it might help a distraught mother win back one tiny piece of her life.

But there were other items on her list, and she was determined to work through them all, regardless of how strongly things stood against Shaun at this point.

She drove absent-mindedly through the thickening Dallas traffic. The sky was darker, clouds lowering with their oncoming payload of rain. *Great*. She didn't have an umbrella in the car.

A call had to be placed. After the voicemail tone, she left a message that couldn't be ignored. "I have important information about your son, Shaun, that not only will affect his case but could affect you as well. If I don't hear back from you within the hour, I will be forced to show up at your work. I'm sorry to do that, but it's essential that we speak. Thank you." Then she left all her contact information. Within five minutes, the call came in, and she set up a meeting.

As she drove, rain staying well ahead of her wipers, she peered ahead nervously, and her thoughts drifted to the color of Detective Nick Webb's eyes and to the soft lines around them, indicating humor, and perhaps a trace of old sorrow. And the compassion that filled them.

Detective Nick Webb pulled up the software on his computer to begin researching the mysterious Trevor. While it was loading, he thought about Dr. Jill Rhodes. He wasn't accustomed to outside parties getting involved in an investigation, and he wasn't sure he liked it. Especially an inexperienced person who could easily hamper their progress. Or throw a monkey wrench into what had heretofore been an airtight, although tragic, case.

Although he had to admit to himself, they hadn't exactly done a lot of investigating with Shaun Thayer's case. It had pretty much been a done deal from the get-go. They'd handed over the evidence to the District Attorney's office and left them to decide the timing and specifics of the next steps, whether he'd be charged as an adult or juvenile. He couldn't help thinking about Shaun, just a kid, really, with his entire future on the line.

But then he thought about Katie, a kid whose life was over.

He steeled himself against empathy for Shaun, which he came by naturally. He had a soft spot for the young, the infirm, the vulnerable, even those who turned to crime for various reasons. Yet his fingers flew over the keyboard. Curiosity got the best of him, and he allowed a tiny thread of possibility to wind its way into his mind.

What if there was more to this case?

CHAPTER EIGHT

Shaun's father, Bill Thayer, had the look of an impatient executive who viewed his time as extremely valuable. They sat in his private office at his architectural firm, his name prominently on the company signage on the building. "What is this about? Your voice message was disturbing, to say the least." He'd wasted no time launching the first missile.

"I'm terribly sorry, Mr. Thayer." *She wasn't.* "I am in the midst of a very rushed investigation with the aim of helping your son, Shaun. I know you want the best outcome for him, and I've got to say, it's not looking good for him. I'm concerned about him, and I know you are, too." *Maybe so, maybe not. The jury was still out on Bill Thayer, though it wasn't looking good.*

Jill's eyes traveled from the lack of concern on Thayer's face to his expensive slacks, silk shirt, and high-end loafers, topped off with a shiny wedding band encrusted with diamonds. But then, his expression registered something else—perhaps a dawning awareness that he should show more concern for his son.

As the conflicting emotions played out over his face, he eased back in his chair and carefully crossed his leg. "Of course, I am concerned. How can I help? And please, call me Bill." Was he truly that apathetic about his own son? Or was he the victim of a carefully constructed persona, one that he'd built along the way in his career as a successful architect? Yes, she'd looked him up online and seen all the accolades and awards earned by his firm.

Sometimes, in the quest for a public-facing persona and the resulting dedication to maintaining it, people lost touch with who they really were deep down. Other times, all the person had was the public mask, never having developed a true persona of their own. *Shallow*. Perhaps that was Bill Thayer. Perhaps not.

"I realize you may not feel comfortable answering some of these questions," she began. "They're rather sensitive, so let me know if you don't feel like you can handle them." It could be overplayed on her part, but most people reacted by going in the opposite direction when told *maybe you can't*.

He pulled himself up, looking slightly offended. *Yes, I can, and I'll show you*. "Of course, I can handle your questions. Fire away."

He gave her a disarming smile at that point, and she could see his charm. That, combined with his looks, his polish, and his obvious success, would make him a magnet for a younger, more beautiful version of his ex-wife. Her eyes strayed briefly to the silver-framed photos of a gorgeous brunette holding a toddler and flanked by an older child. The picture-perfect family.

There were no photos of Shaun.

She thought about Karen, her pain still raw many years after being betrayed by this man. And Shaun, for the most part, abandoned by his father. Good place to start. "Can you tell me about your history with Shaun and his mother? It helps if I hear from both of you, gain a more complete picture."

"It's pretty simple. Karen and I dated in college, then moved in together. I was building my firm, and she had a job. Then, she got pregnant with Shaun, and we got married." Spoken without a trace of emotion. *Either a lack of empathy or a cover-up for guilt.*

"So, you got married because Karen was pregnant. I imagine that was a bit unplanned."

"It was, but I did the right thing, and we did the best we could." *Was he proud of himself for marrying his son's mother? Or, again, covering up his guilt for ultimately abandoning them.*

"Sometimes people do the right thing, even though it doesn't align with how they really feel deep down." She let him think she was empathetic about his sacrifice.

He sighed. "If I'm being honest, I have to say we weren't exactly deeply in love when we married. We weren't compatible, I realize, looking back. She's sort of an earth mother type. All of her focus was on Shaun, all of her energy on being a mom." His mouth twisted in a trace of distaste. "But we were young. Part of the way I built my business was by networking and socializing. I had to do it on my own because she never wanted to go with me. She wouldn't leave Shaun with any kind of caregiver, including her own parents. Or mine." He looked frustrated at the memory.

"And when did you meet your second wife?"

There it was...a chink in the armor. The slightest of hesitations and the clenching of the jaw.

"A few years after Karen and I got married. I'm not proud of this, but the truth is I was getting ready to break up with Karen right around the time she got pregnant. I was already halfway gone. But then, there was Shaun, so I stayed. When Shaun was older, I met Courtney when she came to work at the firm. She's a gifted architect," he added pridefully.

It was an old story—*I'm married, but I'm not happy, and I swear I'm going to get a divorce. Soon.* An affair that goes on for one or two years or more. Sometimes followed by a divorce and new marriage to the one who stole him away.

Sometimes followed by yet another divorce and the single life, the 'mistress' being the transitional relationship. But the woman in the photos, whoever she was, had won—the guy, the ring, and the new family, despite her role in the destruction of his first family.

The wreckage was Karen and Shaun, who had been dumped. It was difficult not to judge, but that was her job. She pushed aside her own feelings of distaste and pressed on. "Following the divorce, what can you tell me about your relationship with your oldest son."

"My relationship with Shaun is fine. It's not easy juggling time with him and time with my younger kids. Shaun doesn't come over and stay with us, so we have to arrange dinner out for a couple of hours at a time, just he and I."

"And how does Courtney get along with Shaun?" she asked, guessing the answer already.

He shifted. "She's not comfortable with Shaun. They don't really cross paths very often."

"How do you mean?"

"Shaun..." he cleared his throat, "makes people uncomfortable. It's just easier to spend time with him myself rather than deal with the issues when he comes over to the house." He stopped there.

She made a note on her tablet to stall a bit. "So, Shaun doesn't have a relationship with his younger siblings, then?"

"They're too little, and he's too old for them to have anything in common, so no, they don't have a relationship at this time."

"I understand. What can you tell me about Shaun as a child growing up? I'm especially interested in any differences you noticed before and after your divorce. Children tend to have a hard time coping with divorce no matter how well it is handled."

"Look, I love my son, okay? But he's always been a little... different. This goes back long before the divorce, despite whatever Karen said to the contrary. She doesn't want to see it, never has. She would rather chalk up his unusual behavior to me. But he started changing around age five. It started with communication, speech. He stopped being the chatterbox he was as a toddler. Then it became touch. He didn't want anyone to pick him up or hold him. Then it was eye contact." He paused, and this time, she saw a trace of something. *Sadness? Bewilderment?*

"I hate saying this, but dinners with my son are uncomfortable," he continued hesitantly. "He looks down at the table, his lap, the food, and of course, his phone the whole time. He only talks in response to my questions, and his answers are short. There is no real conversation. There is no banter like most fathers have with their sons. Sports? No way. He's not interested, and also, he's very... uncoordinated. So, we both suffer through it and can't get out of there fast enough."

This was a not unusual story with kids on the spectrum, perhaps Asperger's. It took steely determination and dedication for any parent to persist, to not be dissuaded by the behaviors. Determination that Thayer clearly lacked.

This next part would be tricky. It was important to get unvarnished truths, not tainted with a built-in point of view. "Unfortunately, we need to talk about the potential for violent behavior. Shaun has been accused of killing a classmate, who was apparently his close friend. Katie—do you remember her?"

"Of course I do. She and Shaun played together when they were really little, but I wasn't aware that they'd continued a friendship into adolescence. Not until after he... when everything happened."

He looked genuinely surprised, which made sense. He didn't live with his son, and when they saw each other, which appeared infrequently, there was no real conversion. Still, it seemed as though Karen might have kept him informed. Or maybe not, given her bitterness. "What about violent behavior? What can you tell me about that?"

"I've never seen him do anything physically violent. I find it difficult to believe he would all of a sudden do something like... what happened to Katie. But the reality is, I rarely see him. Unfortunately, I'd have to say I really don't know what the potential is for that with Shaun." He looked dismayed, and she believed him. "There was that one time with the neighbor's dog," he added suddenly.

"The neighbor's dog?" She'd heard something along these lines before, from Shaun's mother.

"He was taking care of the neighbor's dog, and something happened to it. The dog. Ah, I don't really know the details." He seemed to regret having brought it up, and perhaps knew more, but didn't want to say. *Protecting his son?*

Pretending ignorance, she asked, "What happened to the dog?"

"I wasn't there, but Karen told me about it. Apparently, the dog died while in Shaun's care." He sighed. "I feel terrible for my son; you have to understand that. I don't really know what to do about him. With him, or for him." His jaw worked, and his eyes fell away as though he was remembering things that troubled him.

It appeared genuine. That could be the concerned parent, the more empathetic person deeper down.

There wasn't anything left to ask, but as long as she was here and as long as he seemed somewhat open. *Why not?*

"I don't mean to offend you, but whatever your son has done, or however difficult it is to connect with him, he does need you. He needs a father who is involved in his life. He will have one of two pathways. One, with memories created by a loving dad who spent time with him and who made a continuous effort to connect no matter what. Or, two, not that."

She rose and stood at the door. "Pathway two is never good."

CHAPTER NINE

Jill checked the time. Late afternoon. She sat in the lobby of Bill Thayer's office building and placed a call.

"Hello?" Hillary Ramsay, Katie's mother, sounded impatient. And maybe something else.

"Hello, Mrs. Ramsay, my name is Dr. Jill Rhodes, and I'm looking into your daughter's case. I'm terribly sorry about your loss. I wondered if I could drop by quickly with just a few questions."

"Who are you? I'm sorry, but I'm not aware the D.A. is sending out investigators at this point. They know who killed my daughter," her voice caught then, "and it's just a matter of time before they charge him."

"I'm actually not working with the D.A. I am trying to help with the case, though, and I could really use your help."

"Well, if you're not with the D.A.'s office, then who are you working for? Wait a minute. Are you working with that... *that killer's attorney?*"

Jill sighed inwardly. This wasn't going to be easy. "Actually, yes, I was hired by Shaun's defense team, but I assure you, my investigation is neutral."

"You have got to be kidding! I don't know what you're trying to do here, but that boy *killed my daughter*. You can't possibly think I want anything to do with trying to get him off! Goodbye," she finished.

"Were you aware, Mrs. Ramsay, that your daughter had a boyfriend, an older guy?"

Silence.

"I have information that you may not have, and I could use your insights. I know this is terribly difficult. I promise you, if our conversation goes in a direction that you're uncomfortable with, we will stop, and I will leave."

More silence, then a heavy sigh. "Fine. But you'd better come now before my husband gets home."

A short time later, Jill sat in the Ramsay's living room in a house in the same neighborhood as Karen Thayer's, just a few doors down. She'd noted the undeveloped land near the homes, land that was filled with trees and undergrowth.

The neighborhood was in transition—original homeowners were leaving via downsizing, moving to adult/assisted living elsewhere, or because of death. Newer homeowners were buying and renovating. Existing, younger homeowners were updating their homes.

The Ramsay's home clearly fell into the latter category. It was very modern and featured an expansive, open-concept living, dining, and kitchen. The white leather sofa on which they sat was sleek and elegant, and the large grand piano in the corner topped off a meticulously decorated space. *Did anyone actually play it? Or was it just an accent piece?*

She thought of Karen Thayer, who lived just a few doors down but in a completely different home. A 1980s-era home, one which she couldn't possibly have the means to remodel. Though essentially neighbors, the families were at two different socio-economic levels, clearly.

What impact had their differing family portraits had on the friendship between the two teenagers? One child in an intact family with a modicum of wealth, the other child from a broken family, being raised by a single mom with little means and a disconnected and somewhat uncaring father.

Privileged teenagers could swing one of two ways. On the one hand, were the kids who eschewed showing off their family's wealth and made it a point to befriend the less fortunate.

On the other hand, there were the kids who formed tight circles of mutual affluence, avoiding the kids whose families were not members of their parents' country clubs.

Had Katie been in the first category? Had she continued her friendship with Shaun out of pity, aiming to do her part for the less fortunate? How would being pitied have affected Shaun, especially if he'd also found out about her boyfriend? The complexity of those agendas—pity, jealousy, and love—could have stirred the latent pot of violence.

"Thank you for agreeing to meet. I am terribly sorry for your loss, and I realize all of this is uncomfortable. I'm sorry to have to bring up painful issues, and I appreciate your willingness to talk. As I said, if you don't wish to continue, we can stop at any point."

"You'd better start with that comment on the phone about my daughter having a boyfriend. She wasn't allowed to date except in groups, and definitely not older boys." Hillary Ramsay's emotional strain was evident in her pinched look and clipped tones. Perhaps she was beautiful before tragedy befell her family, but now, her pale skin was stretched too tight, her watery gray eyes were darkly smudged underneath, and she wrapped her arms around her too-slender body as if she might fall apart at any moment.

"Yes, let's start there. I learned from talking to her friends at school that she was spending time with someone by the name of Trevor, and he is apparently in his early twenties." This was a bit of dissembling, but if she said *a friend* instead of *friends*, she'd be giving away Sophie's confidence. Hillary Ramsay, despite her fragile appearance, didn't strike her as the understanding sort, but instead, someone who might immediately finger Sophie as the culprit for something and call her, demanding answers.

"I knew everything Katie did, every friend, every activity. There wasn't *anything* about her that I didn't know. I'm her *mother*. And she didn't lie. We raised her to be honest. She would never hide something that significant from me, from us. Her friends are wrong. Kids gossip and say things about each other based on nothing. I know."

Hillary Ramsay's tone was brittle, her jaw as taut as a bow pulled as far back as it could go, her words like arrows let loose in defense of... *what?* What was she defending, protecting? Possibly her daughter's memory, her reputation.

Perhaps a mother's sense of self, that she'd done all the right things, that the tragedy that befell her daughter was in no way her own fault.

The biggest lie parents told themselves was that they knew

their teenagers intimately, knew what they did when away from home, knew what they thought and felt. And that they didn't lie to their parents. If she ever had her own kids, Jill promised herself she'd have much wider open eyes.

But then again, perhaps it was easier to sleep at night if you fooled yourself to some degree.

Jill sat back and breathed slowly, re-calibrating the tension between them. "You loved your daughter. That is very clear. I work with parents every day, and I have a sense for those who deeply love their child versus those who... I'm sorry to say, there are some parents who are not as invested as others. But when I listen to you, I hear so much love, so much devotion, and so much pain."

Hillary Ramsay jerked, suppressing a sob. "My daughter was a beautiful human being, and she had a wonderful life ahead of her. And it was all taken away by that... *weird boy.*" She spat out the last words. "I tried to talk her out of seeing him, but she wouldn't listen. She insisted Shaun was a good person, but I knew what was really going on. Katie always wanted to rescue every stray animal that crossed her path. She cried over baby birds that couldn't possibly survive. She wanted to take in a baby possum once. *A possum!* Disease-ridden rodents."

Now Hillary's eyes brimmed over with tears. "Shaun was a... a *stray* in her eyes, someone who needed rescuing. And maybe he did, with that clueless mother and absent father. But my daughter didn't need to rescue him. She needed to *stay away from him*. And now, it's too late." Jill pulled a tissue out of her bag and handed it to Hillary, who grabbed it and dabbed under her eyes.

"I'm so sorry. I just have one more question. What was it about Shaun that caused you to want your daughter to stay away from him?" She wasn't going to get anything else about the mystery boyfriend, Trevor, whose presence in the daughter's life wouldn't be acknowledged, not now, anyway.

"He was strange. He didn't make eye contact, so I never could get a sense of who he was. He glommed onto Katie at an early age, and he never made any other friends. At least none that I saw. And then, there was the neighbor's dog."

"The neighbor's dog?" Here it was again—the dog that died while in Shaun's care. *Would she hear a new perspective this time?*

"Shaun had a job taking care of the neighbor's dog while they traveled, and one time, the dog turned up dead."

"What happened to the dog?"

"I don't know, but the owner was terribly upset about it."

"How did you know he was taking care of the dog? I mean, did you see him walking the dog or see anything else?"

"I saw him walking the dog, and I thought it was strange. Who lets a kid like that take care of their pet? I wouldn't trust him," she stated adamantly.

"Can you give me the neighbor's name and number?"

"Sure." She did, and Jill wrote down the information. She rose to leave, but Hillary Ramsay stopped her.

"It was Sophie that talked about my daughter having a secret, older boyfriend, wasn't it?"

"Why do you say that?" Jill asked, stalling.

"Sophie was always jealous of Katie. She's cute, but Katie was beautiful. Sophie had friends, of course, but *everyone* loved Katie. She was a shining star in the constellation of her school's social galaxy." Her eyes shone with an intensity that bordered on disturbed. "I'm not surprised she'd try to hurt Katie's reputation, even after..." There she stopped as tears formed again. "It doesn't mean anything," she continued, "any gossip you hear. It doesn't mean anything."

Hillary rose abruptly and wobbled a bit as she did so. "I think it's time for you to go." At the door, Hillary took Jill's arm just before she walked out, a warning flashing in her eyes. "I hope you're not repeating any idle gossip about my daughter. And some fictitious boy."

"If it is gossip, I won't repeat it." Dr. Rhodes assured her. "Again, I'm so sorry for your loss."

Hillary sagged and let go of Jill's arm, though she seemed reluctant, as though it might be a lifeline. She slowly closed the door.

Jill sat in her vehicle briefly and called the neighbor, who was retired, and agreed to meet the next morning.

She'd dug into Asperger's earlier that day. One common trait was the tendency to become aggressive, especially when feeling thwarted in some way, with the possibility of blind rages. Had something happened when Shaun was taking care of the neighbor's dog, something that triggered rage, violence? Was this a pattern she was seeing? First, the dog, maybe other incidents, and finally, Katie?

As Jill drove away, she was so deep in thought she almost missed the call. "Hello?"

"Hey."

"Hey."

"I know we didn't have plans for tonight, but how about dinner?" Ethan sounded upbeat, and it reminded her of the way he'd called and asked her out when they first started dating.

He was traditional and believed in real dates, not just hanging out hoping for a hookup. At least, that was how it was in the beginning, and she'd relished it.

"Dinner, huh? What's on the menu? Besides me?"

"Well, you are a tasty appetizer, or maybe dessert, but there will be actual food on this date, missy." He told her the name of the restaurant, one of the city's most elegant, on the top floor of a high-rise downtown. Her left eyebrow raised just a fraction.

"Wow. Pricey much? Let's see… it's not our anniversary; it's not my birthday, so what's up?" She pulled up at a light and stopped.

"Do I need a motive to take my best girl out for a nice dinner? Before I forget, it would be nice if you could wear that little black dress, the one we picked out together, with the… neckline that I like so much."

She smiled, and the driver of the vehicle next to hers at the light looked at her funny. "I don't know. Maybe I'll wear jeans and boots."

"Ha, ha. You only wear jeans to the grocery store, and you never wear boots. Do you even own any boots?"

She laughed. "Okay, if you insist on objectifying me, I may as well give you something to look at." She glanced at the clock on her dashboard and thought about her list. "But I'll need you to make a later reservation. Eight o'clock should give me enough time to wrap everything up for the day."

"Really? What happened to office hours? You're normally done by 6:00 at the latest."

"Right, but I'm working on this special case, and there aren't any office hours. I'll see you at eight."

"Wait—I thought I'd pick you up, you know, like a real date, like we used to have." He sounded a bit disappointed

"That would be wonderful, but I'm not sure how long this is going to take." She said goodbye after making another promise and hung up. Right now, it was time for another bit of fact-finding.

CHAPTER TEN

"Hello, Detective Webb? It's Jill Rhodes. Listen, I have a couple of things to run by you, if you have time."

"As a matter of fact, I was just about to find someplace to grab something to eat. You're welcome to join me," he told her. A few minutes later, they met at a small, casual neighborhood restaurant that she knew well.

After perusing the menu, she ordered coffee while Detective Webb ordered a burger and fries. Then, he asked, "How can I help you?" He seemed genuine about the offer, so she relaxed a bit.

"If my memory serves me from the two courses in legal psychology I had in graduate school, the age of consent in Texas is around seventeen. Or is it eighteen? What can you tell me about that?"

"What is this about? Are you still working on the Shaun Thayer case?"

"Yes, I am, and I'm trying to get a sense of both Shaun and

Katie. I have reason to believe that someone may have taken advantage of Katie, possibly that guy Trevor, the one I told you about."

"Taken advantage? Are you talking about an assault of some kind?" He couldn't hide the shock on his face. "Look," he leaned forward, "the autopsy didn't show any signs of anything like that." *Was he humoring her?*

She sighed. "No, I don't mean an assault. What did you find out about him?"

"I did some research and didn't find any prior record on the guy, except for one thing. I found a drug possession case, plea bargained, but it was several years ago. Nothing since." He confirmed Trevor's age, and it solidified one of her suspicions.

But another disappointment set her back. Her earlier theory about Katie getting involved with someone who was involved in drugs was looking thin. Still, though, Cade could be involved in dealing drugs and hadn't been caught. Not yet. She knew she was grasping at straws.

"What were you talking about earlier, about an assault?"

"I'm not talking about rape, if that's what you're asking. I'm speaking in the statutory sense. What exactly is the age at which a teenager can give consent in Texas—in the legal sense?"

"It's seventeen, although the law tends to turn a blind eye if the sixteen-year-old, for example, has sex with a boyfriend who is the same age or one or two years older. In some states, they have what's called the Romeo and Juliet exemption for teenagers having sex who are close in age," he said a bit sarcastically, "but in Texas, there is no such exemption. Still, though, it's almost unheard of for anyone to utilize the laws and prosecute those kids."

"But what if the boyfriend is five or six years older? What if he's in his twenties and she's fifteen?"

"That's different. He can be charged with a second-degree felony, *indecency with a child*." His face tightened. "I think you'd better tell me what this is about."

"I will, but first, can you tell me what happens in a practical sense? If a fifteen-year-old meets a guy a few years older and dates him, who really cares? Girls that age can be very mature." She didn't really see it that way but wanted to push it to see what Detective Webb might tell her.

"If the girl's parents were stupid enough to let it happen, if they knew, then nothing would be done about it. Unfortunately, there are parents who are so clueless they think their teenage daughter knows what's best for her. Too many parents are afraid to say 'no' to their kids. They try instead to be friends, let them make decisions that wreck their lives because they're not old enough to see future consequences."

Interesting. The tone of Webb's voice implied he was protective of women. Perhaps righteously indignant about the rampant exploitation of girls? "From talking to Katie's friends," again the slight fudging, "I believe she was seeing that guy Trevor, and you've confirmed he's in his late twenties. I don't know for sure they were having sex, but I think it's possible." She paused, her mouth twisting. "But I'm not sure. Teenagers, as you know, can embellish."

"Katie was fifteen, not sixteen. The law takes it more seriously when the age disparity is greater, and in this case, it sounds serious. I wonder if her parents knew."

"Her mother didn't, unless she lied to me. She seemed surprised when I told her Katie was seeing an older boy, defensive, even. She insisted she knew everything about her daughter and that there was no boyfriend."

"I think we both know how clueless parents can be about their teenagers' activities," he said.

Detective Webb's food arrived with her coffee, and he took a huge bite of the burger, chewing thoughtfully. Somehow, he managed to keep it from looking sloppy as he devoured his food. She found herself noticing his lips and slid her eyes away, embarrassed. She cleared her throat. "Well, what happens now?"

"About statutory rape, in this case? Nothing. Katie's not here to provide testimony, and her parents, or at least her mother, didn't know it was happening. Typically, the parents bring cases like this to the attention of law enforcement, who then act on the information. Prosecutors make the decision to file charges, and they typically would in a case like this, given the age disparity."

Too bad. Wait. "There's something else. I think Katie's best girlfriend, Sophie Bradshaw, who is probably the same age, was also seeing the guy, and she pretty much confessed they were having sex. What about that? Can you go after the guy with that information?"

"I can if Sophie is willing to testify about it. But you are required by law to report something like this, aren't you? That's a start."

Of course, she was. She knew that. It had tickled at the back of her mind ever since her conversation with Sophie. But she hadn't wanted to take those steps, not yet. But now, Detective Webb knew, and there was no turning back. "How about this? Consider it reported—to you."

He eyed her carefully. "Are you sure enough about the facts at this point to file a formal complaint? Because once we take that step, it can't be undone. Only the prosecutor can decide about charges, not me, and not you or anyone else. We seem to be missing a lot of what we build cases like this on, mainly Sophie's willingness to talk about the fact that this guy had sex with her."

Jill chewed her lip. She didn't really have enough solid facts at this point. Sophie's 'confession' had been given as a result of Jill's—albeit mild—manipulation, and with the belief that it wouldn't go any further than that. Also, Sophie seemed clueless that it was illegal for Trevor to have sex with her.

But what if Sophie were approached by law enforcement? Would she admit it if the police called her in? Or would she clam up, protect her ex-boyfriend? Or clam up out of fear in general?

"If I do file a report, and I think I have to, what happens next?"

"Since she's a juvenile, we would have her parents bring her to a children's advocacy center for questioning." He seemed to note her concern. "Don't worry; the process with children is far gentler than it is with adult witnesses and victims. She would be interviewed on video by people who work with children so that the process wouldn't have to be repeated over and over again, to minimize the trauma of the questioning."

That sounded better. "And then what?"

"Then, we would pick up Cade and bring him in for questioning, in his case, not so gently. I don't mean he'd be hurt," he said at her alarmed look. "I mean, he would be read his rights, and if he refused an attorney, he would be subjected to the same interview process all adults get. If he asks for an attorney, one will be appointed. Depending on how compelling her testimony, charges could be filed whether or not he confesses." He looked at her with concern. "Don't feel too sorry for this guy. He has no business messing around with teenage girls."

"Oh, I don't feel sorry for him," she said, meaning it. "It's Sophie I'm concerned about. It's not okay what he did to her, and possibly to Katie. But now, her secrets will be out in the open.

She may or may not understand why it's important for Trevor to be held accountable for his actions. It's going to be rough on her, either way."

Detective Webb gave her a look of compassion, of empathy, and it touched her. She dropped her eyes, lifting her coffee cup for a sip to cover the flush she felt creeping up her neck. "I have to go," she said, putting her cup down and standing to leave.

"We'll have to fill out some paperwork. When do you want to take care of that?" he asked, peering up at her.

He wasn't going to let her get away that easily. He was like a dog with a bone. But there were other things to take care of. "Tomorrow morning." She glanced at her watch and gasped. *6:25.* "Wait," she said, one more question in mind. "Did you find out where Trevor Cade works, by any chance?"

Driving, she reflected on the so-called boyfriend, Trevor. According to Sophie, Katie had intended to confront him the day she was killed. She'd been thinking Trevor might be the motive for Shaun flying into a rage. But what if it was Trevor that had become enraged when Katie broke up with him?

Or perhaps she'd threatened him with exposure for having sex with a minor. With two minors. He'd be looking at federal prison. That was strong motive.

At home, she peeled off her jacket and shoes as soon as she reached the bedroom, leaving things where they fell. But she took a moment and turned on the television to watch the news while she dressed for dinner. The top story stopped her in her tracks.

News cameras were trained on a candlelight vigil for Katie Ramsay. Their minister, using a microphone and speakers so he could be heard over the crowd, prayed for Katie and her parents. Katie's father, Jeff Ramsay, whom she'd not yet interviewed, spoke of his loving daughter's life, cut tragically short, his voice breaking.

Hillary Ramsay, eyes flashing with conviction, called for her daughter's killer to be charged, asking why nothing had been done.

The camera focused on a well-known City Councilman who stood tall next to Katie's parents, with a commanding presence, his hand on Jeff Ramsay's shoulder. He called for justice, challenging the D.A. to do his job and prosecute the murderer.

And, finally, the Councilman threw out the bait. "We all understand the tragedy this is for the Thayers, and we may have compassion for them, but that is nothing compared to the sorrow and grief of the Ramsays. The D.A. needs to take action and let justice take place." The camera panned the gathering crowd of neighbors. *Justice for Katie* read one sign, thrust high by a woman with an angry expression.

Jill grabbed her phone.

The vigil was at the home of the Ramsay's, right down the street from Karen and Shaun Thayer's home. Justice only had a short walk, three houses down the sidewalk.

CHAPTER ELEVEN

She drove down the street, attempting to get to the Thayer's home, but it was jammed with media and other vehicles. Lights blazed from the Ramsay's home and from cameras trained on the reporters who stood with their backs to the house, speaking earnestly about the unfolding tragedy of two families whose paths had crossed in a terrible way.

The small crowd of people, some waving signs, moved restlessly. As she passed, Jill saw one woman point down the street toward the Thayer's house. The crowd began to move.

There was no place to park. Maybe one street over, or two streets, would work, and she could walk back to the Thayer's. But just as she drove past their home, Karen texted Jill and told her to drive around back. She found her way around the block, into the alleyway, and found Karen at her open garage door, drove in, and parked.

In the modest living room, Karen peered out the front window and gasped. Like a swarm of hungry insects, media people and the sign-waving crowd flowed down the street from the Ramsay's home and onto Karen's lawn. Soon, the intense camera lights were trained at Karen's front door, and the crowd began chanting *justice for Katie*. Someone yelled something rude, filled with expletives, directed at Karen Thayer. Something about their neighborhood no longer being safe.

She turned to Jill, face pale, eyes huge. "Oh, my God! What am I going to do?"

"Where's Shaun?"

"He's at his grandmother's house. I felt like he should be somewhere else now that there's a lot more media attention."

"That was good thinking. Let's start with some hot tea and find somewhere else to sit." She hoped the media cameras would inhibit the crowd from doing anything violent.

They busied themselves with the most ordinary of things. Karen boiled water, Jill selected mint for herself, and English Breakfast for Karen, and they carried steaming cups to the small family room at the back of the house, further away from the lights and the rising buzz of voices.

"How is Shaun?" Jill asked carefully.

Karen Thayer's hand shook as she lifted her cup of tea. "I don't know. He still won't talk except about day-to-day things, and even then, it's just the bare minimum. I don't think he's sleeping at night, not enough, anyway. I'm going to have to figure out what to do about school. He doesn't want to go back, and I don't want to force him. Our lives are in some kind of terrible limbo." Her shadowed blue eyes filled with tears. "I have never cried so much in my life. I'm sorry," she whispered.

"There's nothing to be sorry for – you're having a normal

reaction to extreme events. Getting support is crucial. Did you call the number I gave you?"

"I did, and I have an appointment for tomorrow. Thank you for that."

"Of course. I'm wondering what you need to do tonight to take care of yourself. It doesn't seem like a good idea for you to stay here. No one knows my vehicle, so I can drive you somewhere, and you can recover your car later. How about your parents, so you could be with Shaun too?

"Shaun's with my ex-husband's family. My parents live out of state, and I rarely see them. They're not an option," she explained. "Besides, *this is my home*. I don't want to give it up because of a few reporters. Or those other people." Though her words were brave, her voice betrayed the fear behind them.

Humans need to feel they are a part of the tribe. If the crowd turns on you, you can't help but feel threatened to the core. Even when that crowd isn't your actual tribe, doesn't care about you at all, and only wants to use you to grab the next headline. Social threats are indistinguishable from physical threats to the emotional brain.

But though Karen's fear was palpable, there was something else, something that frightened her even more than the crowd of reporters outside the house.

"There's something else you're worried about, isn't there," Jill prodded gently.

Karen looked down at her lap, at her hands twisting with one another. Seeing them in surprise, as if they belonged to someone else, she stopped, wiped her hands along her jeans, and said nothing. But her hands gripped the sides of her legs.

Jill waited.

"I'm afraid of what's going to happen to Shaun. There's this thing... something that happened a long time ago, but I'm afraid it's going to get out there. Do you remember me telling you about the neighbor's dog that died while Shaun was taking care of him?" Jill nodded, and the story poured out.

A few months earlier

Karen sat at the kitchen table, trying to get her bank account to balance. But that wasn't really the point, was it? What difference did it make if she had two hundred eight five dollars and twenty-three cents or two hundred eighty-four dollars and ninety-nine cents? Either way, there was too much month left for the amount of cash in her account.

She checked the clock. Shaun had been gone for well over an hour. She'd learned to time his doggy-care excursions, mindful of the length of time it took for him to complete each step on the carefully written list. *Enter house, retrieve leash, clip it on, walk Rocco.* That took twenty minutes, tops. *Feed him and refresh his water bowl.* That took ten minutes. *Check the house, making sure all the mail is in, and the papers retrieved and left inside the front door, check all door and window locks, leave, and lock the front door.* That took five minutes at most.

He was always on time, always. He never missed a beat, rigorously adhering to his schedule, which was super important to Shaun. There was nothing wrong with being on time, every time, and the extreme punctuality with which Shaun managed his days was one of the few advantages of being him, of being wired the way he was wired. That, and his near-perfect grades in every science and math class. Thirty-five minutes to do all of it, and it was now well over an hour. *Where was he?*

She abandoned the bank balancing project midway, slid on sandals, and made her way to the neighbor's home on the other side of the street, two houses down. At the front door, she paused, then felt silly. The door was unlocked, so she opened it cautiously. Inside, it was quiet. *Dead quiet.*

She felt strange walking through her neighbor's house. Ellen, a retired widow who frequently traveled, kept a tidy home. She was often seen walking briskly through the neighborhood, smiling, stopping to chat with everyone, Rocco proudly trotting beside her. He was a friendly mixed breed who loved every person and every dog he saw.

Ellen smiled and said good morning when she passed Karen, who sometimes encountered her neighbor while retrieving the morning paper. But Karen had never taken the friendliness as anything more than a superficial greeting.

"Shaun?" But there was no reply or indication that he'd heard her. She stepped quietly past the formal dining room, the main living area, and the kitchen. *Where was Shaun? Where was Rocco?* Anxiety sent small tremors into her belly. *Had Shaun finished and left?* But the front door wouldn't be left unlocked. Plus, he had no place to go. Nothing appeared disturbed or out of place.

Out of the corner of her eye, she saw color on the patio outside—Shaun's royal blue tee shirt. Relief flooded her. She stepped outside, and the relief vanished.

Shaun sat still, Rocco at his feet, body splayed and unmoving. He stared straight ahead; his hands were folded in his lap. He looked up briefly at his mother's approach, face expressionless, then looked back down.

"Shaun, what happened? What's wrong with Rocco?" She

knelt by the dog, ran her hands along the furry body, felt for broken bones, looked for blood. She could see nothing wrong.

"Small dogs, under 15 pounds, on average live to be twelve years of age, although large dogs don't live as long. Dogs often die of the same things people die from—kidney failure, liver disease. Even cancer." He made no eye contact with her as he spoke in a robotic voice. "Sometimes, they die because of the things people do."

"What things, Shaun? What did you… what happened to Rocco? Shaun, do you hear me?" She reached out to shake him out of his distant stare, but he jerked away.

"I happened to Rocco."

"What do you mean? Shaun, talk to me, please. Tell me what happened."

But he said no more, and she never got an answer. Instead, she gently carried Rocco inside, then retrieved her car and drove him to the veterinarian whose name had been left with Shaun. The vet took care of Rocco from there, and when Ellen got back, she called Karen to find out what had happened. But Karen had no answers, and Ellen was now a neighbor she avoided.

When Karen finished her story, she turned to Jill, pain and fear etching her features. "What if the police find out about Ellen, and she tells them about Shaun and Rocco?"

"I don't know." She didn't tell Karen she planned to meet with Ellen the next day. There wasn't any reason to get her hopes up about what was probably a pointless exercise since Shaun had declared himself as the direct cause of Rocco's death. This investigation had turned, once again, into further confirmation of Shaun's guilt. But it also held signs of a couple of back doors through which he might be able to escape doing the kind of prison time that would certainly ruin his life and possibly destroy him. Even as she had that thought, Jill felt a twinge of guilt on Katie's behalf.

Someone rang the front doorbell. They froze, looking at each other. The doorbell rang again, then again, repeatedly. Someone banged on the door, and they heard muffled shouting.

Karen's cell phone rang, and at the same time, so did Jill's. She reached for her own as Karen answered hers. Both listened intently, asking a couple of questions, and ending their calls at the same moment.

"Oh, dear God. They're going to take Shaun to court and petition to try him as an adult. *Tomorrow.*" Karen covered her mouth and sobbed in agony. "That was Peter McClure, my attorney."

And Jill had heard the same thing from Nancy Barrett, who'd just called her. Their window of time to find a way to help Shaun was rapidly closing. It might even be completely closed.

The doorbell rang again, and someone banged on it. Karen jumped. That was enough. Jill went to the door and swung it open, immediately regretting the impulse as the white-hot lights of multiple cameras blinded her. She held a hand up to shade her eyes, and as she did, questions were fired in her direction.

Where is Karen Thayer? Who are you? Not getting an answer, they mistook her for a representative of some kind and peppered her with questions.

Does Ms. Thayer know her son is going to be tried as an adult? Will she take him in willingly? What happened to Katie Ramsay?

And on and on.

Impulsively, Jill spoke. "Ms. Thayer is unavailable for comment.

I urge you all to consider that the Thayer's son is innocent until proven guilty by a court of law. There are new developments in this case, and the investigation into Katie Ramsay's death is ongoing. If anyone has any information about this case, please contact Detective Webb with the Dallas police," she added, doing her best to look directly into a nearby camera. "For now, you can all go home."

More questions were instantly fired, more urgent than before. She tried frantically to close the door, but someone stuck a shoe in the gap and blocked her.

CHAPTER TWELVE

Jill tried again to close the door. "Please move your foot. You are trespassing. I will be forced to call law enforcement if you don't leave immediately."

"Great. Not necessary, though, since I *am* law enforcement." Detective Nick Webb's voice held a trace of irony.

"Oh." It was all she could manage as she looked up in surprise. "What are you doing here?"

"How about letting me in first? Probably not good having me stand here with you like this, with all the cameras rolling."

Reluctantly, she held the door open just wide enough to let him in.

"Wait," he said before she could close the door. "Let me take care of this." He turned and faced the crowd, holding up his hands. When they quieted, he explained who he was and that there would be a press conference the following morning. He asked them to kindly leave of their own volition while conveying an unspoken warning.

Reluctantly, they broke down their equipment and dispersed, although a couple of them shot angry looks at Detective Webb as they departed.

She thanked him, but he waved her off. "Wow. What you did just then was possibly the stupidest thing I've seen in a long time."

Stung, she began to protest, but he stopped her. "And it was possibly the most brilliant too."

Stunned, she motioned him into the closest room, a formal dining room just to the side of the front hallway, out of earshot of Karen. "What do you mean?"

"The thing about the media is that they can be your friend or your foe, depending on the circumstances. As a whole, it's a free-for-all, everyone vying for the most riveting headline. But individually, you sometimes find that rare journalist that is still interested in truth and justice."

"This is kind of like those species that are almost extinct, right?"

He smiled. "Right. But tonight, we don't have the luxury of finding that kind of journalist. Time is running out. In fact, that's why I'm here. I'm afraid Shaun will be charged tomorrow."

Her heart sank. "We have to tell Karen." But she thought of something else. "Wait. You said possibly brilliant."

"If your words make it on the air, and you never know what clip they will show, there's a chance that someone with more information will step forward."

She took that in, saying nothing. Information might be offered in Shaun's defense, helping him. Or there might be information brought forward that damned him for good. And she'd instigated it.

Unsure at that point, she asked him to wait for a moment. She found Karen hiding in the powder room. "Detective Webb wants to see you, Karen." Seeing her hesitation, she said, "I don't think it will help for you to avoid him. Whatever he has to say, someone has to tell you anyway. But don't say anything to him. Just listen." she said, drawing on her extensive experience watching crime shows, channeling her inner legal counsel.

Looking like she might collapse from the stress, Karen Thayer nevertheless cracked opened the powder room door. "Will you be there with me?" she asked.

"Of course."

In the dining room, Detective Webb waited, seated at the table. "Thanks for seeing me, Ms. Thayer," he said, rising and shaking her hand. "This isn't anything formal, just a heads up. The D.A. is going to ask for your son to be tried as an adult. We believe he will then get a warrant for Shaun's arrest, but we can probably sidestep the media scene by having you bring him in for questioning. Either way, he has to come in. I just wanted you to know so you can be prepared." He said it to Karen, but his eyes slid to Jill's as he said it.

Karen gulped and nodded, her eyes pleading with Jill as if she alone could stop the cold march of the justice machine.

But she couldn't. Helpless, Jill did the only thing she could do. "This is very stressful, Karen, but let's focus on getting ready for tomorrow." Her practicality was her go-to tool in times of hardship.

"Are you sure you want to stay here tonight?" she asked again. Resolved to stay, Karen shook her head. "Okay, well, consider taking something to help you sleep, perhaps an analgesic. You'll want your rest for tomorrow. Call your attorney first thing in the morning. Eat. Your body is more resilient if you take care of it, even if you're not hungry. Shaun needs you to be strong for him tomorrow, and you can't do that if you don't take care of yourself."

She walked Detective Webb to the front door. He stopped, and she wound up stuck between him and the door while he watched her carefully. "What time do you want to get together tomorrow to do the paperwork on the other case we discussed?"

She hesitated. "I'm not sure. I think it's fine if we do it later in the day. I have things to do for Karen Thayer in the morning, and it's time sensitive because of what's happening later." She couldn't help exuding tension. Detective Webb was on the other side of the work she was doing for the Thayers. He would soon put handcuffs on a teenage boy, one who may not have known what he was doing.

Was he innocent? Likely not. But he may have been a victim of life circumstances that gradually bent him until he broke. And unless she could help him, his life would be ruined.

Webb nodded sympathetically. "Your call." He continued to stand there, so she pulled open the door.

"Dr. Rhodes," he began.

"Jill, please."

"Jill. I want you to know that I take no joy out of putting a teenage boy in prison. Sometimes the job means witnessing a tragedy, lives ruined all around, while at the same time doing what I have to do, which is to uphold the law."

"I understand, Detective Webb, but—"

"Nick, please."

"Nick. I do understand your job, but I have a job to do as well. I am trying to minimize the damage to a kid who may not be guilty of the crime he's being accused of."

As she said it, something rose up. A feeling, an instinct, a glimmer of something that didn't live in hard data but that was no less real. "In fact, I believe he *is* innocent, and I aim to help prove it." The boldness of her declaration shocked her as though it had come from someone else.

Nick's eyes widened with a look that said, *wow, how naïve can you be?* "I wish that were true, believe me. But I'm afraid you are going to be disappointed. And I hope you don't give this boy's family a lot of false hope."

She pulled the door open wider, flushed with indignation, and stung by the criticism. "I will be in touch." But her voice was cold as ice.

"I'm sure you will." He stepped out, now clearly stung as well.

But she didn't care about that at the moment. She closed the door a little forcefully. She hadn't yet stepped away when the doorbell rang again.

"I *said* I would be in touch, and there's nothing else for you to do here tonight!" she flung as she opened the door but stopped in surprise. Bill Thayer, looking a little pale and uncertain, stood there on the threshold.

"Er...I'm sorry to intrude, but I wanted to find out how Karen and Shaun were doing." He shifted awkwardly. "Um, what are you doing here, Dr. Rhodes?"

"You're not intruding, and I was just leaving."

In the family room, Karen looked up in shock at Bill, who sat down and touched her shoulder tentatively. "I saw Dr. Rhodes on the news in front of the house. I heard what she and the detective said. What can I do to help?"

The dam broke then, and Jill slipped out after a last glimpse of Bill Thayer holding Karen while she sobbed, the two of them putting their heads together in sorrow over their child.

Maybe something good would emerge out of all this pain.

THE EXPERT WITNESS

Jill slowed and pulled over a few blocks away from Karen Thayer's home and checked her cell. It was on silent, but she didn't remember putting it in that mode. She gasped at the small red number nine attached to her text icon and the number five attached to her phone icon.

Opening one, she saw the numerous texts from Ethan. *I'm here...* and later, *waiting for you, Miss better late than never... Okay, 30 minutes... Where are you?!* Several others with various emojis, the tone escalating from persistence to anger. Then the final one, *At the bar now, CALL ME.*

CHAPTER THIRTEEN

Jill made the call to Ethan, but it went straight to voice mail. She left a remorseful apology. But how do you explain entirely forgetting the person you supposedly love? Yes, she'd been caught up in the case and the drama of the media. Yes, she was needed by Karen Thayer, and no, it wasn't something that could have been put off.

But it only takes a moment to send a text message explaining that you will be delayed or possibly be unable to show up.

At home, after putting on sweats and pouring a glass of chilled chardonnay, she tried Ethan again, leaving another apology. She thought about families.

Most of her friends were married with young children. She thought about what went before having children and what happened later, not only for her friends but her clients.

The anticipation of birth—the ultrasounds, the bodily changes, the support, or lack thereof from a spouse, the baby showers, the carefully decorated room with pinks and blues, or neither so as to avoid gender typing, the ridiculous number of choices of parenting advice in book form, or blogs, read and adopted zealously, or ignored.

As a family therapist, she never knew which way to guide new parents but had learned over the years to ask a few simple questions. *What should you do so you feel best about yourselves as parents? How can you love your children to the best of your ability? What did your parents do that was right and you want to repeat? What did they fail to do? What did they do that didn't work, and you want to avoid it?*

Despite her training, she couldn't say she owned the secrets to great parenting. And the reality was that all parents learned on the job, just as therapists did. And all children were different, thus requiring a unique approach.

Who knew which child would be the concert pianist or the Olympic medalist? And which would get addicted to drugs and destroy his life? How did you raise a child to become an adult according to your own aspirations for her?

One of the most frightening things about parenting was the reality of choice. Kids started making their own choices at a fairly young age, and as much as parents tried to guide them, it was inevitable they'd break free and pursue their own desires.

A parent's job is to keep them safe and help them mature. A kid's job was to establish independence. Two jobs inherently at odds with one another.

She reflected on the Thayers and the Ramsays, two families living on the same street but worlds apart. And the unlikely friendship between two kids that should have faded after grade school but hadn't. How the two families had been drawn together early in their children's lives, and now, in the most tragic of ways.

What did these two kids have in common? What had they shared, and how had their secrets and dreams changed as they left childhood behind and morphed into hormone-filled teens? What choices had they made, and how had those choices led them to a nightmare in the woods, to the death of one, and the pending incarceration of the other?

She curled up on the sofa after draining her wine, pulled a throw over her legs, and dozed off. But the buzzing and pounding at her door woke her a short time later. She dragged herself over and let Ethan in.

"Ethan, I'm so sorry. This case blew up into some things I never planned for, and I went over to the home of the woman whose son is about to be charged with murder. I'm sorry you had to sit there and wait for me."

But he didn't seem to hear her. "I know, I know. I saw the news later. But couldn't you have sent me a text? How about a quick call? Jeez, don't I even rate a real kiss-off? You totally ghosted me, Jill!"

"I had my phone on silent. I'm so sorry. But I'm exhausted. Can we talk about it tomorrow? I have another long day ahead of me."

Anger and something else fought for priority on Ethan's face. He pulled her over to the sofa and clumsily pushed her down on it. "I kind of had something planned for tonight, and it should have been really romantic, but now... I know this is a long time coming, and I know you've been waiting for it, and—" He stopped and sat down next to her looking pale.

Dread filled her heart. "Ethan, we're both tired, and you're..." The fumes wafting from him told the story of how he'd filled his evening. But saying it out loud would only inflame him. "Let's talk tomorrow. Come on, let's go to bed. You can sleep here. You didn't drive, did you?"

"Of course not! Do you think I'm stupid?"

"No, you know I don't." She tried to stand, but he pulled her down and stood instead.

"Nope. Gonna do what I came to do." He wobbled but got on one knee. "Jill Rhodes, I love you back to the moon… I mean to the moon and back…" He sounded sloppy now, chuckling at his own faux pas. "Anyway, where was I? Oh, yeah," and now he looked childlike, and that clawed at her heart. "Will you marry me?" He fumbled in his pocket, then laughed crazily. "Whoops! Forgot the ring… the one I haven't bought yet… oh, well, honey, you can choose it later, right? You're so damn picky anyway I'd probably get one you wanted to return." He laughed again at his own joke, smiling up at her, love in his eyes, but not the kind she wanted.

She froze.

He grinned and wobbled on his knees. "I said, will you marry me? Usually, the person hearing that question answers with a yes or a no. Or a *hell no*." His voice was playful, but as the silence stretched, his expression turned sour.

This was all wrong. The timing, his drunken state. She thought about the couple in the restaurant, how blissful they'd seemed, how others had caught the contagious joy, and then, the scattered applause and the smiles. "Ethan, you know I love you, don't you? But now, like this—"

He lurched to his feet, his face mottled with anger, hurt, and alcohol. "I guess I have my answer." He stumbled toward the door, but she rushed and blocked it.

"Don't leave, Ethan. Please. Stay here. We'll talk tomorrow, I promise. I'm not saying *no*; I'm just saying *not now*. Okay?"

But he'd pulled out his cell and ordered a ride. Before she knew it, he was gone, and her living room was silent again, an emotional stew of loss and anger hanging in the air. Her chest felt heavy, and exhaustion dragged at her limbs. She curled back up on the sofa and fell into an uneasy sleep, Nick's gray-green eyes haunting her dreams.

CHAPTER FOURTEEN

As she drove, Jill glanced at her phone periodically, saddened again at the blank screen. After several texts over the course of the early morning hours, Ethan still hadn't responded.

In all her dreams about getting engaged, none of them featured the sad mixture of Ethan's fumbling, ill-timed gesture and her aversion to the way it was done. Overshadowing all of it was the absence of elation, celebration, and the beginning of planning their future. Unfortunately, moments like that can't be undone and tend to leave a lingering sense of loss. She sighed. The path forward for them was shaky at best.

Her thoughts turned to the case. This morning's interview would be routine, but she needed to be certain before going to the next steps. Back in Shaun and Katie's neighborhood again, she parked and sat quietly for a moment.

Sunlight dappled the street, a dog barked nearby, and blue jays called, answered by a mockingbird. It was early and quiet, and a slight breeze moved the tops of the live oaks. Looking up and down the quiet suburban street, you could never tell that tragedy had struck two families. Yet the birds trilled, the late autumn leaves fell, and lives streamed forward.

No one knew what went on behind other people's closed doors or what went on inside each person's mind. What had Shaun thought about, what had he wanted, and what had he done the day Ellen's dog Rocco died?

This investigation was proving to be very different than her everyday practice. People came to her and sat in her office, a calm but sterile environment, and talked about their lives while in a safe cocoon, sheltered by the empathic listening of a professional.

But how much of their lives did they truly reveal to her?

How much had she missed because she never saw the *context* of their lives—the streets on which they lived, the friends and extended family with differing perspectives? The state of their homes inside, which told its own stories about the daily goings on, the cycles of love, connection, joy, disconnection, loss, pain, and grief.

And what of the remainders of their rage? The hollow sorrows they'd left behind them in other people's hearts, never to be spoken of in the therapist's office. Because most people came to therapy to talk about their own worries, pains, and losses. Therapy was, after all, about the person sitting in the chair, rarely about those the patient affected, except to complain about them. Or point the finger at them as the cause of the patient's pain.

"Thank you for seeing me," Jill said after they were settled in

Ellen's tidy living room. The house was neat and clean but clearly a bit dated. "I know this is awkward, but I'm trying to help with Shaun's case. First, what can you tell me about him? I know he took care of your dog, Rocco, some time ago."

Ellen's eyes softened. She was a study in contrasts. She held her lean body upright, her shoulders rounded with muscles, her forearms ropy. She was tightly toned all over, unusual for her age, which Jill guessed around late fifties.

But her expression was kind, her jaws weren't clenched, and her eyes were open and expressive. It was a prejudice, she knew, perhaps born of Jill's overall aversion to exercise, but she equated athletic types with a personality structure of tension and perfectionism, with a bias toward action.

Perhaps not so true in this case.

Jill noticed a dog chew toy poking out from under the sofa, looking well-worn.

"I wondered if anyone would ever ask. You're the first. I thought about going to the police, but I wasn't sure." Ellen sighed. "I try to make friends around me. Life is so much nicer when you know your neighbors. When you feel like you can rely on them, and they on you, isn't it? I tried to get to know Shaun's mother, but I never got very far. She seemed shy or just aloof."

"How did you get to know Shaun?"

She smiled. "That's a funny story. I was walking Rocco one day, and all of a sudden, he stopped and began making this choking noise. Shaun was outside in his yard, nearby, and he started talking about it."

He's coughing, so that means he's getting air into his lungs. You know when a person or an animal is really choking because there's no sound. That means the airway is completely blocked. You have to compress the diaphragm hard after making sure the throat isn't blocked. Whatever is in there will pop out. But your dog is not choking.*

"And, of course, he was right. Rocco stopped making that noise, wagged his tail, and was ready to go. I asked Shaun how he knew so much about it, and he told me he read medical journals as a hobby. *Medical journals*—can you imagine? That would be like reading stereo instructions for me… oh, sorry. I'm old enough to remember stereos."

Jill smiled. Ellen reminded her of someone. *Crystal, her mom.* On one of her really good days. She could be light-hearted, reminiscing about the past in an amusing way.

"Anyway, after that, I noticed he'd be out when I walked Rocco, almost as if he were seeking companionship. I mean, I walked him at the same time every day, so it wasn't hard for Shaun to know. Dogs love routine, you know."

Right on cue, a golden retriever trotted into the room, came over, and nuzzled Ellen first, then, after checking the social cues, approached Jill for pets. Then, she circled once and plopped on the floor next to Jill. "That's Elsa." Ellen beamed at her dog, who looked up, grinned enthusiastically, and huffed once.

"How did it come about that Shaun took care of Rocco?"

"Well, Shaun and I chatted almost daily then, mostly about medical stuff. He was full of facts and data in an unending stream. A couple of times, I made mental notes and looked things up later, thinking maybe he was using Dr. Google as a reference. But I quickly discovered he knew things that weren't discoverable with a quick internet search. He's got one of those photographic memories, I think. Anyway, I could see how much he responded to Rocco, the affection, and how safe Rocco felt with him. Dogs are great judges of character, and Rocco loved Shaun. Our outside walking friendship turned into dog-sitting."

Eidetic memory—the ability to recall images and information in far greater detail and for longer periods of time than most people—in one specific focal area, medicine. Shaun's obsession with learning and sharing medical knowledge was another signpost of Asperger's.

"What happened on the day Rocco died?" Jill asked.

"Well, the truth is, I don't know for sure since I wasn't there, but I do have a pretty good idea."

"I was told Shaun… did something to him, caused his death in some way."

"What?" Ellen looked shocked. "That's crazy! Who told you that, the police? Well, it's a lie, I can tell you that," she said indignantly. "Shaun wouldn't hurt a fly! He would never hurt Rocco, not in any way."

Jill was confused. "But I was told that you were upset after Rocco died and that you blamed Shaun for his death."

"*What?* Where did you hear that?" But knowing slowly crept into her eyes. "I think I know. It was Hillary Ramsay, wasn't it? She's never liked Shaun, despite his friendship with her daughter. She couldn't help herself, even telling me things I didn't care for, clueless that I was Shaun's friend." Her lips tightened.

Jill sat quietly.

"Or maybe it was Karen, his mother," Ellen speculated further. "You know, after Rocco died, I tried to talk to Karen. I wanted to tell her it was okay, that I wasn't upset about Rocco, that it wasn't Shaun's fault. But she just avoided me." Her face reflected her obvious sadness.

"What happened to Rocco?"

"Rocco was old, and I'd been told he would probably go downhill suddenly. But he was doing well before my trip, and I knew Shaun would take great care of him, so I wasn't that concerned. Anyway, when I got back, Rocco's vet was clear. He'd just sort of flamed out from organ failure due to old age."

Jill sat back and thought. *Shaun didn't kill Rocco. Shaun hadn't flown into a violent rage and killed the sweet pet he was taking care of.*

This changed things, but now, a number of things slid into focus, rearranging themselves into a new pattern for Jill. "This is important, Ellen. Are you certain that Shaun didn't hurt Rocco?"

"I'm absolutely certain. He was so gentle, so loving with him. They had a special bond. I tried to tell Shaun it was okay afterward, but I couldn't get through to him. He just stood there, eyes down, with that tic of his—the blinking—and wouldn't say anything. It was hard enough losing Rocco, but I felt like I lost Shaun as well."

After letting that revelation settle, Jill asked a few more questions, seeking more information about Katie and her family. Yes, Ellen had seen Katie and her parents, but only briefly as they drove past her while dog walking. No, she hadn't heard any useful information about them.

"What about Katie and Shaun's friendship?" Jill asked. Since Ellen spent time with Shaun, maybe he'd talked about Katie. But Ellen had nothing to add.

As Jill stood at the door preparing to go, she turned to Ellen. "One more thing. Did you ever see Katie with a boyfriend?"

Ellen thought about it and suddenly snapped her fingers. "Yes, I did, once. And I thought it was odd. There was a guy who let her out of his car down the street, out of view of her house, like they were sneaking around."

"What was odd about it?"

"Well, he looked quite a bit older. In his twenties, I'd guess, maybe close to thirty. Far too old for her. At first, I thought he was a relative of some kind, maybe a cousin or older brother. But Katie was an only child, so I knew that wasn't right."

"What else do you remember about him?"

"He was strikingly good-looking. Kind of a young Brad Pitt — blond hair, blue eyes, well-built, the whole package. I saw them kiss in the car. Then they saw me and pulled apart quickly. After he drove off, Katie came up to me and struck up a conversation. She tried to tell me the guy was her cousin from out of town. I didn't say anything, but I think she knew that I didn't believe her."

Jill drove away from Ellen's house, thinking about everything she'd learned. Ellen's neighbors, or at least one of them, Katie's mother, assumed she was upset with Shaun about Rocco's death. Hillary Ramsay had assumed that Shaun must have killed him. Even Shaun's mother thought it was her son's fault, so convinced of it that she'd avoided Ellen, afraid of confronting the terrible facts.

Shaun's silence about Rocco had left people suspicious about him, unable to offer their sympathy. He may have felt he deserved their scorn after the loss of the dog for whom he'd held such affection. Awash in self-blame, he'd gone silent. His silence then had cut him off from Ellen, someone who had cared deeply for him.

Guilt. Inappropriate guilt, misplaced remorse. Perhaps shame. Wired with a conscience, most people struggled with feelings of shame when their own behavior violated their most cherished values. At times, those feelings spread to encompass over-responsibility, as in believing oneself to be responsible for something that was, in fact, entirely out of one's control.

Survivor's guilt—devastating remorse following the loss of a close friend or family member. *Why her and not me?* That may have led to his mutism. Now, Shaun's silence about Katie's murder might be cutting him off from people in ways that threatened his freedom.

She thought about coping mechanisms, that everyone had theirs. But for some people, coping mechanisms such as silence and lack of eye contact caused unintended consequences.

Then she thought about what Ellen had witnessed, the far older boyfriend. That confirmed what she'd learned from Sophie, but it wasn't conclusive. Kissing didn't automatically equal sex. Still, though, she had to report what she suspected about Sophie.

It also confirmed something that may have been a stimulant for Shaun. He may have seen Katie in the arms of this guy Trevor, just as Ellen had witnessed. Still at play was the possibility that Shaun had had a violent outburst borne of intense jealousy and killed Katie.

She checked the time—8:45 a.m. When would Karen get the call from her attorneys? The one telling her to bring Shaun in for questioning again, an interview that would no doubt end in his arrest.

What did it mean that Shaun hadn't hurt Ellen's dog? It was tempting to draw a correlation, but she knew from her days in the lab during graduate studies that human behavior was rarely that simplistic. The fact that he'd been kind to the dog didn't mean he hadn't snapped with Katie, gone into a blind rage triggered by jealousy, and killed her.

CHAPTER FIFTEEN

Her phone rang, startling her. *Jade.* She'd forgotten about her call. "Hey, sis. I'm sorry I didn't get back to you. I'm in the middle of a complicated case, and I know it's not an excuse. What's happened? What's Mom done now?"

"I'm not calling about Mom. I'm calling about me. Some things have happened that I'm... I'm not sure what's going on. I need you... I need your clear head and calm logic. I know! Usually, I don't," she said, laughing. Jill could all but see the smile on her face.

Jade typically rolled her eyes at Jill's attempts to bring her back down to earth with logic. Her sister leaned heavily into the esoteric, convinced her heart was her best guide in life, or a good psychic, or a dream she'd had the night before. She was a successful artist, driven by creative forces Jill found mysterious and baffling at times.

Yes, they were twins, closer in ways that went beyond typical siblings. But they couldn't be more different in the ways that they operated in life and viewed the world around them.

"Can you come over for coffee? If you don't have patients."

"I wish I could, but this case is hurtling toward a conclusion, and I'm nowhere near finishing my investigation. I'm afraid I'm going to have to take a rain check." She paused. "Are you okay, though? I mean, it's nothing serious. Is it?"

There was a pause before her sister spoke. "No, of course not. It can wait. It's probably just my imagination, anyway." As if her imagination were something to be discounted. It was an odd comment coming from Jade, who normally gravitated toward anything imaginative, imbuing high levels of importance to things that Jill found ordinary and unimportant.

The latest was the color of paint in Jade's sunroom, chosen by her husband, Daniel, and their decorator. *Pale yellow. I think it's making me psychotic,* complained Jade. *Yellow is a terrible color for trying to achieve a calm mental state.*

Change it; it's just paint, Jill had told her sister, who'd shaken her head as if she had no power to do so. But she'd been unable to let go of the significance.

How had the decorator not realized what a mistake this color was, how disruptive it could be? It was the room where she painted, where the light was the best, where she normally felt so creative.

As the silence stretched between them, Jill tried but couldn't feel anything. The thread between them sometimes conveyed the unspoken, but today, she got nothing.

Perhaps whatever was going on with Jade really was a product of her sister's imagination. Not in the usual creative sense, but in the sense of exaggerating something insignificant, making it mean more than it did. The knot in Jill's stomach let go. "I'll call you later; maybe come over for a glass of wine."

"Sure. It's just…" Jade's voice trailed off.

"Just what?"

"Nothing. I mean, yes, there's stuff to talk about. I miss you. It's been a while." She sounded wistful.

"Me too. But I can't promise when. I'll have to call you later and let you know when I'm free."

Jade sounded okay. Or was she covering up, deliberately putting on a facade? If so, it wasn't like her. Jade knew as well as Jill did the transparency between them, the impossibility of concealing anything of significance from each other.

Jill was unclear about where she should head next. If Shaun didn't fly into a rage and murder his only friend, then who did? Was it possible she was investigating a case that was no longer a guilty slam-dunk but, instead, a murder that someone had gotten away with? Someone else who wanted Katie dead?

All along, she'd envisioned the murder as a terrible, emotional scene gone dark, a crime of passion. That Shaun had lost touch with reality, perhaps gone into a fugue state of some kind in which he'd killed Katie but had no recollection of it later. Or he remembered the events that ended in Katie's death but was so consumed with guilt he couldn't talk about it.

She thought about her own revelatory words to Detective Webb. *I believe he is innocent, and I aim to prove it.* Where that had come from, she had no idea. But she believed it.

The unconscious mind—one of the last frontiers of human knowledge—fascinated her. Believed by some to be nothing more than a repository of repressed thoughts, memories, feelings, and unrelated associations. Believed by others to be the storehouse of fantastic mental powers, including the ability to mind-read or see the future, or remember past lives. If only the key could be found that would unlock those powers.

Jill had experienced inexplicable moments of awareness at times, of things about which she held no discernible facts. Sometimes, it was simple things like finding someone else's keys in an odd location without having been there when they were lost. Other times, it was almost a sense of seeing around corners, anticipating future events in her close friends' lives, such as foreseeing a break-up while the romance was still hot and heavy. She didn't think of these incidents as anything significant. But she sometimes wondered if they were the tip of the iceberg, indicators of an ability that she had yet to fully manifest.

What if her unconscious mind was sensing something about Shaun that pointed to his innocence? Even as she had that thought, she flashed to her sister Jade with her mystical thinking and beliefs that had little grounding in reality.

Perhaps this case was eroding Jill's usual analytical approach, veering her off of her usual fact-based path and into the mysterious. She felt a little off-balance, unsure of how to proceed, along which presumptive path to continue her work.

Shaun was innocent.

Shaun was guilty.

Her mind a seesaw, a conflict of facts versus intuition.

Now, however, with no one else doing any further investigating into Katie's murder, she felt an unexpected pull. Perhaps it was up to her to find out the truth about what had happened to Katie. In case what had happened to her wasn't Shaun, but someone else. However low the odds of that, it was a question worthy of further investigation, worthy of digging deeper. In fact, if she were honest with herself, she knew she couldn't let it go. She couldn't stop until she knew all there was to know and felt that solid grounding in the truth.

But she wasn't an investigator. She had no forensic training, in psychology or otherwise. Still, a young life was suspended in the balance.

Jill's phone rang, startling her out of her reverie, and she punched the button on her steering wheel to answer.

"Dr. Rhodes." Peter McClure's commanding voice filled her vehicle. "We need to see you at our offices right away. Something has happened."

CHAPTER SIXTEEN

"As you know, the Thayers are going to be required to take Shaun in, and remand him to custody sometime today. We need a wrap from you on this case, Dr. Rhodes. We'd like to see you at our offices within the hour to collect your notes and get your final assessment." Peter McClure spoke in his typical way, all command, no room for dissension.

Jill twitched. There was something about a dominating male voice, with the unspoken assumption of her compliance, that always aroused in her a sense of rebellion, a desire to do the opposite of whatever was being demanded of her.

But she knew that rebellion for its own sake was merely a force pitted against another force, not necessarily a constructive response. In this case, however, she had a righteous stance. "I don't have a final disposition on the case at this point, Peter," she said, using his first name deliberately. "In fact, I have a couple more interviews. I'm aware of the time issue, and I—"

"Maybe you didn't understand me," he interrupted. "There is no more time. If you have something of value to add to Shaun's case, we need it now. If not, then we're not going to waste more time and, quite frankly, expense."

"I understand perfectly. I have uncovered information that wasn't known previously, and I believe it will change everything about this case."

"What information?" He didn't sound curious or interested. It was spoken like a challenge as if he sought to prove the flimsiness of whatever she'd found.

"Once I've completed the last couple of interviews, I will be at your office promptly to share what I've found. Right now, I've got to make some calls."

"Dr. Rhodes—"

"I promise, I will get back to you," she said before cutting him off and taking a measure of satisfaction from that small action.

She did have calls to make, one in particular. "Hello, Mr. Ramsay, it's Dr. Jill Rhodes. I met with your wife and—"

Jeff Ramsay, Katie's father, interrupted. "You should know by now I'm not going to meet with you or talk to you. That boy *killed our daughter*. And you're trying to get him off! My wife is going through enough without you going to our home and upsetting her with gossip about our daughter, lies spread by teenagers who don't have anything better to do than defame their *dead classmate!*" His voice had risen in volume with each sentence, and she had to lower the volume so she could focus. "If you come near us again, we'll file a restraining order and make sure you lose your license!" He disconnected before she could respond.

She knew it had been a long shot, him willing to talk to her, especially after her visit with Katie's mom, but she was glad she'd made the effort in that particular order. Mothers typically knew far more than fathers about their daughters.

There was something a bit frightening to most men about a daughter's maturity into a sexual being, often prompting paternal distance and reticence. It was sad because the one thing a girl needed most as a teenager was a strong relationship with her father, that being the best predictor of her ability to choose a man wisely for herself later. And not get pregnant prematurely.

A strong relationship with her father... Jill let her mind wander briefly into that territory for herself. *Her father*—if you could call him that. It wasn't wise to think about him because, inevitably, she felt lost, confused, frightened, and angry. And this was an especially bad time to think about those particular memories. She quickly channeled her thoughts into the upcoming interview, one that she anticipated would be even more challenging than calling Jeff Ramsay.

Sitting in the trendy restaurant, she looked around at the Dallas business lunch crowd, grateful again that she didn't have to contend with the overly wide smiles, the earnestness of the pitches, the exchange of business cards followed up by scores of emails, and the exhaustion of having to hold up the façade. To win business, you had to be positive and upbeat, even if your personal life was falling apart at the moment.

While she had a brain for business, she lacked the will to do what it took to succeed in the corporate track. And she lacked the complacency to succeed in anything less than an executive role. She'd toyed with the idea of a corporate career but was grateful she'd chosen private practice instead.

She'd requested this table to get a chance to speak with the waiter. Finally, a twenty-something guy with tousled, sun-streaked hair, riveting blue eyes, and a physique that might grace a screen someday placed her water glass and menu on the table and smiled the kind of smile that probably left most women weak.

"I'm Trevor, and I'll be taking care of you today. Can I start you with a chilled glass of chardonnay or a nice pinot noir? I also have a wonderful sauvignon blanc, which goes great with our special today…"

Jill let him continue, fascinated with the display of personal magnetism, which was considerable. There were rare people who seemed to be born with this trait, with the ability to draw in others with little to no effort, to somehow create the impression of warmth, of a special connection, of the notion that you, and you alone, were the chosen object of this amazing person's attention. She smiled back at him. "Actually, Trevor, I'm here to see you. I know about you and Katie. And you and Sophie."

"Me and… who?" He started, then quickly recovered. "I'm sorry, ma'am, but I have no idea what you're talking about…. But I'll be glad to get a glass of wine for you. Which would you prefer?"

Amazing. "No wine, just water, and it would be wise for you to take a break and listen to what I have to say. I won't take much of your time. Just stand there and smile like I'm putting in an order." She waited while he absorbed her words, wondering if he'd simply walk away. But he didn't. "Good. I am helping with the investigation into Katie's death. I know you had a relationship with Sophie and, later, Katie, who broke up with you." She'd purposely targeted his ego, most likely his main vulnerability.

"Broke up with me?" He gave her a flat laugh. "You've got it all wrong. I broke up with her. It was nothing, anyway. Just a high school girl crush on me." His eyes slid away as he lied, even as he tried to maintain the charm.

Ignoring his denial, she continued. "What happened when Katie broke up with you? I know she went to see you that day, the day she was killed. So, don't bother to deny it." She let that sink in. "By the way, we're talking about two underage girls. In the state of Texas, what you did is a crime, for which you can be charged with a felony."

His skin paled, and his eyes darkened. "Is that some kind of threat? And, for the record, I didn't do anything."

"Not a threat from me, but the police are looking into this. I know Katie was upset that you didn't tell her you were with her best friend, Sophie, right before you started seeing her. She went to you that day, didn't she? *She broke up with you*, not the other way around. What happened, then? What did you do to her?"

Now his skin flushed red, and he no longer resembled the silver screen god he had before. He leaned in close to her, smiling with too much teeth, jaw clenched. "Listen to me, lady. I don't know who you are, but you're barking up the wrong tree."

He leaned in closer again, one hand on the tabletop. "As far as Katie and her... friend go, there's no proof that I did anything but tease them, had a little fun watching them fight over me. It's too bad what happened to Katie, but her weirdo friend is the one you should be talking to." He straightened.

Jill watched, fascinated, as he transformed once again to look like the promise of steamy romance to women or, alternatively, a producer's dream. But she'd seen his dark side now, and she was repulsed. She was ready, already lifting her cell, and snapped his photo before he could turn away.

He reached for her phone, but she'd already tucked it in her bag as she stood to leave. She made sure she drew people's

THE EXPERT WITNESS

attention as she walked away, heart thudding. After a few steps, she glanced behind her to see if he'd followed her. He hadn't.

She strolled past tables and made her way to one of the side entrances to the restaurant, avoiding Trevor since his service area was in the area closest to the front door. It was difficult not to turn her head, to avoid looking behind, wondering if he followed despite her tactics.

She slipped out the door and continued walking. But her Lexus was in the front. She'd have to make her way there around the rear of the restaurant to avoid being seen by Trevor. She made her way to the rear, noticing the thinning vehicles, the lack of others walking to their cars or arriving and exiting cars. No one brushed past her, either in her direction or in the opposite. Soon, she saw nothing but an alleyway and dumpsters.

This wasn't what she'd expected. It was too remote, and her amygdala was keenly aware of that fact as it caused a surge of adrenaline, raising her heart rate.

She'd just turned the corner for the side parking lot when suddenly, there he was.

He moved in close, pressing her to the wall, and put his arm out, placing his hand on the wall, effectively stopping her. "Going somewhere?"

CHAPTER SEVENTEEN

She tried to move past him, but he moved with her and blocked her again. She froze, daring to look into his impossibly beautiful face. "Move. Your. Arm."

He dropped his arm quickly. "I'm sorry. I just wanted to talk to you again. Look, I'm under a lot of pressure, and this job means a lot to me. I'm working my way up to manager, and the pay helps me with my other career." He raked his fingers through his hair, the boyish charm on full display. "I just wanted you to know that nothing happened between me and Katie. She was a kid who had a crush, and I guess I let her have it. It was flattering because she was gorgeous. But we didn't have sex. I swear it."

"What about Sophie?"

Once again, she'd caught him off guard, and now his face registered a mix of anger and fear. "Sophie who?"

"You know who I mean, and unfortunately for you, Sophie is alive and well. She can testify against you." But as soon as the impulsive words left her mouth, she regretted them. *Had she introduced a threat to Sophie?* She had no idea who Trevor really was or what he was capable of.

"I don't know who you mean, but again, teenage girls crush on me all the time. I work in a restaurant. Girls—women," he quickly inserted, "—come here for fun and drinks. I take good care of them, and some try to get my number. And I do have quite the social media presence, so it's not like I'm hard to find," he finished pridefully. "I hope you don't, like, spread false rumors about me, damage my reputation."

He was a bit of an enigma; she'd give him that. One minute, he was the pretty boy trying to get into the entertainment industry, banking on his good looks. The next, revealing a dark side with veiled threats. Then, back to the handsome persuader. His personality flips were dizzying.

"Are you saying both Sophie and Katie had a crush on you? Bet that didn't work out well for you, did it?"

His ego took over, just like she thought it would. "Like I said, it happens all the time. Cute teenagers, divorced moms, even a few older, uh, let's say desperate types."

She nodded as if she understood, though his cavalier attitude towards women made her skin crawl. "Would you say one of the two girls, Katie, or Sophie, was jealous of the other? Because of you?" Playing to his ego again.

"Wouldn't surprise me."

He was no longer denying the connection to Sophie, but he wasn't admitting it either. That thread, the possibility of charging him with underage sex, now lay at Sophie's door and within her discretion. And the odds of her wanting to press charges against the guy she still longed for were extremely low.

His eyes slowly scanned her body, and a slow grin lifted his lips. "Why are you really here? You wanted me to follow you, didn't you?"

She suppressed a shudder at the implication she might be one of those women seeking the thrill of a hook-up with this guy.

"On the contrary, I find you extraordinarily repulsive." Disgust evident in her tone. "Now, if you'll excuse me. I have to go." She moved swiftly past him, head high—confidence, however false, radiating in her every motion. She resisted the urge to look back but sighed in relief once inside her vehicle with doors locked.

Sophie saw the number of the call coming in and gasped. *Finally!* She was thrilled in anticipation of hearing his sweet voice, with the possibility of seeing him soon, which was undoubtedly why he'd finally called.

But when she answered with breathless excitement, there was no reciprocal warmth, none of the things she'd expected.

"Did you talk to someone? I can find out, so you'd better tell me the truth," he demanded.

"I..." Her excitement quickly turned to fear. "This woman came to the school and interviewed everyone. I *had* to talk to her."

The caller swore. "Who was she? Her name."

"Dr. Rhodes, I think. She's an investigator trying to help Shaun's case."

"What did you tell her?"

"Nothing! It's not what you think. I didn't say anything about—"

"Shut up! If you know what's good for you, you'll keep it that way."

"But I didn't do anything, I swear." A tear slipped down her cheek.

"*I don't care.* When are you going to get that? Just keep quiet. And you should be glad it's only me calling you."

What did he mean by that? She felt an inexplicable chill but couldn't stop herself. "Wait! Why didn't you answer my texts? What about Katie?"

But he was gone, and her chest felt achy and full of something terrible. For the first time since all of this started, she wished for her mom, for her comfort. If only she could go back in time when the hardest decision she had to make was which movie to watch with her for the hundredth time. She could all but imagine the big bowls of popcorn in their laps, feel the sticky fingers, and hear the laughter, her innocence still preserved. The ache in her chest expanded. She and her mom hadn't done anything like that in years. And she was no longer innocent.

"Hey, man! What was that for?" Trevor glared at the asshole who'd just thumped him in the chest. He backed away shakily.

"Stupid idiot. Figures a pretty boy like you would have shit for brains. You had her eating out of your hand, and you blew it. Now I'm going to have to take care of this."

"What do you mean? I told her to shut up. She will."

"No, she won't. She's a stupid teenage girl, and she's already said too much."

"No, man." Fear traveled through Trevor. This guy had a look in his eye, one that harbored violence. "Anyway, it's too late now. We just have to be careful."

The man laughed coldly. "Careful? It's too late for that. You just couldn't stop yourself. And now, you're going to help me take care of it." He threw Trevor's phone at him. "Call her back."

"She's not a problem, man, I'm telling you."

"Call. Her. Back." He punched Trevor viciously in the side. "Here's what you're going to tell her." Trevor barely registered the specific instructions while he was doubled over, struggling to catch his breath.

Trevor made the call with shaking hands.

But the guy wasn't done yet. "Now, it's time for you to understand who and what you're dealing with," he told Trevor, who backed off, pleading.

"No, not the face, man. Please, I have to make a living with it!" But the man kept coming, fists raised. "Don't let him do this," he threw his last-ditch plea to the side. But the merciless man watched impassively while the asshole did exactly what Trevor dreaded.

CHAPTER EIGHTEEN

Two weeks ago

Her soft knock at the bedroom door created a warm spot in his chest. *She'd showed up.* Shaun waited for a moment, prompting another knock, this time louder. When he opened the door, she smiled. "Hey, dufus, what took you so long?" Katie pushed her way in, threw down her backpack, and flopped on the bean bag in the corner as he sat on the floor nearby.

His insides beamed, but his face remained mired in concrete. "I'm glad you're here." He knew she got it, but still, she had to tease.

"You might want to tell your face." To his horror, she reached over and pulled the sides of his face so he was forced to smile. Seeing his look, she dropped her hands quickly. "Sorry. I know better than that."

He felt the flush sweep his skin. Nothing was worse than

that feeling, the slow burn of embarrassment, growing deeper because someone else, standing in front of him, saw it.

But Katie knew. "Hey, dufus, don't do that. I'm sorry. I shouldn't have touched you, and I didn't mean anything by it. *Hey*," she ended softly, deliberately not making eye contact, knowing how it helped him to compose himself if her eyes weren't on him.

Carefully, he set up the chess board, letting the music carry the energy in the room. Classical music calmed him, but there was also classic rock 'n' roll. He even enjoyed big band and jazz. Everything from Gershwin to the Beatles. Katie was great about his music. She understood what he needed and never judged. While he set up the pieces, she scrolled on her cell, tapping, and laughing at times.

"I can't believe some of the stupid things people post! Check this out." She turned her phone and played a video of their classmate, Josh, standing on his head while vaping, falling over, and almost choking.

"People are stupid," he said. "Vaping is one of the worst things you can do to your body. It's even more addictive than cigarettes because it's easier to use, and the toxins can lead to significant lung damage and even death. 39 deaths as of the most recent data. Did you know the latest thing," he named a brand that had become hugely popular—"delivers more nicotine than a pack of regular cigarettes? And the particles in the aerosol—which is what it is, *aerosol*, not vapor—can cause cardiovascular injury, with links to negative effects on resting heart rate, blood pressure, and the cells that line the blood vessels. Did you know 11% of users have asthma? Yet they still do it." It truly did amaze him, the lack of common sense of the average teenager.

"Okay, you are *such* a nerd," she said, laughing. Then she turned serious. "But point well made. Maybe you could post this stuff on vaping? Might help some of these people. Just saying. In fact," she said, her eyes bright with one of her *big ideas*, "you get the facts and data together, and I'll do the posting. No one has to know it came from you and that head full of factoids." But she smiled like she was proud of him.

That was so like Katie, wanting to help other people. She was always going around noticing who needed a little extra encouragement or who needed to be defended against the bullies and nasties. In their school's swirl of people and personalities, the social ocean in which he regularly felt he was drowning, Katie was his life raft.

But he'd never post anything on Instagram, or TikTok, or anywhere else. Let them vape themselves into the E.R. Let them fall on their heads. But Katie was different; she was special. The rest of them could take care of themselves.

"Let's play." Shaun started with one of his favorite classic moves, pawn to e4. She obliged with pawn to c5, and he swiftly moved his second pawn to c3. Chess with Katie wasn't the most challenging game in the world but watching her make her moves was what it was all about.

Her slender fingers, tipped by short nails, and no polish, fascinated him. She twirled them over the board before she reached down to pick up a piece. Sometimes, she chose a piece, touched it, but decided not to move it. She huffed out air when he took one of her pieces and said, *"Really?"*

She rubbed a finger over her sculpted brows when she concentrated. She twisted her lips sideways, tapped her front teeth with a nail, and pulled her long blond hair. A range of micro-expressions flew across her face with each stage of the game, some gleeful, some disgusted, some he couldn't begin to interpret.

How did someone have a massive repertoire like that for facial expressions? It wouldn't be good to stare at her too much. Most people didn't like that, especially when he stared at them. Her stunning beauty was the obvious reason to peer at her, averting his eyes when she caught him. Which was rare since she knew not to make too much eye contact.

But it was the play of emotions, the flash of her eyes, the flick of her hand, the slow smile on her lips, the lithe way she lounged on the bean bag chair, that drew his focus.

His innate stiffness, the way his legs didn't fold quite right, the way his arms and hands dangled in the most awkward ways, and the slight cave in his chest created a sharp contrast between him and this beautiful girl whom he couldn't understand. *What made her come over and spend time with him?*

It was different from when they'd played together as children. The only thing that had mattered then was the games they played—who won or lost—and who built the biggest Lego monster, whose mom made the best cookies, and who could throw the biggest fit when they were told their play date was over.

It wasn't until middle school that things changed. Playdates ended for him while Katie's social calendar filled with sleepovers with her girlfriends and after-hours sports. Still, she'd never completely forgotten him, especially when he ran into trouble at school.

Remembering that, grateful for all the times she'd stood up for him, he let her win. She let out a small hoot after declaring checkmate. Then she narrowed her eyes at him. "Hey, dufus, I know you let me win. Why do you do that?" But she'd asked it so softly it felt like butterfly wings.

"I let you win because you like to win," he told her.

"In that case, we don't have to play. We'll just set up the

board, and I'll sweep off your pieces and yell, 'checkmate'! We're done, right?" She teased him because she knew how much he loved to play.

They sat for a while, Katie scrolling and tapping on her phone, Shaun watching her, music gently filling in the quiet spaces. With her eyes still pinned to the screen, she said, "I'm glad you don't follow all this stuff. It's really worthless."

Unbelievably, he watched a small tear roll down her cheek. Pressure built unbearably. He didn't like seeing her upset. But he didn't know what to do. The questions jammed his chest, but none of them came out of his mouth.

"You ever wonder about why people do terrible things to other people? I mean, why is that fun to some people? I can't imagine doing something to hurt someone else and watching them suffer. And don't get me started on social media. There's so much cruelty out there." Her eyes traveled to Shaun and widened. "Hey, it's okay! I'm just rambling on about nothing. Oh, you don't think I mean me, do you? Of course not! Hey, my life is a big bowl of strawberries, dufus, topped with whipped cream."

The false levity in her voice didn't fool him.

"I have to go," she said, standing abruptly. "See ya later, Shaun. You know, dufus," she said at the door, eyes downcast, "you really are my best friend."

And she was gone. The questions remained lodged in his throat, making him feel sick. He put on a headset and blasted the music, submerging the sorrow that ate holes in his gut. Not all of it, but some of it. Much later, he crept cautiously online, finding out things about Katie that made his blood boil.

CHAPTER NINETEEN

Jill drove with shaking hands on the wheel, remembering Trevor and the coiling darkness behind his movie star looks. She thought about the genetic package he'd been given and what that might have meant as he grew up.

Beautiful babies got loads of smiles and showers of love from the moment they first gazed upon a world that would favor them throughout their lives. A world that would give them all the positive regard, adoration, and acceptance they could possibly want.

Not having to try to get what you craved, having so much of it handed to you, sometimes resulted in a personality structure that might be summed up as 'user' or 'narcissist.' Of course, there were many other factors involved in personality formation, but being born exceptionally beautiful was a powerful one.

She flashed through a handful of patients over the years, recalling some who, in spite of their exceptional looks, were unable to see themselves as attractive, awash in low self-esteem. Others could, yet it didn't make them happy.

Beautiful or not, her patients often struggled with life, confusing the right to *seek* happiness with the expectation that it should be so, with little effort. Still, others were blind-sided by the inevitable losses and disappointments inherent in every life, unable to move forward, locked in anger, resentment, or grief.

What had Trevor done with his looks? Had he found ways to exploit others with a magnetic smile, sparkling eyes, glowing skin, and a sculpted body? Even his voice was riveting. How potent had that combination been for a couple of teenage girls? How had that kind of personal power, the ability to easily manipulate the vulnerable, felt to him?

What had he done with it? Power could be addictive, an end that justified destructive means.

As Jill headed toward her destination, the sky darkened, swiftly moving clouds gathering on the horizon. *Great.* Soon, the rain fell in sheets, and the previously sunlit street flowed like a river.

Parking, she sat for a moment, gathering her thoughts and questions, waiting for the rain to let up. There wasn't any point in fighting the downpour, which would undoubtedly be brief. *Don't like the weather? Just wait a few minutes; it will change.* The old saying in North Texas, home of violent storms, twisters, hail, and flash flooding. Not to mention the blazing heat combined with humidity over the long summer.

Her cell buzzed with a text message. Nancy Barrett, one of the attorneys she'd met at the start of the case. *The D.A. called for Shaun to be remanded into custody. We have only a couple of hours. You have to meet with us now. Sorry.*

Jill sprang out of her vehicle, struggling to open her umbrella, and sloshed to Karen Thayer's door. The wind blew the rain sideways, and she was soaked in seconds, but thankfully, the weather had chased away the media because there was no one in sight.

"Oh my God, I'm so glad you're here," said Karen tearfully as she ushered Jill in. "Don't worry about it," she said as Jill tried to deal with the water pouring off of her umbrella, her soaked shoes, and her wet bag.

Karen fetched a towel, but Jill didn't want to waste too much time, so she stepped out of her water-soaked shoes and gave herself a quick swipe or two, and hurried to sit down. "I'm sorry this has to be so rushed, but it's time for me to speak with Shaun," she said. "Alone, I'm afraid."

Karen hesitated. "But I'm his mother. I should be with him while you talk to him."

"When he goes in later today, you will be with him. He will definitely need you for that. I'm going to make this as easy for him as possible. But you have to trust me. Also, no matter what you hear, don't come back in until I call you. It's nothing bad," she added at Karen's alarmed look. "Promise me."

Reluctantly, Karen called her only child, her troubled son, into the room, then quickly left.

Whatever Jill had been expecting, this wasn't it. Shaun was thin, gazed solidly at the floor, and slipped in like a ghost. His tee shirt and jeans were too baggy, and her heart fell. *Was he eating at all?*

Knowing he might be reticent to sit physically close, she'd strategically placed herself at one end of the sofa. Shaun sat as far away as possible, shoulders rounded, hands gripping his upper thighs tightly, neck already reddening as he hunched and gazed at a spot somewhere on the floor.

Jill took a breath and let it out slowly. Then, another. As her heart rate settled, Shaun's breathing began to match hers. "Shaun, I'm glad to meet you. I'm Dr. Jill Rhodes." He looked up sharply, and she hastened to say, "not a medical doctor. I'm a psychologist." He nodded slowly and looked down again.

"I'm hoping you can play a game with me. Not for fun, but so I can help you. I'm going to say some things, theories I have if you will. I need you to give me a signal when I'm on track. Would you rather tap your leg with a finger or tap your nose when I say something right? Or use some other signal?"

She waited for about a minute, which seemed to drag on forever. This might be a terrible way to approach this kid. But she didn't have a Plan B at the moment.

Finally, he moved. Without looking at her, Shaun slid his right hand forward and tapped his knee.

Perfect. Sometimes, giving someone a choice between two easy things opened the pathway to some form of interaction. "Thank you. Just give me one tap if I'm on track. I'm going to tell you what I believe. Katie was your friend, your best friend, and you loved her."

Shaun tapped his knee once.

"You wanted to help her."

Tap.

"She was in some kind of trouble, and you found out."

A long pause, frowning.

"Okay, you didn't know exactly what kind of trouble she was in, but you suspected something."

Tap.

"You didn't have anything to do with her being killed."

His forehead wrinkled in confusion, but he wouldn't look up. No tap.

"Okay, let me try that again. You feel responsible for her death."

Tap.

"I'm going to come back to Katie, but I want to talk about Rocco, the neighbor's dog. He died while you were taking care of him. I think you felt responsible for that in some way."

Tap.

"But you didn't kill Rocco."

His face registered alarm.

"It's okay. I know you didn't."

He slumped even more. If that was possible.

"It's the same thing with Katie. You would never have hurt her, but you were there when she was killed, and you couldn't stop it."

Tap. Hand shaking. A tear slid down his nose and spilled onto his lap. He drew in a hitched breath.

"And you feel responsible like you did when you couldn't prevent Rocco's death."

He nodded, still looking at his lap and crying softly.

"Because you feel responsible for what happened to Katie, you're not speaking up to defend yourself."

Tap. More tears, snot running now.

"Here's the thing, Shaun. You're not responsible for what happened to Rocco. I talked to Ellen. She's not mad; she never was. She just misses you. Rocco was old and was going to die any day. He just happened to die while you were keeping him. That's not on you. And she has an adorable new dog she'd like you to meet. She wanted you to know this so you would stop blaming yourself."

His chest heaved while little moans escaped.

Jill extended her heart to Shaun without moving, not touching him yet holding him in warmth. She whispered loud enough, so she knew he heard it. "It's the same thing with Katie. You aren't responsible for her death. You loved her, and you miss her terribly."

Now, he sobbed, and Jill held her breath, hoping Karen would keep her promise to stay away.

Gradually, he quieted, and she went on, her voice returning to normal volume. "Here's the thing, Shaun. I don't believe you killed Katie, but someone else did. I have an idea about who it is. Would you take a look at this photo and tell me if this is the person who was there that day?" She held up her phone and showed him the shot of Trevor, confident now.

Shaun peered at the photo and shook his head. "I don't know this guy." Jill struggled to remain outwardly calm as if his speaking was the most normal thing in the world. "He doesn't look anything like the man who was there, the one who stuck Katie with my knife, making her bleed out." He looked up at Jill, stricken. "I tried to stop the bleeding. I tried so hard. But she wouldn't breathe. She wouldn't wake up. There is a quantity of blood without which a body can't be viable."

"You're correct, Shaun. I'm sure you did everything you could," she reassured him. "Can you tell me what happened?" Jill asked.

CHAPTER TWENTY

The day of the murder

Shaun moved cautiously through the trees. They jokingly called it *Mirkwood*, from *The Lord of the Rings*, and it had seemed vast when they were little and discouraged them from going there. Now, it was merely a small area of reserve land bordering their neighborhood, no wider than a few home lots, with a trickling creek. Not a forest, not anything much except thick undergrowth with live oak, mesquite, and sweet gum, the usual scraggly trees that could be found growing wild in north Texas.

Fall meant leaves—crisp, dry leaves—underfoot. He didn't care for the sound and aimed for exposed roots to be quieter. He fingered the folded blade in his pocket, a rare gift from his dad. *Since you like wandering around and exploring biology, you could use a tool.* And it had come in handy when he wanted to carefully pry things apart, to inspect the insides, like pods that contained butterflies in the making. Although he'd only done that once, feeling bad about the butterfly that had died, never getting a chance to flutter away. But he used it for other things.

Voices sounded ahead, and that brought him to a stop. He never ran into other people here, which was one of the many reasons he loved it.

He crept closer to the voices, curiosity winning over his social aversion. *Wait.* One voice was familiar. *Katie,* and someone else, a man. Through the trees ahead, flashes of color and a cry. He thrashed ahead, unmindful of the noise, his ears buzzing, his arms flailing. *Katie!* He had to get to her.

A man with a ponytail pinned Katie's arms to her sides as she shouted at him. "I said, I'm done with you! Get your hands off of me!" His back was to Shaun, but something about the way he moved made him look older.

"You don't get to say you're done. You're forgetting—I have all I need to ruin your high school prom-queen life for good. I don't think you want your friends, let alone your teachers and your *parents,* to see you with your legs spread," he told her.

"You wouldn't dare."

He couldn't hear everything that was said. Something about knowing something and Katie threatening to tell. Whatever she'd said must have pissed the guy off because of what happened next.

"Don't ever come near me again—" But she never got to finish because he punched her straight in the face, causing her to fall. She put her hand on her cheek in shock, her mouth falling open. Shaun must have made a sound because her eyes darted to him. "Shaun! What are you doing? *You have to get out of here.* Go away. *I mean it, dufus.*"

He stood, frozen, fingering the knife. "Katie," he mumbled.

"Shaun," she pleaded. "Leave, now! Go home!"

But he couldn't go, just leave her like this. "No," he said, a quiet determination rising through the fog of fear. "Let her go," he said to the guy, his heart now pounding a warning.

He turned to Shaun. "What did you say? Did you actually tell me to let her go?" He stepped away from Katie and flexed his hands while rolling his shoulders. "Oh, this is gonna be fun." He advanced on Shaun, who stood trembling.

Katie flew at the man's back, throwing herself at him, screaming, "Leave him alone!" She punched him with her small hands and pushed him, but she was no match for him. He shoved her onto the ground as if she weighed nothing and turned to Shaun, who pulled the switchblade and popped it open.

"Oh, what have we here? Did your daddy give you a big knife?" He laughed at Shaun, who swiped the knife clumsily through the air, missing the guy by a mile.

Before Shaun could register what was happening, a blow came out of nowhere. He dropped instantly into darkness and the rustle of leaves.

A blackbird called and was answered by a blue jay. His head hurt because it was lodged on something hard. Slowly, the bird calls pierced his awareness. His eyes opened to the canopy of leaves overhead and a haze of cirrus clouds in the sky above that. He was on the ground in the woods, his head awkwardly resting on a large rock.

He held something in his hand. It was cold and a little slippery. He dropped it as he rolled over and sat up slowly, touching the swelling on his temple. For a moment, he had no idea where he was or how he'd gotten there. *Katie!*

He stood and swept his eyes over the area. *Where was she?* A shape on the ground a few yards away drew him. It was Katie—on her back, terribly still. His eyes swept back and found the object he'd dropped. His knife, the blade extended and covered in blood. *What had he done?*

He dropped beside her, put his ear to her mouth, and listened, but the blood thundering through his own veins drowned out everything else. He put his hands on her chest and pushed hard, once, twice, three times. And more, but it was no use. Her beautiful eyes stared upward as though she yearned to fly with the birds far away from this terrible place.

Later, he found himself at home with no recollection of getting there, standing in the family room behind his mom, keening at the story on the news. *Katie…*

When they came for him, he sat mute while they peppered him with questions, first at home, and later at the police station, his mom sitting with him, urging him to talk. It was nice to have a superpower, and his was the ability to turn human voices into white noise, no discernable consonants or vowels, just a low-level buzz. Easy to ignore. In fact, at times, while they buzzed, he actually slept.

Later, back home, when his mom begged him to talk, his superpower failed him, and her pleas unleashed the sadness. He sat with her, still mute, tears coursing down his cheeks and forming an unlovely mess on the front of his tee shirt.

But his words were frozen, stuck inside him, and after a couple of days, his mom gave up asking about Katie. They spoke only when absolutely necessary about small things. *Time for breakfast—what do you want? You need to take a shower, Shaun.*

How about staying home today? And tomorrow... But he never went back to school. The days were indiscernible, his studies neglected.

None of it mattered because Katie was gone. And it was his fault.

"And you're sure you don't know the man? You've never seen him before?"

Shaun shook his head miserably. "But I don't know what really happened. My mind has erased it. Maybe the man wasn't real. Maybe I'm the one who hurt Katie."

"Shaun, listen to me," Jill told him. "I don't believe for a minute that you hurt Katie. But you are going to have to go back in for questioning later today. You can still help us find the man who did this to Katie. She would want that. She would never want you to take the blame. Tell your attorney what you've told me, and after that, answer questions only when your attorney says it's okay. Otherwise, don't talk to the police." She wasn't sure if she was qualified to give that kind of advice, but she felt it was necessary. "Shaun, we are going to get justice for Katie. *You are*, with your words, by telling the truth."

He lifted his head then, and the look of hope in his eyes pierced her heart. She saw two distinct visions of Shaun's life going forward. One was flawed but filled with potential. The other was a never-ending nightmare. A weight fell on her shoulders, made worse by the lack of clarity. *Had she promised something she couldn't deliver?* Who had been the guy in the woods? Without his identity, Shaun's future was bleaker than ever.

CHAPTER TWENTY-ONE

Jill left the Thayer's more confused than ever. She'd been so sure of her theory that Trevor was the real killer, that he'd been the one who'd murdered Katie. She'd broken up with him, and in his narcissism, he couldn't take it. He'd flown into a murderous rage.

But now, she believed Shaun. That meant someone else had met Katie in the woods that day. Someone else had taken Shaun's knife and used it to take her life.

At least she'd answered one question. Whatever jealousy Sophie had felt, it hadn't led her to kill her friend. That was a relief, but the uncertainty about the rest of the case troubled her deeply. She'd been so close to solving the case, handing over Shaun's testimony, which she'd recorded with her phone, to provide a good reason for law enforcement to do a real investigation now to prove Trevor's guilt.

But who would believe him now? He couldn't point the finger at a specific person. He could tell his story, but not knowing who the mysterious 'other guy' was would cast serious doubt on him and his veracity. They were back at square one, and the saddest part of today was the devastation in Karen's eyes as she prepared to turn in her son, again.

An urgent text message arrived, announcing itself over her car speaker. She left the route she'd intended quickly.

A few minutes later, she sat in the conference room at McClure and Associates, facing three attorneys. Michael Fischer looked slightly embarrassed but tried to give her a supporting smile. Nancy Barrett looked at the table and her notes, anywhere but at Jill.

Peter McClure glared at her. "Dr. Rhodes. It's so kind of you to take time from your busy day to meet with us."

"I'm sorry I was delayed, but it was for a good reason," she retorted. "I've met with Shaun, and his story lines up with the theory I've developed about what happened to Katie. It seems he—"

"Wait. Shaun *talked* to you?" McClure's face tightened.

"Yes, of course. Now, from talking with Katie's best friend and with Shaun—"

"You shouldn't have interviewed Shaun without one of us present," interrupted McClure. "*We're* his legal counsel, not you, and it's inappropriate for you to solicit anything from him without us." McClure's voice rose. He splayed his large hands on the table, his eyes narrowed at Jill, his breathing shallow. "That interview is not privileged with only you present! It's discoverable—regardless of your license—once this moves into a criminal indictment. You may have just compromised the entire case." He was in full fight-or-flight mode now.

What was the source of all this anger? She'd been hired to help with the case, to potentially help with Shaun's defense, and she was doing exactly that. Why wasn't McClure grateful? Why wasn't he listening and taking notes? She glanced around the table at Fischer's embarrassed expression and Barrett's avoidance.

Of course.

This was ego. McClure was livid that she'd accomplished something they hadn't done as a legal team. Somehow, it made him look bad in front of his associates. Apparently, his ego overrode other pressing priorities.

Well, so what? Shaun needed help, and she aimed to give it. "If this information is discoverable, so be it. I know I said at the start I didn't want to go to court, but if that's what is required, I will do it."

"We're not going to pay you a penny more," McClure said. "You'll be spending your day there on your own dime."

"Wait a second, Peter. We haven't even heard what she has to say. How do we know if her testimony as an expert witness will harm or support the case? If it comes to that." Michael Fischer braved McClure's withering glare and refused to back down. "I say we listen to Dr. Rhodes and figure out later what needs to happen regarding her testimony."

"I agree," said Barrett, looking up, her voice gathering strength.

McClure glared at his associates but then turned to Jill and gave her a *"well?"* look.

She told them everything, or mostly everything. She didn't mention going to see Trevor since that hadn't yielded any new information other than his obvious defensiveness. But since Shaun hadn't identified him, it was pointless anyway.

"So, after all this legwork, what we have is Shaun's story of a mysterious man who supposedly killed Katie." McClure's derision hadn't lifted one bit.

Ignoring the shot, she went on. "It's more than that. I'm convinced on multiple fronts that Shaun is harmless, incapable of committing an act of violence, let alone one as brutal as this. As I said, I'm willing to provide expert testimony in his defense." She prodded him. "It seems like we're further along than before. Shaun is talking and is willing to tell his story to the police today. At the very least, it introduces some doubt into the case, doesn't it?"

"It doesn't change the evidence, though," said Barrett regretfully. "With no idea who this other man is, and with the evidence that places Shaun at the scene, we're still at square one."

"But can't you get the police to investigate more? Can't you get them to dig into Katie's life, see if they can find the man? It could have been a stranger, I realize. But it also could be someone she knew, someone who left evidence behind in her life, threads that can be picked up."

Both Fischer and Barrett thought that might be possible, but McClure shut it down. "We don't have the resources for an investigation like that. The main thing we have to do now is work on keeping Shaun out of jail, get reasonable bail while we wait for trial, and then get ready for that." He turned to Jill without warmth or gratitude of any kind. "You're dismissed from the case, Dr. Rhodes."

Stung, she gathered her things.

Michael Fischer followed her out. "Dr. Rhodes. I'm so sorry. He can be a real jerk at times, but he means well. He'll make sure Shaun gets a vigorous defense. You did a great job—I hope you realize that. I'm so grateful for your help, and I'll make sure you get every penny you are owed, if you are called to testify as an expert witness."

She brushed that aside. "I don't care about that. I care about a teenage boy who's lost his best friend and may soon lose his freedom."

As she drove away, her teeth ground in frustration. And something else, a sensation of being mired somehow, frozen, or stuck. That was foreign to her as a person who preferred to move forward. Not rapidly. Carefully, perhaps. But always forward.

She'd made significant progress on Shaun's case, opened the door for the potential of creating enough doubt in the eyes of law enforcement and in the eyes of the District Attorney's office, so that perhaps he wouldn't be indicted today. *Why hadn't that made a difference to his attorneys?*

Even worse, what could she do at this point? She'd been kicked off the case.

She spotted Jade from across the crowded patio. The sun had warmed the chilly day, providing a great opportunity to sit outside, a rare day for that in Dallas, with its often inhospitable too-hot or too-cold or too-rainy weather.

She paused for a moment and watched Jade before joining her, noting the drawn expression, the hands in her lap worrying the fabric of her skirt, the frequent sips from what was clearly an alcoholic beverage, despite the early hour.

But as soon as Jade spotted Jill, she shifted into her usual sunny expression. Jill's sister made it her mission in life to inject positivity wherever she found herself, no matter how challenging that might be. Jade's life was far from perfect, but most people had no idea that was the case.

Jill slid into the chair after hugging her sister. "Hey."

"Hey," returned Jade.

Jill studied her sister, refraining from asking a potentially invasive question.

"So, what is this case you're working on?" Jade quizzed her instead, genuinely interested as always in Jill's work.

"I wish I could tell you everything. Believe me. I could use your perspective." At Jade's surprised look, she laughed. "I know! It seems like we're switching roles lately. You—seeking my analytical take on whatever it is, me wanting more of your... mystic brain."

"Wow. I never thought I'd hear that from you," Jade smiled. "But you're the one with the amazing intuition. You can practically see around corners. My 'mystic brain' is good artistically, but it doesn't do me much good beyond that." A trace of self-deprecation or perhaps melancholy in her voice. "Anyway, what can you tell me?"

"All I can say is that I'm helping with a legal case," she said, careful not to utter the word 'criminal,' given Ethan's rapid deduction and consequent realization she was working on the well-publicized case. "And at first, all the facts lined up one way. Then, I had this odd... intuition, if you will, that the facts didn't tell the whole story. I followed that thread and found out some unexpected facts that—" She stopped, realizing there was little she could add without tripping over confidentiality issues.

Now Jade studied her. "I see. You're getting signals that don't automatically line up neatly, and that gives you an unsettled feeling. You're not sure if you should listen to that part of yourself or instead to what you're hearing around you. You're maybe afraid that if you do, you'll go in a direction in which you can't predict what will happen next. It's uncertainty, and I know how much that scares you."

It was as if Jade had reached out and touched her solidly in the center of her body, around the solar plexus; so strong was the sensation. She literally pulled back for a moment, her body reacting physically. She reached up unconsciously and placed her hand over the space below her chest and above her naval.

Slowly, she pulled her hand away, suddenly self-conscious. "What does that even mean?"

Jade pulled a sideways grin. "And now that you're on shaky ground, you're faking bafflement. Some things never change."

It was true. She avoided uncertainty like the plague. Had for as far back as she could remember. She read voraciously, studied endlessly, and made sure that she knew where she was going before she took a step. Only Jade knew the truth, could touch the tender spots in her psyche. No one else knew the source of her fear of uncertainty, and she was careful not to share the full story with anyone. The last thing she needed was pity.

But she'd come here for a different purpose. "Actually, what you said does resonate. It makes me stop and consider something I've been toying with. It's this idea of the unconscious mind as a harbor for another level of awareness. But let's drop my shop talk for a minute. Something's going on with you."

Jade dropped her eyes. "It's nothing, really. I think I'm imagining things. Or maybe I have a guilty conscience," she said, looking up with a shaky laugh. Jill recognized the slightly wobbly tone of voice when her sister was drinking. Jade rarely imbibed, and when she did, it was in moderation. Today, it seemed different.

"A guilty conscience?" A blooming awareness of something uncharacteristic of her sister began to rise.

"Um. Let me ask you something. If Ethan cheated on you and someone close to you found out, would you want them to tell you?"

Jill's eyebrows shot up. "What? Are you telling me you know Ethan's cheating on me?"

"What? No! He's not. Or, at least, I don't think he is. This isn't about you and Ethan. It's just a hypothetical question, you know, one of those things people ask when they're slightly paranoid and maybe a little bit drunk." She smiled a bit too much, and Jill recognized the cover-up. *Not ready to share what's really going on.* Not alarming, but not entirely characteristic of her either. Not when it came to their usually wide-open relationship.

Jade was looking at her with such earnest eyes. This was the person who knew her better than anyone. And the person whom she knew better than anyone. "I know it's more than you're saying. I'm here when you're ready."

Jade's eyes filled with tears which she quickly brushed away. "I'm not ready yet. But I will be."

Jill pulled her into a quick hug and left, a part of her own heart still at the little outdoor café.

CHAPTER TWENTY-TWO

Jill blew into her office, surprising Lauren, her assistant. "Whoa! I thought you were out today. I canceled all your appointments as per your request."

Lauren was an undergraduate, heading toward her own bright career as a psychologist. She still sported her *I'm a freaking Millennial and proud of it* look, with unnaturally bright red dyed, blunt-cut hair. A color Jill found unfortunate, given Lauren's striking combination of olive skin and light hazel eyes. Her natural hair color, deep chestnut, would have been better, with perhaps some highlights. And then there were the required tattoos. At least she'd kept them minimal and easily covered by more conservative clothing. Which she clearly wasn't ready for, as illustrated by her low-cut top and bizarrely striped leggings.

But her heart always warmed at the sight of Lauren, who radiated goodwill and humor, and who pulsed with the desire to help. Right now, Jill was lucky enough to be the recipient of all that barely tapped caretaker energy, which Lauren would need to tone down a bit later as she built her own practice to avoid rapid burnout. But she had years ahead to learn and prepare for the rigors of private practice, assuming that would be her path.

Then there was Lauren's personal life. "Back online again, so soon?" Jill asked. Lauren was a rapid serial dater. As soon as one guy departed the stage, and sometimes while he still fumbled his way offstage, a new guy would be lined up.

Lauren turned over her phone on the desk while giving Jill a guilty look. "Just checking out the scenery. I heard what you said—let some time pass in between so I can," here she paused and made air quotes, "*learn from my mistakes.*"

"You can't learn anything if you're already in hunting mode," she said. "But I've led this horse to the water enough. Some people have to learn the hard way."

"Am I the horse in this scenario?" Lauren's face twisted with mock horror. Then she grinned and laughed. "Message received, and I formally register a protest against the slur on my ability to learn. I do have a 4.0 just so you know."

"Different kind of learning. But on to other things. Where's Dr. Kelly? I thought he'd be back by now." Jill's practice partner and mentor had taken a much-deserved long vacation.

"He's out today, jet lag and whatnot. Probably on duty to pick up the dogs and get the house squared away."

Preston Kelly's wife, Donna, loved her two labs almost as much as her husband, doted on them, and wouldn't waste any time retrieving them after a trip. Jill pictured their peaceful home, dogs lounging on their own personalized luxury dog beds. Preston telling a joke while pouring wine, deliberately keeping the conversation light. Some things didn't change, and one thing that never changed was his ability to separate himself from work. Dr. Kelly never ever spoke about work while away from the office.

Their number one rule as partners was that getting together socially was for fun, the office was for work. She wished he was here today. His counsel was sorely needed at this point, but she was out of luck.

"Hey, where are you going?" Lauren twisted her neck as Jill passed by, raising her voice, "You know, I can talk about your case, too." While a sounding board would help, Lauren wasn't yet trained for the kind of case Jill was working. And she had a slight tendency to gossip—another behavior she'd have to learn to entirely curb.

Jill blew through the hallway door and past Lauren into her private office. She pulled open a drawer of her filing cabinet and stared at the disorganized mess. She'd been telling herself for months to stop and take the time to put her client files in order, to straighten things, to throw out old insurance documentation since she had Lauren to handle that part of the business. She slammed the drawer shut and stared at her laptop incriminatingly. She hadn't worked on her book in weeks, either. It wasn't exactly writing itself.

Perhaps McClure was right. Maybe it was a mistake, her running around playing amateur sleuth or amateur forensic psychologist; however, you saw it. She didn't know what she was doing, and consequently, she was bungling things right and left. After almost two days of work, she'd come up with little. At least nothing concrete. She still had more questions than answers.

Yes, she'd gotten Shaun to talk, but where had that gotten him or her? Had there really been a mysterious man there, someone who'd killed Katie? Was Shaun suffering from delusions? Was he a terribly good liar? Or was he telling the truth about the worst day of his life so far?

If her instincts could still be trusted, he wasn't lying. He was shattered by Katie's death. Witnessing her get killed, unable to stop it, feeling responsible, unwilling to defend himself—these were the hallmarks of survivor's guilt. *Why had he been spared while she had not? Why hadn't he been able to do something to save her?* Shaun needed counseling, not a jail cell. He needed support, and care, and a pathway back to wholeness, not prison.

Maybe she could help him that way, be his therapist. Get back into her comfort zone, and do what she knew she was good at. Time to settle down, get back to work, and forget the criminal end of the case. The case she'd been fired from, anyway.

She quickly envisioned her professional life settling down, getting her back into her usual rhythms. The uneasiness that had dogged her the past two days began to lift.

She could go see Ethan, say 'yes,' and get on with her personal life as well. She rubbed her left hand, the still-empty ring finger, and thought about Ethan's disappointment. He was a good man, and he loved her. He was ready to commit, and she'd been ready for a long time. If not now, when?

She tried to envision herself engaged and planning a wedding. But she didn't feel the emotions she'd expected herself to feel. A knot formed in her stomach as another face floated in view, not Ethan's.

She heard the front office phone ring, heard Lauren's voice. In a few moments, her intercom buzzed. "What?" It came out uncharacteristically sharp. "Sorry. What is it?"

"There's someone on the way here. He says he's with the police." Lauren sounded excited, speaking in sotto voice like they were spies or something.

"Okay. Send him in when he gets here."

"*And?*" Lauren waited expectantly. "Wait, I'm coming back there." She hung up before Jill could stop her. She breezed in a moment later and threw herself on Jill's sofa. "Okay, spill. Who is this guy, and why is he coming here?" Lauren's brows raised. She fairly tingled with excitement.

"He's no one, and you know I can't tell you why."

"Sure, you can. Everyone that comes here signs a HIPAA agreement stating clearly that case notes are shared between all practitioners in this office."

"Well, I can tell you he's not a patient, he didn't sign anything, and you're not yet a practitioner."

"Ouch. Little things like a final degree and license and you go all dotted i's and crossed t's on me." Lauren huffed in mock indignation.

"He's probably coming here about this case I'm working on, the one on which I'm acting as a consultant to a legal practice, about a teenage boy who is accused of a crime. Or, at least, I *was* working on it. I believe I've been fired."

"Accused of what kind of crime? Hey, is this about that kid who killed a girl? Stabbed her to death? I heard he's only fifteen and already a vicious killer. Social media's been blowing up about it." Lauren's eyes went wide. "Wow, can I help you on the case? Maybe I can go with you to talk to people, take notes for you, and hold your briefcase. Get your coffee. Rub your feet. Anything!"

"Calm down. He's not a vicious killer… and I can't say anything else right now."

A voice called from the reception area. "Hello? Anyone here?" *It was him.*

Lauren flew out to let him in, and after following him to

Jill's office, stood behind Detective Webb and made gestures to indicate how hot she found him.

"Thanks, Lauren." Jill closed her door a little too hard and turned to Webb, who fixed his gray-green eyes on her. She was silent. Their last encounter hadn't exactly left her in a good place.

"I want to start out by apologizing," he said. "I shouldn't have spoken to you that way."

"It's okay," she said, keeping her tone neutral, though his apology made her feel a little lighter. But something built within her, and her next words shocked even her. "Listen, I know it sounds impossible, but Shaun did not kill Katie! He was there, he witnessed something, and he wasn't able to save her, and that drove him into some kind of shock, silenced him. But he's talking now, and he can give a description of the killer. We have to help him—"

Webb reached out and put his hands on her shoulders, and the warmth transferred to her body almost did her in. "It's okay. Calm down. I'm here because I believe you. I want to help Shaun, too, if that's possible."

Relief flooded her. She pulled away and talked while she paced. "I got Shaun to talk. He told me what happened that day. He witnessed someone, a man he couldn't identify, with Katie, although he says he was knocked unconscious after that. When he woke up, Katie was lying there. He tried to revive her unsuccessfully. That's why he had her blood all over him." She stopped and looked at Webb. "I believe him."

"Go on."

"I think that guy Trevor Cade is involved in this somehow, even though Shaun didn't recognize his photo."

"Wait. Where did you get his photo?" Nick Webb's eyes darkened.

"I went to see him at the restaurant where he works. I guess I rattled his cage a little because he got pretty steamed. He told me to back off." No need to tell Webb how threatening the altercation had really been. "I snapped his pic before I left."

Webb wiped his hand over his face and shook his head in exasperation. "What were you doing? Do you know how dangerous it can be to confront someone who may be connected to a murder? That's *my* job, not yours… People who do terrible things can get desperate when confronted if they think someone's getting close to finding out."

"I was perfectly safe. It was a crowded restaurant." No need to alarm him further with the full story. "Did you find out anything more about him?"

Webb pulled out his phone, tapped it. "I did. Trevor Cade is 28 years old, which makes his so-called relationships with the two girls a felony," he held up his finger, "if we can prove he had sex with them. He finished high school but no college, as far as I can tell. And he's held a number of jobs since then, most of them in hospitality—restaurants and bars. But here's something interesting. About a year ago, he bought a late-model sports car, one that costs a pretty penny. He moved to a high-rise, luxury apartment. Yet, his only job seems to be waiting tables."

"What do you think it means?"

"Not sure. It could be drugs. Lots of drugs get peddled through staff at restaurants. Plenty of exposure to buyers if you know how to spot them."

"But at a high-end restaurant? I can't picture patrons at a place like the one where Trevor works trying to buy drugs from the waitstaff."

"You'd be surprised. Addiction isn't just for the down and out. But, it may have nothing to do with the people who eat there, but instead with the waitstaff. In a high-end restaurant, they make a lot in tips, much of it cash, and it would be easy to use some of that cash to buy their next round of party favors."

"You never know the real source of someone's wealth," Jill pointed out, "even when it seems sudden. His parents might have bought the car, and maybe with his looks, he does get large tips, big enough to afford the new apartment. He hinted that he's into modeling on the side. He's quite good-looking."

"Possibly. Anyway, I think it's time to lean on him with the threat of child indecency charges, even if we can't make those stick. That may scare him enough to talk. Unless we can get Sophie to talk. Either way, I'll let you know what I find out." He turned to leave.

"I'm going with you," Jill said.

"Not necessary, but thanks," he said.

"Not asking. I'm going to see Trevor, and if you're there, great; if not, fine. But *I'm going*," she said.

He huffed in exasperation, then suggested they might as well ride together.

As they walked out together, Lauren's eyebrows almost hit the ceiling.

Sophie's heart lifted as she pocketed her phone. *Finally*.

How could she have doubted him? The way he'd looked at her, his smile, the way he'd lifted her off the ground with his arms tightly wound around her waist, kissing her in that special way. How every inch of her body had melted with him. She was a smitten kitten in his arms, opening herself body and soul to whatever he wanted.

Even when it was... those things she'd never dreamed she'd be doing. But she quickly pushed it out of her mind now, like she had then too.

He wanted her. She'd missed him so much. Even when he'd told her about Katie... well, of course, he'd liked her, but it was Sophie he loved. He'd just told her. Well, texted her, but that was just as good. *I'm sorry about everything. I got confused. But I miss you; I need to see you. Can you come over? Now? Love ya, T.*

She searched her mind for a good reason to not go home on time. With Katie gone...her parents had been much more restrictive. But of course—it was right in front of her—practice, cheerleading. Her mom already thought that was where she'd be. She just wouldn't show up to practice, and instead, she'd go to Trevor's. *Perfect.*

A few minutes later, she passed the concierge, who looked at her strangely as he grabbed a phone. She flipped her hair and walked haughtily by. She was Trevor's girlfriend. Why did that old guy think he could look at her that way?

She stepped off the elevator and made her way to Trevor's unit. Two men walked past her, going the opposite direction. As they passed her, the younger one gave her the once-over.

What was with the older guys today? She looked away. But something tickled in the back of her brain. He looked familiar, but she couldn't place him. The older guy was well-dressed and carried himself with importance, but there was something chilling about the way he'd looked at her, looked *through* her, as though she didn't matter. She thought she heard one of them whisper, *that's her*, but she must have been mistaken.

At Trevor's door, she paused and put on her sexiest smile, then pushed the doorbell. She heard it ring inside. Nothing. She pressed it again and again. But she heard no sounds inside. She pulled out her key and used it to open the door. What she saw didn't make sense at first. But it all coalesced into something unthinkable. Then she screamed.

CHAPTER TWENTY-THREE

Jill and Nick Webb found the door to Trevor's apartment open, everything quiet. Too quiet. They stood in the entryway while Webb spoke in a loud, firm voice. "Trevor Cade. This is Detective Nick Webb with the Dallas police. We're here to ask you some questions."

Silence.

"Wait here," he told Jill as he moved cautiously into the unit. He checked out the kitchen first.

But she couldn't just stand there. She walked boldly forward, rounded the sofa, and gasped. "Detective Webb, you'd better come here."

"Jill? What are you doing? I told you to wait until I made sure to clear the—" Now he saw what she saw. "What the hell?"

She'd already knelt and felt for a pulse. "Call 9-1-1." She had little medical training, but she knew how to check for life. Trevor was obviously severely injured, possibly a brain injury based on the beating he'd taken, but he was still alive.

The paramedics strapped Trevor in, giving him an I.V. and oxygen. Jill and Nick Webb talked softly as they took him away. "Who would do this?" Jill wasn't expecting him to answer. All her theories were out the window. Trevor, the killer. Trevor, *not* the killer. Now, Trevor beaten almost to death, and possibly fatally. *By whom? And why?*

"Not sure. But this is looking more and more like something tied to the money that leased this space and bought his new car. I think we're back to the drug angle. It's time to talk to some of the people at the restaurant where he works as a starting point."

But something didn't sit right with her. "Okay, so let's say Trevor Cade is dealing drugs, mixed up with the kind of people who supply the drugs, bad people. What does that have to do with Katie's murder? And why, after all this time, did someone come here and try to kill Trevor? If she was killed over drugs, and so far, there's absolutely no one in her circle who says she ever did them, then why go after Trevor?" She shook her head in exasperation. "None of this makes sense."

"No, but it will at some point. Most of my work is connecting dots that are so big and so obvious anyone could solve the case. But sometimes, there are cases like this, where nothing makes sense until it does. I just have to keep looking."

"You mean we. *We* have to keep looking." She knew she had no standing to make such demands. She'd been fired by the attorneys, and she wasn't a detective. But she wasn't going to let this case go, not now.

"I know you want to be helpful, but this case is escalating. If Trevor's assault is connected to Katie's murder, someone is getting more desperate. The vast majority of the time, murder is a one-off. Someone flies into a rage, and someone else dies. Or someone plans a murder to gain assets—money, property, drugs, you name it—and someone dies. But it's extremely rare to see a chain of events like this, first a murder, then an assault. That smacks of a cover-up of some kind."

"Covering up what, though?" She'd said it out loud, but mostly she'd asked herself. Shaun didn't seem capable of a Machiavellian plot to kill his best friend, then her supposed boyfriend. If he'd been jealous of Katie's relationship with Trevor, and he'd flown into a rage over it and killed her, why go after Trevor now? Especially since he was being watched by his hovering mom and about to be indicted. No, there was no way Shaun was involved in Trevor's assault. In fact, as far as she was concerned, this assault solidified her belief in Shaun's innocence.

"Whatever it is, *I* have to pursue it, and I'm sorry to say this Dr. Rhodes, but you'll only get in the way at this point. I can't do my job while making sure you don't get hurt along the way." He had the decency to at least look contrite as the words left his mouth.

It rubbed her the wrong way, his assumption that she needed his protection. Should she point out that she was perfectly capable of taking care of herself? Should she be offended that he was so focused on getting her out of the way that he ran the risk of losing her insights, her help?

Of course not. Being defensive only added unnecessary conflict and friction.

Instead, she chose to ignore the last comments from Webb, along with her rising sense of indignation. "Can I ask you something?"

"Fire away."

"Do you believe, in your gut, that this assault is connected to Katie's murder?"

He rubbed his chin thoughtfully. "Yes, I do, even though there's no clear chain of evidence. But it's far too coincidental, and I don't believe in random events that coincide for no reason."

"First, I agree with that. And in that case, there is one thing that this proves," she said.

"What is that?" he asked.

"Shaun wasn't here today. He didn't assault Trevor. Whatever is going on now, it isn't Shaun's doing. He's been with his mom 24/7. Since this wasn't Shaun's doing, that means that whatever this is about, including Katie's murder, was someone else's actions. *Shaun didn't kill Katie.*"

"You're probably right. But again, this is where we part ways on the case."

"I don't think it's up to you to decide—" she began.

"Hey," called a familiar voice from the doorway. It was Rick Stone, Webb's partner. "What's going on here?" He turned cold eyes to Jill. "What is *she* doing here?"

Webb filled in his partner while Jill looked around. She could hear Stone's voice, dropped low, protesting. No doubt trying to get her kicked out of the scene, but by now, she was used to it. First, the attorneys, now Webb's partner. Webb himself.

So, what? None of those people could possibly care as much about Shaun as she did. More than ever, she felt strongly that Shaun had nothing to do with any of this. He'd been a victim, too, in the wrong place at the wrong time. Even Webb seemed to have moved over to her line of thought. He might not welcome her on the case, but if she were able to connect more of the random pieces, pull things together, he'd have to acknowledge any facts she might find and use them for his case.

"I'm going down to interview the concierge. People have to pass him to get on the elevator, so he's bound to have seen whoever was here," Webb told his partner after a few minutes of heated conversation.

Stone looked pissed, but he agreed to stay and secure the apartment. "This is a crime scene, anyway, and she can't be here." He shot daggers at Jill.

"He's right. Let's go," said Webb.

Jill headed toward the door, but something dragged at her consciousness. She looked around the room again, slowly. But whatever it was that had reached out a finger and tickled her mind eluded her.

Slowly, Sophie became aware of light. Then, the throbbing of her face grabbed her attention, especially her jaw. She moaned, opening her eyes, then panicked. *She couldn't see! Why was it so dark? Where was she?* "Help," she said, but it came out like a faint croak.

She tried to think, to remember where she was and how she'd gotten there. But her head swirled with pain and disorientation. *Wait.* She'd been on her way to practice, and something had distracted her.

She felt around in the space in which she lay. The space was tiny, just big enough for her, possibly with shelving above. Was she in a closet? Had she fallen in her own closet while getting ready for practice, hit her head on something, and blacked out?

But as she fumbled around, nothing felt familiar. Her closet was littered with shoes strewn everywhere, but this floor was bare.

"Help!" She tried again, but that attempt wasn't much better, and it made the pain in her head intensify to an unbearable level. Now, real panic set in. She tried to roll over, but her limbs felt too heavy, and the space was too small. She was trapped. Pain swirled, and darkness began to overtake her.

Just before she passed out again, she heard voices, none she recognized. She was trapped somewhere with strangers nearby, and no one was coming to help her.

The concierge, a fifty-something guy, seemed eager to help but also intensely curious. "What's going on up there? What happened to Mr. Cade?" Concern shadowed his face. "I had to call the HOA President and report this, and she's on her way here now."

"I understand, Mr. Soldane," said Webb, reading the guy's name tag. "I'm Detective Nick Webb," he said, showing Soldane his badge. "This is Dr. Jill Rhodes, a… consultant. Unfortunately, Mr. Cade has been hurt. I'm not free to provide any details yet. But we could really use your help."

Mr. Soldane stood up a bit straighter. "How can I help? I know everyone in this building, and I see everyone who comes in. At least, during my shift."

"Thank you. We're interested in who came in within the last hour. Especially anyone unfamiliar, non-residents. Do people have to sign in or out?"

"They don't have to sign in or out. Protocol is the resident tells me in advance that they're expecting someone. Then I let them pass."

"What if someone walks in without any notification?"

"Then I ask who they're here to see. I call that resident and confirm the visitor, and then they can go on in."

"Did Mr. Cade tell you he was expecting anyone in the last few hours?"

Soldane didn't think for long. "Yes. There were two gentlemen who came in a couple of hours ago after Mr. Cade called down and notified me. One is a friend of Mr. Cade's, but I don't know the other guy."

Webb took out his notebook and pen. "Who was the guy you recognized?"

"Oh, that was Mr. Andrews. Uh, John Andrews. I think he's somebody important."

Nick cut his eyes briefly to Jill, who registered the unspoken message. John Andrews sounded like an alias, not a real name.

"What makes you think he's somebody important?"

"He's always dressed like he's a banker or something—real nice suits. And just the way he carries himself. Like he doesn't put up with any kind of bull— oh, sorry," he said sheepishly, glancing at Jill. "You get the idea."

"And the other guy? Any idea who he was? What did he look like?"

"No idea who he was. But he was with Mr. Andrews. Kind of a rough-looking guy, long hair, works out, some tattoos. He didn't really look like someone who would be with Mr. Andrews."

"How long were they here? Before you saw them leave."

"Not sure. I don't always notice when people leave."

"What about anyone else who could have gone up there? Maintenance people?"

"No one today. And I know all those people."

Nick rolled the pen he was holding. "Anything else you can think of? Especially anything unusual."

Soldane didn't have anything more.

They stepped away from the concierge desk, Jill tugging at Nick's arm. Something didn't quite add up from her point of view. "Do you think he's really telling the truth? Someone went up there and assaulted Trevor Cade, and according to this guy, no one unusual passed by. Maybe Cade's so-called friend isn't really a friend."

"I agree," said Webb. "It doesn't add up. But I have other leads to follow, namely Cade's fellow employees." He turned to go.

Jill stayed planted, frustrated. And something more. She turned back to the concierge. "Mr. Soldane, are you sure that absolutely no one else came through here in the last, say, two or three hours or so?"

"Well, sure. People come through all the time. But that detective said in the last hour, and anyone unusual. That's what I gave him," he added a bit defensively.

"It's okay. We really appreciate your help. But anyone else in the last few hours that you were maybe surprised to see, but maybe you knew them?"

"Sure. His girlfriend." At that, his face reddened, and he clammed up as though the words had slipped out despite his better intentions.

"I see. And why were you surprised to see her?"

"She hasn't been here in a few weeks, so I figured they broke up."

"But today?" she prompted.

"Well, she breezed by here like she owned the world, so I guess they made up."

"And about how old do you think she is?"

His face deepened in color. "I don't know."

"It's okay," she assured him. "You're not in trouble for whatever Mr. Cade might have been up to."

He looked a bit relieved. "Well, if she were my daughter, I might be the person that put him on that ambulance today." His indignation swelled. "She's probably no older than sixteen or seventeen. Way too young for someone like Cade." He looked down for a moment. "Should I have reported him for that?"

Not knowing how to answer that, Jill pressed on, gaining a description of the girl. She and Webb exchanged a look of recognition. Then, she continued with Soldane. "When did she arrive?"

He glanced at his watch. "She came in at 4:00. I remember because the mail always gets delivered between 3:00 and 4:00, and Mrs. Schwartz checks the mail at 4:00 on the dot every day. She stepped off the elevator to go to the mailroom right after Mr. Cade's girlfriend walked by."

Out of the corner of her eye, Jill saw Nick Webb making notes. She continued. "And when did she leave?"

Soldane's eyes widened. "I haven't seen her leave." He looked embarrassed again. "I'm pretty sure I would have noticed if she—"

Jill turned to Webb, no longer listening to Soldane. "Sophie." They ran to the elevator.

CHAPTER TWENTY-FOUR

She'd passed out again. But as her eyes opened this time, she was determined to stay awake, despite the pain. As she slowly sat up, she became aware of voices not far away. She froze, suddenly remembering who had put her there.

Where had they taken her? She could be anywhere. They might have gone somewhere remote, planning to kill her later. Her heart raced, and the pain rose again. She felt around, hoping to find something to use as a weapon, but it was pointless. She felt weak, unable to stand, let alone fight or use a weapon. What weapon, anyway? A coat hanger? She scoffed at herself.

How had all this happened? It had seemed so innocent, she and Katie going off secretly. It was supposed to be super fun and glamorous, the greatest adventure of their high school years. It was something she'd looked forward to for later when she could bring the magazine to school or Instagram her photoshoots, to show off to the other kids.

Katie had talked about creating a blog, setting up her own brand, a platform for her future career as a model, or actor, or possibly a social media influencer.

But Katie was gone. A tear slid down Sophie's cheek. How stupid they'd been. Two silly, thoughtless girls running around, putting themselves in danger. Why hadn't they been satisfied with the life they'd had? They were both popular—they were cheerleaders, and they could have dated anyone. They were best friends.

Instead, they'd both fallen for Trevor, and trusted him completely. Now, he was dead, Katie was dead, and she was about to be dead.

She heard the voices again, but this time, she picked up something different. *A woman's voice!* One she found familiar somehow. She tried to call out but couldn't.

She fell back in exhaustion as the voices faded. They were leaving. Surely, a woman would help her. But trying to call out wasn't working. She felt too weak to do anything. An odd lethargy descended, and her eyes closed.

Jill entered the apartment first, brushing past Detective Stone, who tried to block her entrance. Instinctively, she headed for the bedroom and, once inside, stopped and looked around. Nothing seemed disturbed. The King-sized bed was made, there were no clothes strewn around. There was no sign of a struggle here.

As Nick Webb caught up with her, she slowly turned. Her skin tingled. Then, she saw it. Just the smallest edge, tucked under the bed.

She reached for the handbag, opening it. She pulled out a

wallet, flipped it open, and gasped. "Sophie! This is her bag." She turned to Webb with wide eyes. "She was here. And Trevor was left for dead. She might have walked in on the assault. *Where is she?*"

Stone walked into the bedroom, fuming. "What is she still doing here? This is a crime scene, and—wait. What is that?" He stabbed a finger at the handbag, still in Jill's hands. "That's evidence! And now you've touched it." He turned to Webb. "This is on you. This scene is contaminated now, thanks to you letting this... *shrink* follow you around like an amateur detective."

Webb held up his hand. "Wait just a minute. Something's not right. We've got a teenage girl's handbag, but no girl. We've got the concierge downstairs who says she came up here a couple of hours ago, but he didn't see her leave. We think she's Trevor's girlfriend. It's possible she walked in on the assault, and now, she's gone missing." He turned to his partner. "I know this doesn't look good, Rick, but we have a bigger issue than the fact that Dr. Rhodes touched this handbag. We need to get to the hospital and interview Trevor Cade as soon as possible."

The air fairly tingled with the sense of urgency. Jill knew enough about abductions to realize that time was of the essence if there were to be any hope of rescuing Sophie. Assuming she needed rescuing. And it looked as though she did. But the notion of an abduction didn't add up. "She must be here," she said. "Wouldn't Soldane have seen her leave otherwise?"

But Stone and Webb had already gone into action, looking under the bed, pulling open the bedroom closet door, checking every inch of the small condo unit. After just a couple of minutes, it was obvious she wasn't there.

Nick spoke to his partner. "I don't see how someone could have gotten her out of here, but there must have been a way. They might live here, too, and took Sophie to another apartment.

Or there's a back way out. We have to question Soldane again." He turned to Jill. "You have to leave now," Nick Webb told her, once again dismissing her. He sounded apologetic but also impatient.

But something had her feet nailed to the floor. "No. There's something more, I feel it," she said, unable to let go of the idea there was more here, in this apartment.

"We have to go for multiple reasons. A team is on the way, and believe me, they'll find whatever evidence is here. Look, I really appreciate what you did back there with the concierge," Webb told her, and she knew he meant it. "But I've got to do everything I can to find out where Sophie is. She's our priority now."

"Of course." She turned to leave, but just as she crossed the threshold, she heard something and stopped again. It sounded like a muffled thump. She followed the sound, or where she thought the sound was coming from, back into the bedroom. She looked around but saw nothing and heard nothing. Shrugging, she walked away, leaving again.

Thump!

She rushed back into the bedroom, ran to the closet door, and pulled it open. Following the sounds, she pulled clothes aside frantically, finding nothing. Then she saw it, a flush panel. *A hidden safe room.* She quickly pulled it open. *Sophie!* Her face was red and swollen, and her jaw looked even worse. Blood flowed down the side of her head. Sophie's eyes widened, one of them shot with blood, and Jill hurried to reassure her. "It's okay, Sophie. I'm here, and help is on the way. Just lie still since we don't know the extent of your injuries."

She turned to see Webb in the doorway, looking at the two of them in awe. "Damn. Remind me to trust your instincts in the future."

The future? An odd comment she filed away for later reflection.

Right now, there was an injured girl who needed help and who might be holding the keys to unlocking this baffling case.

In the rush to help Sophie, Jill barely registered the metal strongbox sitting on the shelf in the safe room, but all she could think of at the moment was making sure Sophie got medical attention.

At the hospital, Jill and Webb waited to speak with Sophie, his badge giving them special privileges. It seemed forever before they were ushered into a critical care room, where Sophie lay on a hospital bed, her head and jaw bandaged and her eyes drowsy. *Pain meds.* This would make for an interesting interview.

"Hey, Dr. Jill." Sophie's eyes roamed over Nick Webb with a look of concern.

"It's okay, Sophie. This is Detective Nick Webb. Tell us everything you remember about what happened at Trevor's apartment."

"It's kind of fuzzy," she said, eyes half closed. "My head hurts."

"I know. But it's really important, so we need you to try. Anything at all will help us find who did this to you."

She sighed and slowly began to talk, struggling at times to remember.

Earlier That Day

She hadn't noticed that the two men in the hallway had reversed their direction and were now headed straight for her.

After ringing the bell again, she slipped out the key Trevor had given her and fit it in the lock. She walked in. "Trevor? I'm here. Hey!" Maybe he was in the shower, but as soon as she rounded the sofa, she screamed. "Trevor! Oh, God!"

He was lying on the floor, unrecognizable, his face bashed in, his looks destroyed. She dropped to her knees and shook him. "Trevor! Trevor, are you okay? Wake up! Please," she moaned.

Oh, God, what should she do? Should she check his pulse? But where? She reached out a shaky hand, felt his wrist but had no idea what she should feel. *Oh God, what if he's dead?* Her heart jumped in her chest like a small bird in a cage. Her throat felt like it was closing like it did when she got anywhere near peanuts. *Call 9-1-1.* That was the right thing to do.

She fumbled for her cell phone, but her hands shook so much that she dropped it. She reached to pick it up but suddenly realized she wasn't alone in the room. She turned then, facing the two men she'd passed in the hallway, and the look on the older man's face made her heart almost stop.

The younger guy spoke. "Who are you, and what are you doing here?"

"I'm... Sophie... I'm Trevor's girlfriend. Trevor! He's hurt," she told him. "Please, you have to help him," she pleaded, relieved to have adults to whom she could turn over the responsibility for Trevor. They would know what to do.

He exchanged looks with the older guy, who nodded. "It's okay, we'll help him. But you have to leave now so the... paramedics can get to him. Come on," he said, holding out a hand.

Shakily, she took his hand, and he pulled her up. Once she got on her feet, she got a whiff of his aftershave, and she backed away instinctively, horrible memories flooding her mind.

The warehouse, Katie egging Sophie on. Don't be a prude.

After all, it's just our bodies, and if we can't show them off now, then when?

She was almost sure it was Steve who'd just pulled her up—the guy who'd told them what to do on the modeling job, who had smelled exactly like this guy. But he looked different now. Steve had worn a backward baseball cap, had long, unbound hair, smiled a lot, and was nice to them that day. This guy's long hair was pulled back into a ponytail, he had a mustache, and his eyes were anything but warm. But the aftershave was the same, and it was strong like before as if he never got the memo about subtle scents.

His hands. She'd noticed lots of rings on Steve's hands that day, and even bracelets, like he was vain and had to wear flashy jewelry. One ring that kept catching her eye that day had been a large horseshoe studded with diamonds.

She slid her eyes to his hands. *The horseshoe.* That was when she noticed how red his knuckles were, skin broken on a couple of them. *Was that blood?* Her skin crawled.

She quickly jerked her eyes away, but Steve, she was sure now, had already caught her staring at his hands. He grabbed her arm. "Listen to me. We're going to leave now, quietly. You will not say anything to anyone. If you do, believe me when I tell you it's the last thing you'll ever say." He jerked her arm so hard it almost pulled out of the socket, and she whimpered, believing him.

They started toward the door, Steve aggressively pulling Sophie. She was so filled with dread that her legs felt heavy as concrete, her limbs unbelievably loose. She felt like falling down but was afraid of what might happen if she did. "Wait," she gasped. "What about Trevor?"

"I don't think any of us needs to worry about him anymore,"

Steve said. "He's sleeping with the angels now. It's his own fault, too. In fact, he's—"

In a low voice that cut through like a knife, the older guy told Steve to shut up, sending a look that made him stop mid-sentence.

Steve pulled Sophie's arm even harder, propelling her toward the door. *Oh God, was Trevor dead? Did this guy Steve kill him?* Sophie was shaking so hard she wondered if her bones were rattling.

An intercom next to the door sprang to life. "Mr. Cade, this is Tony Soldane in the lobby. You have two visitors on the way up, a man and a woman. I think one of them is with the police. I'm sure that's not a problem, but you'll have to tell me later. The HOA doesn't like trouble in this building. Later."

The two men stopped. Steve spoke first. "Shit, man. What do we do now?" Real panic in his eyes. "There's only one quick way down, one elevator. A cop! What are we gonna do?"

"Shut up while I think." The older guy turned to Steve and told him what to do as Sophie's fear rose.

"No!" She tried to scream, but something hit her hard in the jaw. Darkness descended.

CHAPTER TWENTY-FIVE

Sophie's story was incomplete, but they had the main picture. A teenage girl is lured to her much older ex-boyfriend's apartment. She walks in and finds his body, then becomes the next victim.

"He called me and said he wanted to see me. I thought he wanted to get back together. When I got there, he was on the floor, beat up. I feel so stupid," she said, and tears welled. "He's dead, and it's my fault," she exclaimed and burst into tears.

"No, he's not dead. He's *not dead*," Jill repeated because Sophie wasn't getting it, but then she did and looked relieved. "But he is in critical care, and we're not sure he's going to be able to help us. It's not your fault. Someone did this to him. We think it's the same person, or people, who hurt you."

Webb stepped in. "Did you see who hit you?"

Sophie looked frightened but resolute. "I saw them both, and I recognized one of them. He was there that day when Katie and I did the—" she faltered.

"What did you and Katie do? I think it's time you told us all about that, Sophie," Jill said.

Sophie looked at Webb and clammed up. He understood and offered to step out as long as Jill recorded their conversation.

"Okay, Sophie, it's just us. What were you referring to?" Jill asked, though she already had a good idea. "Is this about you and Katie?"

Sophie hesitated, but not for long. "Katie went into modeling after school when she was supposed to be at cheer practice. She was good at that, hiding things. Not bad things," she rushed to her best friend's defense. "It was just that she didn't want her parents to stop her. It was her dream, and maybe later, acting." Sophie's eyes welled up with tears again.

"Why did Katie think her parents wouldn't want her to model?"

"They're super conservative. Modeling isn't something they would approve of. Katie once told me her parents didn't want her to start dating until her senior year! Can you imagine that? *No dating until your senior year...*" she trailed off, looking down, studying her lap.

"And who did she model for?"

Without looking up, Sophie frowned. "I'm not sure. She said it was an agency she found online or something like that."

Odd. Surely, Katie would have told her best friend all about the modeling, including the name of the agency. There was a famous agency based in Dallas—Kim Dawson. Katie would have bragged about that.

Unless it wasn't exactly bragging rights. And maybe she didn't need to tell her best friend because she already knew.

"And you did some of the modeling with her, right?" Jill offered it quietly, gently.

Sophie looked surprised but caved immediately. "After Katie got involved in it, I went with her. But I quit after just a couple of sessions, so I wasn't in it for long. That's where we met Trevor, and after that, I didn't care about the modeling anymore. It wasn't really my jam like it was Katie's."

"So, Katie was all for it?"

"She loved it. It was no big deal, anyway. But Trevor—" She flushed again but didn't say more.

Time to get to the bottom of this. "I need you to be really honest, Sophie. About the modeling. Which one of you took off your clothes in front of the camera first?"

Sophie's eyes went wide, and her face flushed deep crimson. "I...she did. I never took off my clothes. Not all of them, anyway, just the top. I didn't want to keep going after that. Please," she stammered. "Don't tell anyone. My mom would literally *kill me* if she knew."

"I think you'd better tell me all about it, Sophie."

"It was just something fun to do. We didn't mean for it to happen like that. Katie wanted to do modeling, so we looked online and we found a website. It started out with headshots, and they promised us we would get paid work later. But after a few weeks went by, they contacted us and said they needed us for a job. When we got there, it turned out to be something a little bit more...well, you know." She bit her lip.

Rather than probe that line of questioning further and risk Sophie clamming up, she went for a different angle. "Where did you go to do it, the agency?"

"I don't know. They picked us up after school and drove us to this warehouse-looking place. There weren't any signs, and they paid us in cash. I went one time after the headshots, and that's when they asked us to take off our clothes, but I refused to go past my top. Katie laughed at me, but I wouldn't do it. I was done at that point, but she went back the next day and a few times after that. I asked her about it, but she said it was no big deal."

What an insane thing to do. Jill felt a chill thinking about two teenage girls getting into a vehicle with strangers who took them to a warehouse, no doubt somewhere remote enough so no one would have heard their screams.

It could have been far worse than a scheme to get nude shots of teenagers. Shots that were no doubt plastered all over the internet utilized by those who fantasized about sex with kids. And those who acted on their fantasies.

For two vulnerable teenage girls to get caught up in something like this was unthinkable from her perspective. From theirs, it was a thrilling adventure into which they'd fearlessly marched. But the executive function of the brain wasn't fully developed at age 15 or even age 20. And that meant a lack of the ability to envision the outcome of today's stupid choices.

It was truly a miracle that most teenagers made it out okay, given their pension for risk-taking and lack of foresight. And when they didn't think ahead, when things went sideways, when they put themselves in too much danger, and luck wasn't on their side…

Then, their stories were trumpeted in the media, vivid images blasted on living room screens, and parents shuddered in horror. High school and college girls who disappeared while on a routine errand or walking home after practice, their bodies found later. Or never found.

No wonder so many parents hovered over their kids today.

"How did Trevor fit into all this?"

"Well, he was there the first day we went to the warehouse. He talked us into doing what we did; in fact, he was in some of the shots with us. He told us all about his modeling career, how much money he was making, that he was starting to get calls for auditions, television stuff. It sounded so exciting. Katie was thrilled."

"And after that?"

"He wasn't there after that, and we didn't realize until later he was hitting on both of us."

"Hitting on you?"

"Well, more than that. Hooking up. With both of us."

"And you were angry about that, weren't you, Sophie."

"I wanted to kill her."

CHAPTER TWENTY-SIX

Weeks earlier

Where was he? Sophie had texted him multiple times. He never took this long to get back to her. But as the hours wore on endlessly, a cold wash of fear and self-doubt swept over her.

That was when she looked at his Instagram account and saw the photos of him and Katie. *Of all the girls in the world...* Trevor's arm was slung around Katie's shoulders as she beamed. They looked like the perfect couple—model boy and cheerleader girl.

Later, at practice, she couldn't make eye contact with anyone, especially Katie, who finally trapped her as she was leaving. "Hey, Soph! What the hell? You haven't said a word to me."

Katie's warm eyes searched her face so innocently. How did she do that? Who morphs overnight from best friend to liar and boyfriend-stealer? Two realities collided in Sophie's mind, and liar won out. "You must be kidding. As if you don't know." She turned away from Katie, determined to make an indignant exit, to drive the point home that they were no longer friends.

But Katie followed her. "What? What are you talking about? Don't know what?" She actually sounded distraught. An Oscar-winning performance, for sure. "Sophie! Stop." Katie tried to grab Sophie's arm, but she pulled away, kept walking.

"Sophie, I'm not going to let you walk away from me. I don't know what's happening, but I swear, I don't know... Sophie, talk to me, please."

Unbelievably, Katie continued to follow her, wouldn't stop babbling about not having a clue. Finally, Sophie pulled out her phone, stopped, and showed the Instagram photos to Katie, who still looked puzzled. "Really? You're going to pretend you don't know who you're with?"

"Of course, I know who I'm with. That's Trevor. But why are you so upset? I thought you'd be happy for me."

"*Happy* for you? Happy that you stole my boyfriend? God, you are unbelievable. I can't believe I thought you were my best friend." And contrary to her wishes, tears popped out as the pain in her chest burst. Her hands balled into fists. She'd never hit anyone in her life, but a vision of Katie's smashed face entered her mind.

Katie's face paled. "Oh, my God! Sophie, I had no idea. I knew you were with someone, but you never told me his name. I would *never*...you have to believe me. He told me he wasn't with anyone."

And that's when it hit her... she hadn't told Katie his name at Trevor's request. *Hey, babe, let's keep this between us for a while...some people might not understand since I'm older.*

And she'd fallen for it, fallen for all his moves and lines, the whispered words that made her feel loved and safe. She'd promised and given whatever he wanted. But what difference had their ages made? True, he was maybe 20, or 22, something like that, and she was 15, but Katie was pretty much the same age, just a few months older. *Why hadn't he wanted anyone to know about her while he posted shots of him and Katie?*

Katie's skin was flushed with anger. "I can't believe that jerk. How did he think he could get away with this? He knows you and I are besties...He actually met us on the same day! How did he think we wouldn't figure this out? Anyway, I'm done with him. Don't worry, Sophie, I would never...I'm going to go tell him right now."

She pulled out her phone and sent a barrage of texts. "And good riddance, sleazeball." She looked into Sophie's eyes. "We're good, right? We're BFFs. Pinkie swears—come on." And when Sophie's arm wouldn't yet lift itself, Katie reached down, curling her little finger around her best friend's, and the warmth of that move broke open the grief. She felt Katie's arms wrap around her, and she sank into them.

Later, she wondered about the text Katie had sent Trevor. Was it the breakup text? Or did she set up time to go see him? To break up, or for other reasons?

Days later, walking numbly on shaky legs to Katie's coffin, seeing her best friend so still and white, she wondered what had happened with Trevor. He was notably absent at the funeral. A chill had traveled down her spine as she thought of the possibilities.

But thoughts of Trevor and Katie were completely overshadowed by the specter of guilt. Her last moments with Katie had been the ugliest, her anger overwhelming. The thoughts she'd had that day of hurting her best friend haunted her still.

Sophie looked devastated. "He killed her, didn't he? I knew something was wrong with everyone thinking it was Shaun. But I didn't want to believe it was Trevor. She went to break up with him, and he... Oh, God! I was...I was with a murderer!"

"Actually, we don't believe Trevor killed Katie," said Jill, trying to de-escalate the hysterics. Once she had her attention, she continued, "We think someone else did, and we think you may know some things that can lead us to that person. Is there anything else, anything at all?"

Sophie chewed a nail and slowly nodded her head. "One day, I asked Katie about the modeling. She seemed different, kind of shut down. She said it had gone a lot further. And it wasn't just still shots. It was video. She was afraid some of it might be on the internet. And she told me one day that she'd lost time, couldn't remember everything that had happened. But she kept saying it was no big deal."

Of course. Why would anyone who was capable of taking advantage of two teenage girls stop at still shots, half-nude, tame shots? That was nothing and wouldn't be worth much. But getting them engaged in sex, pornography, that was probably worth something.

Maybe Trevor's role had been as the lure, with his movie star looks and charm. Maybe he'd been well-paid for his role but later had become a liability.

She stepped out into the hallway to confer with Nick. She passed along the information about the pornographic scheme, Trevor's role in luring the two girls into it.

"Do you believe her?" Webb asked.

"I do. She's devastated by Katie's death, feels terrible about the last time they talked, when they fought over Trevor. But she believes Katie intended to meet Trevor that day to break up with him. That's the confusing part, that she was supposed to meet Trevor, but according to Shaun, some other guy met Katie in the woods that day."

Webb was thoughtful. "We seem to keep circling back to the same question. Who was with Katie that day in the woods? Was it the same person who assaulted Trevor and Sophie?"

"I'm not sure, but I think there may be more to Sophie's story." Jill brought Webb back into the room for the next part.

"Sophie, Detective Webb and I want to find out more about the guy you recognized at Trevor's apartment."

Not meeting Nick's eyes, her face flushed. "Steve was the guy who did the photography. I didn't recognize him at first, but then I did. He's the one who hit me." Sophie went on, with careful prompting, to describe him in great detail to Webb, including the jewelry and horseshoe diamond ring.

"What about the other guy?"

She described him, and Webb asked a few more questions, taking notes. But Jill felt a slight nudge inside. "There's something more about this guy, isn't there?"

Sophie looked doubtful. "Not really. At least, I don't think so. Nothing important, anyway."

"Even if you think it's not important, it could still help. Think about Katie, about everything she told you, everything you thought about when she was talking, even if she didn't actually say it," Jill pressed. "Close your eyes and picture where you were when you talked." Webb looked at her strangely, and she knew what he was thinking. *How can you be a witness to things you didn't actually hear, things you felt?* But Sophie's eyes were already closed in deep concentration, so he just went with it.

After a moment, her eyes sprang open. "Now that I think about it, I remember her saying something about another guy that day when she lost time. Someone she recognized, not right away, but later."

"Did she say who it was?"

"Not exactly. She said he looked like a friend of her parents from the country club. Did that help?"

She looked so anxious to please, Jill couldn't help but reassure her. "It helped a lot." Still, though, Sophie couldn't recall the name of the country club friend of Katie's parents. Nor did she have details to supply about the guy—why he'd been there that day or what he'd done.

The door to the room flew open, and a harried woman rushed to the bed. "Sophie! What happened?" She rounded on Jill and Webb and fairly shouted. "Who are you, and what happened to my daughter?"

It took valuable time, but Webb calmly explained the basics of what had happened to Sophie, leaving out the connections to Shaun's case. No need to pour gasoline on that fire.

As he and Jill made their way out, they heard the understandable anger pouring from Sophie's mother. *What were you doing in some man's apartment? What kind of trouble are you in? What have you done?*

Fear can quickly morph into anger, even toward the person you love who has been hurt. And who you are terrified may be hurt again. The instinctive drive to remove the threat by controlling the person's risky behavior. A dynamic exponentially greater with a child.

Out in the hallway, Jill and Nick Webb paused. Though they

didn't agree at first, slowly, they formed a plan. Theirs was a partnership of sorts, formed shakily and with a duration that endured minute by minute.

CHAPTER TWENTY-SEVEN

In the hospital parking garage, two men loitered. The man with the ice-cold stare spoke quietly to Steve. "Do I need to go over this again with you? No, I didn't think so. I gave you two jobs. One was to corral Cade, use him as the bait. The other was to make sure he behaved with the girls. That's two strikes. Third strike was killing that girl."

Steve fairly vibrated with anxiety. "Hey, man, I didn't sign up for all this, and that girl brought it on herself. She fought me like a tiger, and the knife slipped—"

"Shut up with your stupid excuses. It doesn't matter now. But since you started this, you are going to finish it. Cade is in the hospital since you couldn't handle him. Our only luck is he seems to be hanging by a thread, so he's not talking... yet. And he won't get the chance because you're going to make sure he doesn't."

"No way, man. I'm out. I want my money, and you can get someone else for your dirty work." Steve's defiance deflated quickly as he was swiftly reminded of a few things he'd chosen to ignore. The guy had stuff on him, things that could be used to land him in prison for a very long time. He burned with resentment, but at least he could finish this job and get paid. He would deal with him later.

"What did Cade's girlfriend know? Katie. What do you know about his *relationship* with her?"

"I don't know—" he began but quickly had a change of heart as the man advanced on him. "I get it, man. Look, he didn't tell me anything, but I think he had loose lips. He probably told the dead girl some stuff, and you know how girls gossip." He momentarily felt a twinge of guilt about Cade's deceased girlfriend, but he shrugged it off. She'd gotten herself in trouble with her own stupidity.

But the ice-cold guy seemed to be on another track now. "If Katie knew things, she may have talked to her parents or dropped hints that could be picked up later." He paused, and for a moment, Steve thought he was off the hook.

But that relief was short-lived. "I don't think we can count on Shaun taking the fall for Katie's death now that it's no longer an open-and-shut investigation. Plus, he was friends with Katie, and she may have told him things. By now, he's talking to that psychologist. That means there are two other loose ends," he continued. "Here's what you're going to do. I think you know what happens if you fail."

Minutes later, Steve crept through the hospital after finding scrubs on a cart and slipping into them. This was impossible. He'd never make it into the ICU, where Trevor hung onto life, let alone be able to do anything about it without getting caught. A dim part of his brain wondered if this was a set-up, if maybe it was part of Joe's sick plan for him to take out Cade, then be taken out himself by law enforcement.

Well, that wouldn't fly with him because if he got arrested, he'd sing like a bird in exchange for leniency. He'd be the one to take Joe out.

Hopefully, they wouldn't end up in the same prison. The guy was more sinister than his designer suits implied. He was the scariest guy Steve had ever known, and he'd been around some nightmarish dudes before, like the time he'd gotten picked up for drug possession while cruising through the Texas hill country. Those small-town cops weren't messing around, and the local jerks he'd been thrown into a cell with weren't messing around, either. Luckily, he'd gotten out before receiving any permanent damage.

As he approached the ICU, he halted. Ahead of him walked the woman who was working to help that weird kid who'd been accused of the girl's murder. The one he should have taken care of that day in the woods. He'd seen her on T.V. He wasn't sure about the guy with her, but whoever he was, this couldn't be good. *Crap.* They could get to Cade first, and if they did, he might talk. If that happened, Steve's life as he knew it would be over.

Outside the ICU, Jill Rhodes and Nick Webb waited. Finally, a nurse approached them and informed them that they couldn't go in, not unless they were immediate family of the patient. After Webb established his credentials, the nurse paused, uncertain. Then, he said he'd check with his supervisor. He turned away and, surprisingly, left Jill and Nick alone in the corridor outside the sliding glass doors to the ICU.

But Jill couldn't wait. "Let's go in," she said. Webb protested momentarily but quickly caved. They found Trevor alone, his once beautiful face now unrecognizable. Monitors to which he was attached blinked, indicating life. But he lay still, even after Jill softly called his name.

"I don't like this," Nick said, staring at Trevor. "He's not conscious, and he's not going to be able to help us."

She sighed in frustration. "You're right. Wait. Did his eyes move?"

Trevor Cade's eyes moved beneath his eyelids, tracking left and right, not rapidly, but definitely in the pattern of REM sleep, the state of sleep in which we dream. If he dreamed now, that meant his brain was functioning on some level, and if that were the case, he might wake up and talk. Jill felt slightly guilty thinking of Cade in only this objective, clinical way, interested in him only for the light he might shed on their case. Where was his family? Friends? How terribly lonely it would be to suffer severe injuries and wake to find no one there to care for you, to care whether you lived or died.

Trevor's right eye opened slightly, but his left, severely swollen, remained closed. He looked at them in complete disorientation and let out a small moan. "Wha anneye…"

"I think he said, 'where am I,'" said Nick. He leaned slightly toward Cade. "You're in the hospital. I'm Detective Nick Webb, and this is Dr. Jill Rhodes. Can you tell us who did this?"

Trevor moaned again and worked his mouth, but it was clear that his injuries prevented clear speech. It appeared several teeth had been knocked out or were loose, and his mouth was severely damaged and swollen, with a couple of deep lacerations that had been stitched.

"It's okay," Jill said reassuringly. Her eyes traveled to his right arm, which appeared uninjured, and his right hand. His fingers twitched, and he seemed to be attempting to clench his fist. She looked around the room but didn't see what she needed. Then she turned to Webb. "Do you have a notepad and pen, by any chance?" Almost no one carried such things, except maybe police detectives.

He nodded and pulled them out of his jacket pocket. "Why?"

She took the notepad and pen and placed them near Trevor's right hand. "Trevor. If you can hear me and understand me, raise your right index finger."

His finger raised.

"Okay, good. Can you hold this pen?" She slipped it between his index finger and his thumb.

Slowly, he wrapped his hand around the pen.

"Can you write down the name of the person who did this to you? Nod if you can."

He nodded slowly and touched the notepad with the pen tip, beginning to scratch out something.

The door swished open, and a different nurse stood there scowling, only his eyes exposed above a surgical mask, his hair covered with a paper cap. "You have to leave now. This patient is not supposed to have visitors."

Webb pulled out his badge and began explaining, but this seemed to provoke an escalated level of anger from the nurse, who ordered them out, along with a threat to call security.

"Let's go," Jill said, gently taking the notepad from Trevor. They'd just reached the door when the nurse stopped them.

"What is that?" he demanded, indicating the notepad with faint writing visible.

"It's nothing," Jill said, attempting to slide it into her bag.

But he snatched it away before she could, claiming it as hospital property. He ripped off the top sheet, threw the notepad back to Jill, and then practically shoved them out of the ICU, Nick Webb looking explosive.

Jill took Webb's arm and pulled him away. "It's okay. I saw it before he took it."

"But it's evidence. I can go back and get it. I can charge that nurse with obstruction."

"It won't help, anyway. All he wrote was two first names."

"And?" Webb asked.

"Steve, which is most likely the guy Sophie spoke about. And Joe. No last names."

As they headed for the elevator, something pulled at Jill, something that seemed out of place, out of sync. She stopped, thinking. It was the nurse, the second one who'd hastened their departure, who'd exuded hostility. She didn't exactly spend a lot of time in hospitals, and in fact, couldn't remember the last time she'd entered one unless it was to visit a friend who'd just given birth. But never had she been spoken to in an environment like this with hostility. It didn't fit.

Not that nurses couldn't have bad days. She could imagine the stress piling up until their typical gentle demeanor with people broke, frustration spilling over. That could happen to anyone, in even the most caretaking professions, including hers.

But this was different. The sensation grew rapidly into a suspicion. And as it did, she turned back toward the ICU as Nick watched her, puzzled.

She stepped quickly back toward the ICU, and as she did, she saw the confrontational nurse slip out the sliding glass doors and rapidly leave. As he did so, alarms went off, and people began hustling toward ICU. To Trevor Cade's bedside.

Jill pointed at the retreating nurse, and Nick Webb set off in hot pursuit.

But he returned minutes later, frustrated. "He got away."

They stood out of the way and watched while every effort was made to save Trevor, but soon, they turned off the monitors and covered him with a sheet.

CHAPTER TWENTY-EIGHT

Hillary Ramsay opened her eyes in surprise at the sound of the doorbell. Then, she remembered she was expecting a few deliveries that day, just small household things. Why they didn't simply drop the packages and leave was beyond her.

She rolled over and looked at the clock on her bedside table. 5:23 p.m. She slowly sat up, noting the dull headache that never seemed to leave her. She picked up the bottle of Alprazolam and noted how few tablets were left. Her doctor was probably going to give her shit about asking for a new prescription. Hell with him. He hadn't lost his only child.

She picked up the glass of water and drained it, her hand shaking slightly, then sat back against the pillows forgetting all about the doorbell. She hadn't eaten since breakfast, and that was only a slice of toast with multiple cups of coffee, before taking another couple of pills. Followed by watching television and sleeping most of the day.

No one, absolutely no one, including her husband, understood. She reached for Katie's framed photo, one of her favorites. She was dressed for cheer, striking a pose with a huge smile. She was stunningly beautiful. She was Hillary's reason for being—the one person in all the world for whom she would willingly die. In fact, why hadn't it been her instead of Katie?

For not the first time, she fervently wished it had been her, that Katie was alive and well, and that she was the one that was gone. Death would have been a relief compared to the never-ending grief, the hollowness, the emptiness that pervaded her every waking hour. Waking hours that were gradually diminishing due to her lack of interest in life without her daughter.

She lay back, allowing lethargy to overtake her, but was startled to hear the doorbell again. And again. She sighed, picked up her phone, and opened the front door video app. Surprised but pleased at the guest, she turned on the speaker and said hello, then made an excuse to give herself time to dress.

A tiny surge of energy emerged out of the emptiness. This wasn't a story-hungry reporter that hounded her family almost daily. This was a friend, a trusted person in the community. Someone she could talk to, someone to absorb a little of her sadness.

"Thank you for coming to see me," she told him. They stood in her impeccable living room, a beautiful space that had once given her joy but now provided stark testimony to her loss. She couldn't walk into the room without seeing Katie and her cheer friends sprawled around the room, eating pizza, laughing, and talking. It had never bothered her that they left crumbs on the sofas, empty soda cans on the furniture. Those were the happiest moments, and she had never minded cleaning up after them. "It has been hard, as I'm sure you know." She allowed herself a tiny surge of indignation. "After the press came here, you would think that boy would have been arrested by now." She looked up at the man who'd been by her and her husband's side ever since tragedy had befallen them.

"My understanding is that will take place today, but perhaps tomorrow." The authoritative manner in which he spoke comforted her.

His ice-blue eyes were fixed on her, and even though he towered over her, she felt reassured. "What is taking so long? Can you tell me what the D.A.'s office is saying? I just don't understand all this delay. What if he takes off? Kids run away all the time. What if he does? I have to tell you, I don't like it, and neither do the other neighbors—he's living here close to all of us. And his clueless mother doesn't get it that he's a danger to us and even to her!" She drew a shaky breath. "Where are my manners? Let me fix us some hot tea." Her voice quavered with embarrassment at going off like that. *What must he think of her?*

As she re-entered the living room bearing steaming cups, she heard him say, cell phone to his ear, back turned, "That's one. Right. Are you sure? Okay. Don't expect me to congratulate you. Just get the next job done. Remember what I told you." He ended the call and turned to her, surprise registering for a brief flash. Then, his charismatic smile took over. "Thank you for the tea."

What an odd conversation that sounded like to her. Well, who knew what went on for someone in his position. No doubt, there were always people who needed to be reminded of their jobs, pushed to get them done.

She understood that. She'd been the mom who corralled all

the other cheer moms, got them to do their part to support the girls. All the programs, the after-school activities, the coordination of costumes, so many details, and so many people to constantly push to do their part.

And then, there was her job as a cheer mom, a voluntary role as both beautician and cosmetologist. She'd had to get up at 5:30 a.m. starting when Katie first got into cheer at age 8, just to do her hair, to get that bump just so, and to make sure it stayed in for the entire performance. When you threw in the tumbling, dancing, and the stunts, it was truly an act of hair architecture to get that ponytail in high enough, to make sure there were no fly-aways around the face, and to ensure the hair looked as good and perky when the music ended as it did when the music started.

Then there was the makeup! An all-star cheerleader competes with hair AND make-up, which must be done flawlessly so that it doesn't run or smudge with sweat, and sparkles in the lights of the mat at competition for the judges. The eyelashes, the glittery eyeshadows, and the sparkling lipsticks, all so that her girl stood out at competition. She'd even mastered the cat-eye liner effect.

Of course, Katie had done extremely well, up until the last few months, when she'd lost interest in competing. After years of hard work and success, how could she have given it up? Sure, she'd still gone to practice. Or had she? There had definitely been some days when she hadn't been sure where Katie was or what she was doing.

As soon as she had that unwelcome thought, Hillary brushed it aside. There wasn't any way her daughter had gotten involved in anything questionable, and there wasn't any way she'd have not known if she did. They were incredibly close.

Yet her heart pulsed with a deep ache as all these thoughts raced through her brain. "She didn't have a boyfriend, I'm sure of it. I don't care what that psychologist said," she mumbled to herself. Her mouth felt dry, so she took a sip of hot tea. She looked up and realized she'd spoken out loud.

He was looking at her strangely. "What psychologist?" he asked.

She told him all about the visit with Dr. Rhodes, the questions, the insinuations. He listened intently, asking questions here and there. At first, she thought he was on her side about the psychologist's ridiculous notions, but then his questions began to make her uncomfortable.

"I know you and your daughter were very close, and I know this is painful. But is it possible that there was something else, something she didn't tell you, but she told her best girlfriend? Sophie, right? You said they were in cheer together."

She was confused. *Why was he asking these things?* It was obvious what had happened to her daughter. That strange boy, the one she'd tried so hard to keep Katie away from, had killed her. Had destroyed not just one life but two. Because her life was destroyed. "What difference does it make even if she did? Which she didn't." Against her own will, her mind flashed to the text messages she'd found on Katie's phone, most of which she had deleted before talking to the police. Obviously, it was innocent banter, pretending a level of maturity she hadn't yet reached.

But just for good measure, she'd turned off the phone and hidden it, reporting it had been lost. It was no one's business. Maybe Katie had flirted and teased, sent a few photos of herself. *So what?* All the kids did that sort of thing these days. But people—strangers—could take the smallest thing and turn it into a federal case based on nothing. No one would ever expose Katie in that way, not if she had anything to do with it.

She looked up and suddenly felt vulnerable.

"Mrs. Ramsay, it's very important that you tell me what's

really going on. Sometimes, there are things you know that you feel funny about telling, but if you do tell, it helps with the case." *Could he read her mind?* "What if Katie had a boyfriend, and this boy Shaun found out? Maybe he killed her out of jealousy. I'm terribly sorry to bring up these painful things, but we want to make sure he is indicted and held accountable. Don't we?"

His resonant voice mesmerized her, and she found herself nodding. It had never occurred to her that Katie's cell phone might have the information needed to put that boy in prison. Of course, he would have been jealous if he thought Katie had a boyfriend. What if he'd looked at her phone and seen the texts? The dull ache that never left her chest bloomed into anger and then determination.

"There is one thing," she told him. A few minutes later, she handed him Katie's cell phone and simultaneously felt a wave of relief. What a burden it had been, keeping all those secrets. This was someone who would do something to help. She'd known him for years, trusted him, and furthermore, he had authority and power.

A tiny measure of the crushing guilt lifted. If only she hadn't taken Katie's phone away from her that day. If she'd had it, she could have called for help. If she'd had it, she might still be alive today.

He promised her he would take care of everything, that he'd make sure that anything on the phone that would contribute to Shaun's arrest would be shared with law enforcement. The rest of it, the parts that might damage Katie's reputation, would not.

Outside the Ramsay home, the well-dressed man rapidly scrolled through the cell phone given to him by Katie Ramsay's mother. He felt a sense of satisfaction that the connections leading from others back to him were slowly being severed. Steve had finished the job he'd left him to handle. But there was one more. Later, he'd take care of Steve.

He thought of Hillary Ramsay and her stupidity. She'd withheld a piece of evidence that would have possibly exonerated the boy, Shaun. Mistakenly believing she needed to shelter her dead daughter's reputation.

He removed the sim card and destroyed it. As he drove away, he briefly slowed down to drop the phone into a large trash receptacle on the curb, several blocks from the Ramsay home.

It had all been rather harmless, after all, at least in the beginning. Teenage girls so willing to show off their bodies, to engage in sex at an astonishingly early age. It was a sideline for him. He didn't much care for it, but it had kept Steve on the hook in more ways than one. And Steve was supposed to keep that pretty boy moron Cade on the hook.

But Cade had turned out to be a loose cannon, starting with getting involved with the two girls. Then, Steve was supposed to make sure the Thayer girl didn't talk, didn't reveal what she'd overhead when she was supposed to be too out of it to hear anything. He wasn't supposed to kill her, and now, thanks to him, the level of heat surrounding her murder was burning far too close to him.

No one would understand what he'd done or why he'd done it. They'd hang him from the nearest lamppost if that was allowed. This was Texas, and people had long memories for anything they perceived as wrong or unjust.

He couldn't allow that to happen. Exposure was not an option, so it was a matter of taking the next steps. Or making sure that idiot, Steve, took the next steps, starting with the boy and ending with the pretty psychologist he'd seen on television. The one who was keeping the heat on by defending the boy and talking to people, turning over stones, finding out who knew what, casting suspicion elsewhere.

Too bad he and Steve had been forced to leave the girl, Sophie, alive. But with the cops on their way up, they'd had to skedaddle. Maybe something could be done about her later, just in case, she knew something. But then again, the trail of dead bodies was about to be extended as it was.

He might have to move on, start over somewhere else. But he reflected on his beautiful home in one of Dallas' finest neighborhoods, on his country club membership, and on his standing in the community. A lot to give up.

No, he'd have to find a way to clean all of this up and stay.

CHAPTER TWENTY-NINE

They were in Jill's car, leaving the parking garage, silent at first, both stunned by what had happened.

Webb grappled with the sense that they'd witnessed a murder, the second one in this troubling case. To their dismay, the doctor who'd worked on Cade had declared his death to have resulted from his injuries, despite their testimony. He'd listened skeptically, but ultimately brushed aside their conclusions.

Then again, perhaps what they'd seen had been misinterpreted. *Could they have seen a harried nurse going off shift?* Was it possible that he hadn't realized his patient was going into cardiac distress or something else life-threatening?

Webb wondered for the umpteenth time if they were tilting at windmills. Jill Rhodes was a neophyte to criminal cases. In the eyes of the untrained, all these events could be spun together into a web of conspiracy and as such, stimulate too much unfounded speculation. It was exciting to engage in the pursuit of criminals when it wasn't your regular job. She was intelligent; there was no doubt about that. But she was untrained, and he'd been letting her lead the way far too much.

The truth was that whoever had beaten Trevor might have done so for reasons that had nothing to do with Shaun or Katie. Though Sophie had recognized one of the men at Trevor's and remembered him from the photo shoot, it didn't rule out a connection to drugs. Drugs usually meant serious money, and that was the typical motivation behind most of his cases.

Jill Rhodes turned to Detective Webb. "Surely, by now, you realize there's a lot more to Katie's murder. Can't you do something at this point? Can you stop the wheels of justice from grinding up Shaun?" Jill's eyes pleaded and demanded.

He wanted to say yes, that he could, but he was far from certain that there was enough to prevent Shaun from being charged that day. Or even that Shaun wasn't guilty.

He reviewed the various threads of this case. First, there was Katie, getting into porn, maybe not intentionally up front, but being lured into it. Along with her friend, Sophie, she'd gotten tangled up with the apparent bait, Trevor Cade.

But then, she'd wanted out of the so-called relationship and the porn scheme. Had that been the trigger? Had she been a threat to the photographer, so much so that she'd been murdered to silence her?

But it didn't add up. Why not let her out, if she wanted out? Surely other girls had gotten involved and later exited. Why was that such a huge thing worthy of murder?

Senseless murders took place every week in Dallas, Texas, as they did in all major metropolitan areas. He'd worked cases like that his entire career. They were senseless because they were typically perpetrated by people with no impulse control, or while high on drugs, or due to severe mental health issues. Often committed for no good reason other than opportunity. Or simply because someone did something perceived as egregious, and the anger spiked uncontrollably. Someone had a gun or a knife, and some other unlucky person happened to be there.

Contrary to popular belief, pre-meditated murder was rare, and even rarer when committed by rational people who could foresee the risks if they were caught.

Then again, people often did non-rational things for the most baffling of motivations. This was probably no different. His job was to peel back the layers of an investigation, to uncover motivation, then tie the rest of the pieces of evidence together.

His gut bounced around as he considered the threads of this case not coming together the way he wanted, the way he usually developed certainty in his cases before he made an arrest.

One, someone killed Katie. It could have been Shaun. It might have been someone else. Katie was involved in porn and who knew what else since those who exploit teenagers often engage in other illegal activities, including distribution of drugs and prostitution.

Two, a guy named Steve had beaten Trevor to the point that he'd later died. Steve was involved in the same porn scheme that had ensnared Katie, but it wasn't at all clear if those things were related.

And the biggest dangling thread—who was the second man, the one who had accompanied Steve to Trevor's?

They waited their turn in line to pay and exit the parking garage. "Oh, no! I hope that didn't damage my car," said Jill after a thump against her rear bumper.

"I'll take care of it," Nick said, but she swung open the driver's door.

"Relax, it's just a bump. I can handle it on my own."

It was spoken in that authoritative voice that he saw now for what it was. *I don't need your help.* So independent.

He watched her closely in the rear-view mirror, her small sway, wide-legged pants swirling, heels clicking, her body language radiating determination.

He found her intensity far too attractive. She spoke formally, her diction precise considering her age. Her use of language was a throwback to an earlier time when people took pride in their ability to thoughtfully convey complex ideas. Before it became so desirable to speak in the empty and often vitriolic shorthand code of social media.

He'd noticed her eyes, the silkiness of her hair, and her skin. He sighed inwardly. She was a shrink, for Chrissake. He was a detective, a cop. Worlds apart. But he wondered about her relationship status, even as he reflected on his own.

He saw Jill talking to the driver of the other vehicle. He saw her intense look as she spoke, then listened, nodding. She walked forward and examined her rear bumper, went back to the other driver, and smiled.

Jill turned suddenly and headed back, and as she did so, she frowned. *Had she seen him staring at her?* When she climbed back into the driver's seat, he felt himself flush a bit. "All's well with your car?" he asked by way of cover.

Jill looked over at Nick, noting his distant expression. "Yes, the car is fine. Now, what can we do to keep Shaun from being arrested?" She was determined to push that agenda. It was one of her best qualities. Once on a mission, not to be deterred, she'd find a desirable conclusion, no matter what.

Of course, she'd never been on a mission quite like this one. High stakes, yes, but that was usually within her family. This was different. People she barely knew were going to be affected in the worst possible ways unless she succeeded.

"I don't think we can do anything about Shaun. We're not getting anywhere, and I think we're trying to connect things that may be unrelated. I've got to get back to my partner and review what's happened, but I don't think he's going to go along with trying to get charges against Shaun dropped."

"How can you say that?" She was stunned. They'd both found Trevor and Sophie and witnessed Trevor's death as a result either of his injuries or possibly an assault by a fake nurse. "What about Sophie's testimony? Surely that's enough to continue the investigation."

His expression reflected his conflicted emotions. It was obvious he didn't fully buy into her theories, that he doubted her. He sighed. "It's true. He hasn't heard what Sophie had to say. I can go see him, play the recording, go over it."

"Meanwhile, an innocent teenage boy is going to be subjected to significant trauma, not to mention his mother." She thrummed with frustration. "What is your partner's problem, anyway? He doesn't exactly seem like an open person. Can't he see what's right in front of us?"

"He's a good guy, actually. I've known him a long time. He can be stubborn, but he always winds up doing the right thing. He needs to see the alternative clearly before he'll change his mind. Don't write him off. I think I can get him to look into it, but first, we have to get all the puzzle pieces to fit, and right now, they don't."

CHAPTER THIRTY

Back at Trevor's condominium complex, they sat in her car and talked.

Webb had a few questions for her. "What do you think of this kid, Shaun? I'm wondering what your clinical perspective is." And he was wondering that, but he also wanted to sort out his own confusion about the kid.

"He's been through so much. All the trauma of losing Katie, witnessing her murder, then being suspected of being the killer. Then the questioning, first by law enforcement, then his legal team, and later by me. Shaun has been dealt trauma and loss at a scale most people don't experience in their entire lives, and he started out with less capacity than most."

"What do you mean, less capacity?"

She continued. "I believe Shaun has Asperger's Syndrome, or ASD as we often refer to it. It's on the spectrum of Autism, a severe developmental disorder. ASD people struggle to navigate the basics of relationships in life, beginning with their own families. We're so hard-wired for connection that when someone can't, it's jarring. So much so that others pull away, uncertain, confused, and later, less able to empathize, to hang in there with them, to help them cross the bridge of human bonding. This creates a negatively reinforcing cycle for someone with this disorder—innately withdrawn, others backing away, leading to more isolation and less trust in others, leading to a suspicious view of people, which friends and family would pick up on. More social avoidance, and so on."

"So how is it that he and Katie supposedly were close friends? It doesn't sound like he was capable of that kind of a bond."

"Just because he struggles with connection doesn't mean he's incapable of bonding. But you just put your finger on the biggest problem Shaun has defending himself. Because of the way he's wired, he appears disconnected and even uncaring. People are going to have a hard time believing that he cared deeply for Katie and would never have hurt her." She sighed. "And that includes a jury of his so-called peers. Which they won't be—his peers, that is. If he goes to trial as an adult, he'll be judged mainly by middle-aged people who are retired and have the time for jury duty."

"Why would you and I believe Shaun was capable of the kind of friendship he supposedly had with Katie? I admit I'm still struggling with that."

"Shaun has had a tremendous amount of support from his mother—she's been the one person who'd been there for him. With her love and continuous effort, Shaun is higher functioning than most. Right behind her was Katie, a remarkable girl who managed to hold together the bonds she'd formed with him as a child. I've found that it only takes one very supportive person in someone's life to make a profound difference. Shaun had two. But he's lost Katie, and the devastation I saw in him is real."

He thought about what she'd shared. It was compelling, as was her way of explaining it.

"I have a question for you," she said. "I wondered if you and your partner looked at Katie's cell phone. There might be something in it that backs up Sophie's story and possibly helps Shaun."

"She didn't have a phone on her that day. Her mom said she'd lost it. We didn't think it was worth following up since we had all the evidence we needed against Shaun." He sounded sheepish, perhaps at the idea of being called out about missing a potentially important detail.

"That's odd. If she'd lost it, you'd think her mom would have gotten another one immediately. Teenagers, well, most anyone, can't function without a cell phone. The last time I had one crash, I replaced it within two hours." She paused, thinking about that wrinkle. "Anyway, I'm on my way to the Thayers to spend some time with Shaun; maybe see if there's anything else I can help with before he has to go in."

"Don't do that. Please." He sighed audibly. "Let me finish the trail of the investigation. I think if we can bring together some of the missing pieces, and I'm hopeful we can, it could help Shaun. Jill, are you listening?"

But she'd turned away, hands on the wheel, ready to roll. "I hear you, but I have to do what I think is right."

He sighed again and exited the Lexus. She took off almost before he shut the door. In his own vehicle, he thought about what she'd said. Maybe it was time to review the case again, sort out facts from theories and suspicions.

Fact. Katie was murdered that day in the woods. Shaun was

found later with her blood on his person and the murder weapon in his possession.

Theory: Based on Shaun's testimony, someone else killed her that day, but he didn't actually witness the murder because he was unconscious when it happened. That led to two different potential trails. One, Shaun lied because he actually did kill Katie. Two, he told the truth but doesn't know the identity of the killer.

Fact. Trevor Cade was beaten and left for dead. He later died under suspicious circumstances in the hospital. Sophie was assaulted as well but recovering.

Theory: According to Sophie, both she and Katie had a relationship with Cade that stemmed from getting into questionable modeling, perhaps pornography. Also, according to Sophie, Trevor Cade was assaulted by a guy named Steve, who was the photographer for the modeling. Further statements from Sophie revealed that there was another man present at Cade's apartment, identity unknown.

What was the bottom line? It was still too early to form any concrete conclusions, but at this juncture, he had two possibilities.

Possible conclusion one: Katie's murder was completely unrelated to the modeling, Trevor Cade's assault and death, and Sophie's assault. Cade was involved in something else—drugs, most likely, based on his day job as well as his affluence that waiting tables couldn't afford. He'd cheated someone out of their due, whether products or cash, and it had caught up to him. The modeling was simply the way Katie and Sophie had crossed paths with Cade. Sophie had shown up at the wrong time and in the wrong place, and whoever had assaulted Trevor Cade had silenced her temporarily so they could get away. The mysterious Steve hadn't realized that she had recognized him. If he had, well, Sophie might well have also ended up dead.

Possible conclusion two: all these events were connected, not coincidental. There were still missing pieces, and his job was to find them and put them together.

He thumped the wheel in frustration. The facts were few, and the theories were many, all based on the testimony of teenagers.

Then there was the interesting and attractive Dr. Jill Rhodes, still running around in the middle of the case, possibly interfering with evidence, and keeping him on his toes.

And they were running out of time to help Shaun. He grimaced inside. How had he gone from an open-and-shut case to wanting to help the kid he'd originally been convinced had killed Katie Ramsay?

He punched in the number and spoke rapidly to his contact at the D.A.'s office. After much wrangling and compromise, he'd secured a promise that Shaun wouldn't be brought in until the following morning.

They had a few hours left today, but he had no idea how they were going to accomplish enough to keep Shaun out of jail.

Jill glanced at the clock and pressed a bit more on the gas. She hoped fervently that Shaun hadn't yet been forced to turn himself in.

With Shaun's freedom at stake, and a real killer out there, Trevor Cade had been their best hope for resolution. It wouldn't have been too difficult for Detective Webb to lean on him about the underage sex and get him to spill the names of the people behind the porn scheme. But he was lost to them. All they had was two first names, both very common. Steve and Joe.

Shaun had lost the one person his own age who'd understood him and loved him. Jill was determined to help, to push him if necessary so he wouldn't be subjected to the horror of prison. He'd never survive that.

She longed for the insights she would normally seek from her practice partner. But he'd just returned from a long vacation, still had a couple more days off, and was entitled to ease back into his regular work. If she contacted him now, it would take far too long to bring him up to speed. Plus, his vacation would be abruptly over.

She thrummed her fingers on the wheel, her right foot unconsciously pressing harder. A siren whooped, and she looked up in shock at the swirling lights in her rear-view mirror. *Dammit.* She vibrated with impatience while the cop slowly spilled out of his vehicle and ambled to her window.

"License and proof of insurance."

She handed it over. "What is this about?"

"Do you know how fast you were going? 50. This is a residential neighborhood; max speed limit is 35. What's your hurry tonight?" He looked at her with the tired eyes of skepticism, having heard every story imaginable.

"I'm sorry, officer…Duncan? I'm Dr. Jill Rhodes, and I'm on my way to see Detective Nick Webb. I'm a consultant on a murder investigation he's doing."

He peered at her uncertainly. "Really." He strolled back to the patrol car, still holding her license.

Crap. If the cop called Detective Webb, he might get an earful about what she'd been doing, going outside the boundaries of the investigation. Or, maybe, a request to hold her there while he made his way. Webb could stall her here indefinitely.

Only one way to get out of this. A loud tap on her window startled her. She thought about hitting the gas but didn't. She rolled down the glass.

He handed back her license. "Aren't you missing something?" His tone implied he'd known what she'd been thinking. She felt her neck flush. "You are free to go; Webb confirmed your story. I'll follow if you want to go a little faster to get there, but not over 40." The cop looked at her with a new respect and a spark of interest, almost like he was looking at a minor celebrity.

She thanked him and eased away, then gathered speed, with more care this time. *Webb had her back.* She felt an odd sense of pleasure, but it was short-lived. Her phone buzzed. "Hey, thanks for—"

"Don't thank me. You just lied to an officer of the law, Dr. Rhodes." His exasperation with her was becoming a habit. "You're headed to the Thayers, despite my request that you not do so. You are truly stubborn, aren't you?"

"I'm trying to help a devastated family, Detective Webb."

"I'm on my way there." He disconnected, apparently no longer willing to engage in conversation. So be it.

CHAPTER THIRTY-ONE

Shaun's eyes followed his mom pacing the room, talking in a low voice on her cell phone. She'd already made him change clothes twice, both of them unsure about what to wear. How should one dress when about to go to jail? He laughed inwardly at the absurdity of the question.

He shook inside at the thought of being pushed into a police cruiser, driven to jail wearing handcuffs. His mind drifted to that summer when the two families had gone on vacation together, he and Katie in the far back seat of the Ramsay's oversized SUV, playing video games, Katie shouting and doing fist pumps when she beat him. He not minding.

Of course, his dad hadn't been there. He was already gone, making a new family. The permanent sting of not being good enough, of forever feeling so flawed and inadequate that his own dad had left him. What did those other kids have that he didn't? And the shame of it burned in his throat again, leaving it dry and raw.

He thought about the pitying looks his mom had endured from the Ramsays so he could have a fun vacation. She'd put up with so much to make his life easier. Shielded him from whatever she'd gone through when his dad had left and started a new family. Never bitter out loud, at least not with him. Let Shaun form his own opinion of his dad. Worked hard every day to provide for the two of them. So exhausted at times, he wondered if she'd hold up.

What would happen to her without him? Yes, she took care of him, but he also took care of her. He knew he was the reason she got up every day, put on a smile, and did the best she could.

"Shaun?" His mom looked so scared. "How about something to eat?" Without waiting for an answer, she began pulling things out of the refrigerator and putting them haphazardly on the countertops. "I have some leftover lasagna here, but also, since I know you don't like it made the way it is... what is so hard about understanding vegans? They know you're vegan, but still, they showed up with all kinds of casseroles with meat in them. What am I saying? They're only trying to help. I'm sure I can find something else." She stopped and put her hand over her mouth to suppress a sob. "Oh, Shaun! What will you eat—"

"Mom, would you stop worrying about what I'm going to eat in jail? I'm sure everything won't be made of animal products." But he wasn't at all sure of that. He swiveled his head away from the painful scene of his mother's anxiety popping out all over her as if she had an infectious disease of the emotional kind. He did his best with her, but sometimes it was overwhelming.

Did anxiety have a color and shape? He wondered. His eyes were plastered to the television as he thought of the puzzle of doctors treating things like anxiety, disease states that weren't visible to the human eye.

A moving headline on the screen caught his eye. It was another press conference about Katie. A lot of important-looking people were lined up, speaking into multiple microphones.

He recognized the Ramsays standing together, faces shattered yet determined. He thought about the many times he'd sat in their family room, eating cookies, playing games with Katie, always welcomed, even if sometimes with a touch of hesitancy that had grown over the years. They hated him now, and he didn't blame them.

What would he do in prison? Would he be able to take his books, his computer, keep up with his schoolwork? Though he'd dropped everything for weeks, he wanted to get back into the daily rhythm of his classes. He needed to catch up. His thoughts drifted to the pleasant idea of going back to school, quickly followed by the piercing reality that awaited him. If he didn't go to jail and could somehow resume his old routine. Which would never be the same.

He pictured himself walking the hallways, looking around for Katie, missing her. He could almost hear her. *Of course, you have to get back to school, dufus! How the heck are you going to get into medical school if you can't finish high school?* He could hear her low laugh, see her sparkling eyes, pulled slightly down by the sadness that had crept in recently. *You have to get over this and get on with your life. I'm counting on you for that.*

"Well, if you wouldn't have let her run wild, do whatever she wanted, none of this would have happened." Sophie's dad said, keeping his voice low.

"Me? You're blaming me?" Her mom hissed back. "You're never around. You have no idea what it's like, trying to keep a teenage girl on the straight and narrow. I don't want to speak poorly of a dead girl, but Katie was a bad influence. Talk about running wild! She didn't have nearly enough supervision; her mother so focused on cheer she forgot to pay attention to what was going on outside of cheer. And how hypocritical is it for them to get on television like that when they're just as much to blame as—"

"Good God. Now you're criticizing two parents who have lost their only child?! I don't understand you at all. Where is the compassion? Anyway, that's not the point. We have to deal with our daughter now. And stop shouting. She can hear everything you're saying."

"That's fine with me!" Her mom voice at a shriek.

If Sophie ever managed to grow up and have a husband, she would never, ever shout at him like that. Her insides vibrated. She was trapped here in the hospital, unable to escape to her room like she did at home. She put her pillow over her head, and that action stopped her parents' whisper-shout fight. Their voices were muffled now but were directed at her.

"Sophie, answer me," her mother mumbled through the pillow.

She slowly pulled it away, sighed heavily, and opened her eyes. *Wow.* That hadn't helped. Now two voices spoke at one time, at her, about her.

"You have got a lot to answer to, Sophie. What were you doing at that boy's apartment? Excuse me, that man's apartment! You had better tell us everything unless you want to have no phone, no screens, no car, *for the rest of your life.*"

"Stop yelling at her. That's a surefire way to get her to clam up. For someone who's with the kids all day, you don't seem to know a hell of a lot about how to talk to them."

Sophie tuned them out again, this time without the help of a pillow, just her innate ability to create white noise over her parents' frequent and pointless fights. Her eyes wandered to the television screen on the wall. She caught her breath as the headlines scrolled on the bottom. *Shaun and Katie's case.*

The sound was off, but the closed captioning was on, and she read as fast as she could. A press conference, the District Attorney addressing the media, Katie's mom and dad standing by his left side, another man standing to his right.

She was so caught up in reading the captions she almost missed it. But the cameraman zeroed back in on the man to the right of the D.A.

She gasped. *It was him*! The man with Steve in Trevor's apartment. Was he also the man Katie had recognized from the country club? His ice-blue eyes looked right at the camera at that moment, and she knew. Her heart fluttered. "Mom? Dad?" Sophie slowly pointed a shaking finger at the screen. "It's him."

Her parents stopped arguing and gaped at her. Her dad spoke first, "Him who? What are you talking about?" Her dad looked at her mom.

"He's the man at the apartment, the one with the guy who hit me. I think Katie recognized him, too." She pointed again.

"You must be mistaken, Sophie. That man is a prominent member of the community. We know him from the country club. He's on the city council. You've had quite a shock today, and you're not completely recovered. Why don't we call the nurse and get something to calm you down?" He pointed to the door with a look at her mom, who scurried out to find a nurse.

Her dad spoke soothingly, but in the kind of voice you use for a little kid who's ready for their nap, the way she talked to the little ones when she babysat. She had to make him see. "No! I'm sure, and I'm not that hurt, just my jaw aches. There's nothing wrong with my eyes. I recognize that man. We have to call the detective, or Dr. Jill, or someone, now!"

Now that she knew who the guy was, other pieces clicked into place. *What if Katie had threatened to tell?* An important guy like that had a lot to lose if people found out he was taking videos like that of girls their age. And what about Shaun? He'd been accused, but in reality, he might be in danger.

Her heart swelled large with a sense of justice, a sense of making things right that had gone terribly wrong. She'd been angry with Katie over that loser, Trevor. And because of what she'd told Katie, her friend had set off to confront him. Katie had meant to break up with Trevor, but maybe she'd also intended to get out of the modeling that day.

What if she'd gone to see Trevor like Sophie had today? What if those two men were there like they were today? And Trevor—he'd been the one who told Katie about the modeling. He'd been involved from the start! They'd left Trevor for dead and no doubt had meant to drag Sophie away to do who knew what. What had they done to Katie?

Then, she remembered something else. Out of the fog came a conversation with Katie after she'd begun to shut down. She couldn't remember the exact words, but it was something about how she'd overheard something one day. It was the day she'd lost time. Maybe they'd given her something to knock her out. But she'd woken up and crept to the crack in the office door and listened.

THE EXPERT WITNESS

They were talking about lots of money, city contracts, how to handle things so no one would know. Sophie, it scared me.

But when she'd tried to make sense of it later, Katie had brushed her off, said that it wasn't anything after all. Now, though, her mind clicked through the pieces of this puzzle. Katie overhearing something she wasn't supposed to hear. Tiring of the modeling. Mad at Trevor, going to meet him. Trevor working for the ring guy, Steve. *Katie-Trevor-Steve-Country Club guy.*

She kicked off the blankets, struggling to get out of the bed. "We have to go. We have to warn Shaun, tell the police."

Her dad pushed her back onto the bed, and not too gently. "You're not going anywhere, little lady. Not until you're discharged by the hospital."

"Stop it!" She pushed against her dad's hands. "Let me go!" They struggled awkwardly, neither willing to be violent. *Who physically fights their dad?*

The nurse rushed in with her mom and took control. "All right, Sophie, what's the trouble here? We're not ready to discharge you, not until we get all the scans back and make sure you don't have a concussion. I'm going to give you something to calm you down." She quickly pushed something into Sophie's IV line, and a banket began to fall over her.

She fought it, but the heaviness was too much. Her eyes dropped, and soon, she was asleep.

CHAPTER THIRTY-TWO

Outside the Thayer home, a darkly dressed figure made its way to the back of the house. The tall wooden fence had presented a challenge but was easily overcome by breaking the gate lock with his tools. As expected, he could see clearly into the family room through uncovered windows, large ones.

Most people didn't bother covering the windows in the back of the house, thinking themselves safe within the flimsy security of fencing. They left themselves open to view, confident in their security systems, whether wired in place or covered in fur with a loud bark.

He reviewed the plan in his head. This had to work. There was too much at stake. He remembered the cold, flat eyes of the man who could bring his life crashing down at any moment without hesitation.

But what if the plan didn't work? He didn't have a plan B other than to hightail it home, grab a few things and get the hell out of

Dodge. He could disappear after that. He'd have to disappear if this plan didn't work because if he didn't, he would disappear in another very painful, much more permanent way.

He peered in at the three people. The woman who'd been running around interviewing people with that detective, the one whose vehicle had led him here, aided by a small tracking device. He scoffed inwardly, remembering the google-eyed detective scoping out the psychologist in the rear-view mirror, making it all too easy for him to slip on the device.

Fortunately, she'd come here, so his targets were all in one place. The mother and the boy were sitting stiffly. All of them were talking. *What about?*

Joe had said he thought this kid knew who he was, could identify him. *Could he, though?* Steve couldn't remember ever seeing him around until that day in the woods, and Steve was the one who'd been there, not Joe.

He was the one who'd taken care of the girl, although not the way he'd planned. *Who could have known a tiny girl like that would fight so hard?* One minute he was intimidating her, moving in for a good time, and the next, she was dead, and he still wasn't entirely sure how that had happened.

The knife was there, she was fighting him, and then she was all bloody. *She'd done it to herself*. Yeah, that would be his story if he got picked up later.

She'd said she knew who Joe was, threatened to expose both of them. Apparently, she'd overheard some stuff, the business things Joe was involved in, things he thought Steve was too dumb to understand. But he wasn't. He knew what it meant when people did contracts under the table—when large sums of cash changed hands. *Who paid for things in cash unless they had something to hide?* Venmo, credit cards, bank transfers. That was how regular business got done.

Stupid. She should have kept quiet and given in to him. She deserved what she'd brought on herself.

He burned inside thinking about Joe. You'd think he would be grateful for what Steve had done for the two of them. He'd kept Joe out of it so far. Until today, with Cade, who'd never tell anything to anyone, ever again. And the other girl didn't know who they were. At least, he didn't think so.

Was it really necessary to take out *three more people*? Why couldn't they just get on with it, get back to the business they'd had going? He stirred restlessly, fingering the handle of the bag he'd brought.

This was going to bring down even more heat on him than he already had. Sure, he'd pulled together a thin disguise, but if you could believe those stupid forensics crime shows, he'd left massive amounts of his DNA in Cade's apartment. Wasn't it just a matter of time before they matched it to him? Wait, maybe they didn't have his DNA on record. Fingerprints, yes. But if they picked him up, they could get his DNA.

His brain swirled with all of it. Anger roiled in his gut. This should be Joe out here, not him. Joe was the one who'd suggested they go after Cade and his little girlfriend. Joe, with his camera-ready smile and immaculate grooming, putting on that do-gooder act of his, hanging out at the country club.

And did he ever invite Steve out for one of his five-course, bourbon-infused dinners with his cronies? Hell, no. Not that he wanted to hang out with those pompous pricks, anyway. But still.

Steve's phone screen lit. He had it muted, but he could read the text that had just popped up from a number he didn't recognize. *Call this number when it's done.* The text went on to remind him of a few things that sent a chill tracing down his spine.

When this was over, he was going to find a way out from under Joe's thumb if it was the last thing he did.

CHAPTER THIRTY-THREE

Dr. Jill was back, talking in low tones with his mom. Shaun thought about the other things he knew, but the words stuck in the back of his throat, as usual. *How did everyone else do it so freely? Why did words flow for others while his got gummed up, balled up in clumps so large they couldn't escape?*

"Shaun, what is it?" The concerned eyes of Dr. Jill were suddenly focused on him, and his heart thumped. "It's okay. Take a deep breath," she directed him. "Now, another one. And another one. See if the words will come out now."

And they did. He told her and his mom about finding Katie online, on websites he wasn't supposed to visit, and mostly he didn't, but that day he'd been looking for his friend. He flushed crimson and looked at his lap, but he got it all out. The sadness for Katie threatened to overflow.

Dr. Jill sat still, just listening and nodding. When he ran out of words, she spoke to him in a low voice. "That's important information, Shaun, and it will really help us get justice for Katie. Now, I want you to listen carefully. None of this, what happened to Katie, is your fault. You're sad about your friend, and that's going to take a long time to get better. But it will get better, I promise you. Meanwhile, we need to keep you out of the legal system."

His mom sent him to do his final packing, and the voices of her and Dr. Jill faded as he left the room, but he found himself repeating her words over and over to himself, whispering. *It will get better, I promise you.*

Shaun's story about Katie and the internet porn backed up what Jill already knew, but with disappointment, she registered that it didn't add anything helpful. If only they knew who the second man was, the one who'd been present at Trevor's apartment. With Trevor gone, they had little hope of discovering his identity. Unless they could find the first guy, Steve.

Maybe Detective Webb was right. It was time for her to bow out and let him do his job. She'd run out of options at this point, lines of inquiry to pursue.

Shaun moved slowly, carefully choosing what to pack, uncertain about which books. They were all rather large, biology, science, and a couple of Sci-Fi novels. His cell rang, and he looked at the unknown number in surprise. No one called him, except spammers, pretty much ever. Unless you counted his mom or dad, which was rare. He hesitated, almost let it go to voicemail, but something made him punch the button.

"Shaun? It's Sophie. Remember me? Listen, I don't have long. My parents are in the other room, and they don't want me to talk about this, but I am. I'm telling you so you can tell someone else, maybe Dr. Jill or your mom." Sophie's voice sounded slightly slurred, as though she'd just awakened from a heavy sleep. "Um, this is weird, but I know things about Katie, about what she was doing after school, things I think got her in trouble—"

"I know. She let them take photos and videos of her."

"Of course, you would know, too." She sounded resigned but not angry. "Listen, there were two men there today, at Trevor's, and—"

"Trevor?"

"It's a long story, one I don't have time to tell you about. But one of them I saw just now on TV. His first name is Joe, and my parents said he was on some kind of council. I think he's important."

"City council? I saw the same press conference just a few minutes ago, right?"

"Yes! That's the one. Anyway, this guy Joe was there today at Trevor's apartment, and I think he was with Katie during a photo shoot. I think she got in trouble over that, maybe threatened to expose him. She overhead some things, illegal business things he's not supposed to be doing. My parents know him from the country club, too." She told him the man's full name and who he was.

Shaun was silent, thinking about it. He could hear Katie's voice again in the woods as he approached. *I'm not doing anything more for you and that other creep, and, by the way, I figured out who he is. My parents know him, too. I heard all about his shady business stuff, too.*

He had a pretty good idea what she'd planned to bring into

the open, based on the things he'd found on the internet about Katie, things that still caused him to feel uncomfortable. And now, he realized it was more than the embarrassing stuff Katie had done, and that the person who Sophie was talking about was someone important, someone with a lot to lose.

"Shaun! You have to tell someone, okay? Just do it. I have to go—" She'd covered her phone, and he heard muffled voices. Then, silence. She was gone.

He thought he heard a sound outside, movement of some kind. A wild animal? No, it wasn't anything he typically heard, not outside their home. He spent hours upon hours in the woods nearby, studying wildlife, trees, shrubbery, every kind of ology he could within the limited biodiversity of their suburban neighborhood. He was keenly aware of the sounds, where they came from and could identify every single one.

This was different.

Shaun stood in the doorway carrying his backpack, feeling uncertain. Dr. Jill motioned him over. "What is it?"

"Sophie called—from the hospital, I think. She said her parents don't want her to talk about it."

"About what?"

"She saw the man who was there today at Trevor's apartment—whatever that was about. His name is Joe Willis, and he's on the city council. She said he was there, at a photo shoot." He couldn't bring himself to say more about that. "She thinks maybe Katie was going to expose him for stuff she overheard. Things about business he wasn't supposed to be doing. Things that he wouldn't want people to know."

"Are you sure?" Karen looked skeptical, her eyes shifting back and forth between Shaun and Dr. Jill.

"I'm sure about what Sophie told me. I just repeated every word exactly as she told me," he said. "Also, I heard something outside my window. It wasn't an animal. It was something different."

Karen left the room to investigate.

Jill tingled with excitement. This could be the break they'd been looking for. If a City Councilman was part of the porn scheme with underage girls, and if he was doing something else illegal, the exposure would be devastating to him and to his life. Jill vaguely recalled seeing him at the press conferences for Katie's case. Speaking on behalf of her parents, showing everyone his concern.

Diverting all suspicion from himself. Who would ever believe a prominent businessperson like that would be behind a teenage porn scheme? Not to mention engaged in other illegal activities. She thought about those stories that sometimes popped up in the news, about someone in local politics taking bribes, feathering a nest at the taxpayers' expense. And he was probably the person behind Katie's murder. If Katie recognized him, if she'd confronted him, that could be a powerful motive.

Add up all the potential charges against this guy, Joe Willis, and you were looking at decades in prison. Threatened by that prospect, he might do anything to avoid getting caught.

A chill traced itself down Jill's spine, partly fear, but mostly the thrill of seeing the rag-tag elements of this case pull together into a coherent picture, one of exploitation, greed, and violence. With one person at the center of it, and that person was definitely not Shaun.

From the back of the house, they heard a crash, followed by a scream. The smell of smoke immediately permeated the air.

CHAPTER THIRTY-FOUR

Jill pushed Shaun toward the front door. "Go! Get out and call 9-1-1. I'll get your mom." He hesitated, but only for a moment.

Flames cast an eerie light into the hallway of the house as Jill covered her nose and mouth with the crook of her elbow. She coughed and stumbled, trying in vain to get a stronghold along the wall. "Karen? Karen! Say something. Where are you?" But she heard nothing.

The smoke was getting thicker, and it was getting harder to breathe. She pulled open a door, but it was an empty bedroom. *Why wasn't Karen answering her?* She called out again, coughed loudly, and barely managed another call out.

She fumbled around her pants pocket, trying to find her cell phone. Her heart dropped. It wasn't there. She remembered now that she'd left it on the kitchen countertop. Her eyes began to sting. She narrowed them and blinked several times.

She pulled open another door. Bathroom also empty. Oh, God.

She wasn't going to find Karen, and now, she might not make it back out herself. She ducked into the bathroom, pulled open a cabinet, and found a washcloth. She rapidly doused it in water, wrung it out, and placed it over her mouth and nose, holding it in place as she ducked low and moved quickly toward the flames.

Shaun stumbled out the front door, coughing. He quickly dialed 9-1-1. An operator answered immediately, asking the nature of the emergency. "Fire," he gasped. He tried desperately to get the words out about the crash, the smoke, and the fire. "My mom is in there! And our friend!"

But he heard the nonsense spewing from his mouth as the operator asked question after question, all contributing to his growing disorientation. His feet tangled, and he fell, his cell phone flying from his hand, burying itself somewhere in the grass he hadn't mowed in weeks.

Even more disoriented, he scrabbled around, searching desperately for his cell, finally giving up. He struggled to his feet, headed back to go in the house. He had to help get his mom and Dr. Jill out of there. He steeled himself for the inferno, shaking, but the thought of those flames reaching his mom, and Dr. Jill, drove him forward.

He imagined Katie cheering him on—at last, the hero she'd needed on that terrible day. Something surged, an energy, a sense of light, a warmth, not from the fire, but from within. He drew on that energy, prepared to do whatever it took to get the two women out of danger.

He grabbed the door, but someone grabbed him from behind and whispered in his ear, telling him what to do. He struggled and fought, but he was overpowered. Dread filled his chest, and all words fell into the void.

Jill heard a moan and moved toward the sound. She coughed and struggled to fill her lungs through the wet cloth. It was getting more and more difficult to see, smoke lifting to eye level in the small hallway. She put her hand on the wall and felt her way forward. "Karen! If you can hear me, make a noise. I'm on the way."

Then, a small hoarse voice called for help. The master bedroom was filled with flames and smoke, and Karen Thayer lay on the floor. She was conscious, but there was blood on her forehead, a gash. She called out to Jill but lay prone, moving a little but not able to sit up.

Jill grabbed her arms and pulled with all her might, dragging her into the hallway. *"You have to get up, Karen. We have to get out of here,"* she told her, tugging her into a sitting position.

"I'm trying, but I'm not sure I can," Karen gasped weakly. She slumped over, coughing and gasping.

If Jill tried to carry Karen, she'd fail. She summoned every ounce of energy and directed it at the overwrought woman. "Karen! I'll help you, but *you have to get up*. I can't carry you, and we'll both die if we don't get out of here now." Jill used her most commanding voice, pushing the will to live at the woman in the hallway, a woman who'd been through so much, who might have a small part of herself that was tired of fighting.

She'd seen it before. While some people re-bounded from losses, stronger than before, others gradually caved in on themselves, losing the will to move forward in life. Sometimes, finding a way out of life. Driving too fast on the freeway and getting into a fatal accident. Drinking themselves into an early grave. Eating their way to an early death.

This woman was needed by her son, who didn't have anyone else. "Get up! "NOW!" she shouted. Jill yelled again, pulling Karen's arm. She coughed and wobbled but finally stood. Jill tugged her along, holding her up.

She supported Karen while feeling her way back down the hallway. The smoke was thicker than ever. She could hear sirens in the distance. *Where were the first responders?* How long had it been since she pushed Shaun out of the house? Her limbs grew heavier with each passing minute, each minute dragging impossibly long, her lungs struggling to get air.

Then, they were out of the hallway, and she could see the front of the house. With a final burst of energy, Jill dragged herself and Karen to the door.

They made it out, and as soon as they did, Karen fell onto the lawn, coughing and crying.

"Are you okay?" Jill asked her.

Karen nodded and gasped. "Someone threw something, and it crashed through the window. I was trying to run out of the room, and I tripped. I must have hit my head because I was out for a few minutes," she said, gasping.

Jill only half-listened as she checked Karen for injuries. Her sleeve was burned away, leaving flesh that had already begun to blister. She was probably in shock and couldn't even feel the pain of the burn that, when she did feel it, would be devastating. "We have to get help," Jill said, coughing a bit. But realized quickly she had no cell because she'd left it inside. Then, *Shaun.*

Where was he? She scanned the front lawn and the street, but all she saw were neighbors pouring out of their homes. She heard shouting. "Call 9-1-1!" she yelled at the nearest neighbor who was already making the call. "Tell them to send an ambulance for my friend—she needs medical attention for burns."

She stood for a moment, trying to determine where Shaun might have gone. Maybe to Ellen's, to get help. But she saw Ellen running toward her and quickly discovered she hadn't seen Shaun. "Ellen. Can you help Karen? Get her away from the house, the fire."

Ellen quickly took over care of Karen, who had begun to moan. She exuded calm and reassurance as she easily pulled Karen to her feet, then supported her weight, guiding her away from the house.

Jill was in a frenzy, but there wasn't a way to direct the sense of panic she felt for Shaun. *Where was he?* If not here, where would he go? She'd clearly seen him bolt out the front door, so he wasn't in the house.

Or was he? Had he gone back in, trying to help the two of them? She turned back toward the house, dreading the journey back in. Did she have it in her to pull another person out of that inferno?

The sirens were getting louder. She moved up the sidewalk to the house, pausing outside the door, which was open and billowing smoke. Just as she began to plunge in, someone grabbed her by the waist and pulled her back, holding firmly.

"You can't go in there!" The fireman had her in a solid hold.

"I think there's a teenage boy in there!" She struggled, but he wouldn't let go.

"We'll find him. Please step back." And he plunged into the house, protective gear and equipment making him appear enormous. Meanwhile, other firefighters pulled a large hose from the fire engine, connected it to the nearby hydrant, and began spraying the house with water. Soon, it was a soggy mess, but the fire had been contained.

She waited frantically, pacing around the lawn. Finally, after what seemed an eternity, the first firefighter emerged, pulled off his facial protection gear, and gave her the news.

There was no other person in the house. Not Shaun. Not anyone. She took a deep breath, and another, desperately trying to clear her thoughts. *Where could he have gone?*

Then, it came to her.

There was one other place Shaun might head, perhaps out of fear, perhaps in a daze of shock from the fire. It didn't quite make sense to her, but her instincts pushed her. She headed toward the wooded reserve at the end of the street.

CHAPTER THIRTY-FIVE

Shaun woke slowly, lying on the ground, awareness of his surroundings gradually dawning. *The woods.* The man who'd grabbed him paced nearby, talking on a cell. Shaun carefully slitted his eyes, remaining as still as possible. The light from the man's cell lit up his face. Anger coursed through Shaun's veins as he recognized him.

"I told you I took care of it, man. They were both in there, the psychologist and the mom. I got the kid, too." He listened. "It's almost done! Look, I'm getting out of here. I want my money now, and I'm gonna hit the road. What the—what do you mean I've already been paid? Because you're not gonna—holy shit, man!"

He punched off his cell and cursed, fists tightened. He turned to Shaun, who lay as still as death.

The last time he'd seen this man, he'd lost Katie forever. *It was him.* He was the one who'd done it, who'd killed his friend. And he'd gotten away with it so far. Shaun had tried to defend himself that time, but he'd been defeated with one blow. The humiliation of it would never go away.

But things were different now. His words often failed him, and his feet got tangled, but he wasn't the same boy who'd been felled in the woods, who'd been unable to save his best friend. He couldn't bring her back, but he could avenge her. He could see to it that justice prevailed. He heard Dr. Jill in his head. *You are going to get justice for Katie, with your words, by telling the truth.*

Sometimes words weren't enough. Sometimes bold action was required. He waited, feeling without touch the location of his pocketknife, the one the police hadn't found. It was his old one before his dad had given him a new one. He reviewed the movements in his mind, preparing, using all his senses. He was ready this time. He felt the air change, knowing an arm was reaching for him, the hairs on his own arms raising, the sense of a predator near. He struck.

"Ow! You little shit! What the hell did you do?!" The man spun away, pressing his hand against his neck as blood flowed between his fingers.

Shaun sprang to his feet and sprinted away. He thrashed through the brush and leaves, winding around trees, unmindful of the noise, believing his attacker was now on the forest floor, bleeding out, as he'd left Katie. He felt strong, justified, his pulse pounding as he ran.

Then, he heard the sounds of pursuit not far behind him. He pushed himself harder, panic now striking. He headed toward the small creek bed where he'd lingered so many times, watching the small creatures who lived in or near the water.

Turtles, small frogs, cottontail rabbits in the bushes spotted only after sitting still for hours at a time. Blue jays and blackbirds in the trees overhead, the occasional territorial mockingbird endeavoring to drive off the other birds. Usually, that meant a nest nearby.

Nick Webb pressed the gas harder as the piercing sound of multiple sirens drove him to urgency. He could see smoke rising in the darkness ahead. Karen Thayer's house, which he'd recognized from the call over the radio. *Where Jill had gone, against his express wishes.* He gripped the steering wheel tighter and ground his teeth in frustration. He slammed on the brakes at the curb, threw himself out of the vehicle.

"What happened?" he asked Karen Thayer, who was being strapped into a gurney. "Where's Shaun, and where is Dr. Rhodes?" He tried to keep the desperation out of his voice so he wouldn't frighten her into silence. Her eyes were rolling in panic as it was.

"A firebomb of some kind, I think. What do you mean, where's Shaun? He's here, isn't he?" She tried to get off the gurney as paramedics held her down. "Shaun! Oh, God, where is he?"

Webb took a deep breath. "It's okay. I'm sure he's here, but tell me, *where is Dr. Rhodes?* Shaun may be with her."

But Karen Thayer had passed out, and that was when he noticed the burns on her arms. Paramedics took over first aid with her, and Webb scanned the area. An older woman approached him. "Excuse me?" she asked tentatively. "Are you looking for that psychologist?"

"Yes, I am."

"She headed that way," she said, pointing toward the end of the street, where he recognized the access to the small, forested reserve behind the homes. The same one he'd stood in weeks earlier, looking at the body of a dead teenage girl. He ran that way, drawing his gun. He barely heard what she'd added—that no one had seen Shaun since the fire started. He had a terrible feeling in his gut.

Shaun never went into the woods at night. Now that dusk had fallen, visibility was poor. He thought about turning on the flashlight app in his cell but realized that would make him an easier target. He held his pocketknife at the ready, gripped tightly. He knew what to do if he had to do it.

Since Katie's death, he'd watched YouTube videos on self-defense, practicing moves in his bedroom at night. He'd begun working out, a little at a time, feeling the oddity of deliberately using his muscles for the first time in his life. But it was starting to feel better, and he was beginning to feel stronger.

The pursuer was gaining on him, he could hear the thrashing sounds getting closer, and the thrumming in his chest grew faster and stronger. He heard a voice but couldn't discern the words. It didn't matter anyway because he would never allow himself to be put in a helpless position again.

He'd made his way to the creek, and waded across it, then continued into the trees until he reached a particular spot. As soon as he did, he rooted himself, unable to go further. The small clearing was familiar, deadly familiar.

He thought of Katie, and his chest caught with grief. He yearned to scream at the heavens to give her back to him, to wake up tomorrow realizing it had all been a bad dream. *Dufus quit that*, a quiet voice whispered in his head. *Focus on getting away. Run!*

He did, but it was no use. The pursuer was right behind him now. He whirled and slashed with his knife, meeting nothing but air.

At first, it was quiet. Then, Jill heard the sound of thrashing through the trees. She headed that way, but it was slow going. Her heels sank into the soft ground, recently soaked by rain. She threw them off and kept going, her feet sending sharp signals of pain to her brain, telling her how stupid this was.

She saw brief flashes of blue—the color of the tee shirt Shaun had been wearing earlier. "Shaun!" she called out. He was probably disoriented.

She pressed forward, small limbs lashing her face, and suddenly, he was there, in front of her, holding a pocketknife, his eyes wide. He lunged at her with the knife, and she put up her hands in defense while calling his name softly. Thankfully, he drew back at the last second and missed her.

He sobbed and shook. "It was here. This is where Katie died."

She stood still, talking softly. "Shaun, it's okay. Your mom is fine, she's on her way to the hospital with some injuries from the fire, but she's going to be okay. Come on, let's go."

She held out her hand gently and beckoned as if to a frightened animal. Relief flooded her. Shaun was okay, and they would soon be with his mom. The case was whatever it was. What was important was that they'd all escaped the fire; they were all alive.

The case against Shaun was crumbling. She felt that in her gut, that all the tumblers in the lock were falling into place, and soon, he would be free again to live a normal teenage life. As normal as it could be after losing his best friend to a killer, who would soon be identified and arrested. She was sure of it.

At that moment, she thought again of Detective Webb, his gray-green eyes and auburn hair, of the way he looked at her, even when he was frustrated with her. That was interesting, intriguing to her—his focus on her. Was it more than professional? It shouldn't matter, but somehow, it did.

But her pulse raced with Shaun's next statement. "A man, he's here. He grabbed me, and he's after me. I think he started the fire."

CHAPTER THIRTY-SIX

People were stupid. They had no idea who might be watching, who might be approaching with dark intentions. The small Molotov cocktail he'd hurled through the window had worked beautifully until the kid and the shrink had gotten out. *Duh. Should have blocked the front door, and this whole thing would have been done.*

He could still get the job done. That kid and his meddling psychologist were ahead, and now they were his targets again. Steve crept slowly and stealthily toward them, registering how focused they were on each other, talking quietly.

Sure, the kid had thrown him a curveball with that knife, but just like the other time, he'd missed. Well, he'd gotten him but not badly, a weak swing. Still, he had to admire him for that fake-out pose and the quick lunge. The kid was getting some guts, after all. Maybe he'd have grown up and become a real man eventually.

Too bad he'd never get the chance.

THE EXPERT WITNESS

After this was done, he had some final work to do, and anger surged as he thought about Joe, setting him up at the eleventh hour of this stupid job he never should have taken.

Well, Joe was about to regret all of it. He pictured showing up at Joe's fancy house, the shock on his face as he opened the door, his adorable family behind him, welcoming smiles dropping into fear.

He had no idea Steve knew where he lived, but of course, he did. How stupid would he be if he hadn't figured out where his 'boss' lived? Just in case of scenarios like this. In case he'd have to force his payday, extract some extra interest in the process. Oh yes, Joe was going to pay and then some.

As he got closer, he could make out the silhouette of the woman with the kid, her shapeliness unmistakable even in the gloom. Man, she was something. He anticipated putting his hands on her like he'd put his hands on that spoiled teenage beauty queen not long ago, although that had been interrupted. Like he'd wanted to put his hands on the girl back at Cade's apartment. He would have, too, if Joe hadn't been there and the cops hadn't been on them.

He pulled his gun as he reached his target.

Jill's mind whirled. *Someone was in the woods with them, pursuing them?* Something cold swept over her, like wind, but icy, and the trees didn't move. No leaves shook in its wake. The shock of the chilled air and Shaun's widening eyes stopped her from asking him for more information.

He pointed to something behind her, his mouth open and words spilling out, but before she could register what he was trying to say, she felt her arms pinned to her sides, something cold and hard pressed against the back of her neck.

A mouth pressed to her ear and told her what was about to happen if she didn't allow herself to be subdued. She froze, and the worst fear she'd ever experienced flashed through her entire body like lightning.

"Well, well, what do we have here? *Drop that knife bucko* if you don't want to see this lady die. Now!" He shouted at Shaun, who dropped the pocketknife while whimpering the words *don't hurt her*.

Then, they were marching through the woods, she in the iron grip of Katie's killer, Shaun walking ahead of them, disarmed and defeated.

The sparsely forested reserve wasn't huge. It wasn't deep woods, like the kind in Colorado or in British Columbia, where she and Jade had hiked for miles one year right after college. *Jade*. What was happening with her? There hadn't been any opportunity to get back to her sister. Her mind whirled away from that puzzle and focused on the now.

Where was he taking them? He had a gun, but unless he had a silencer, the sound of it going off would attract the first responders back at Karen's house. He wouldn't get far.

But maybe that wasn't registering. He was agitated. She could feel it coursing through the grip on her arm. In fight or flight, he wouldn't be thinking clearly, adrenaline cutting off his logical brain, forcing him into primal reactions.

That made him even more dangerous.

Could she use that to her advantage? Was there a way to turn his own fear against him? She worked on the puzzle in her mind, taking deep breaths.

She thought about the problem of escape, of overpowering

someone far bigger and stronger. Of the hopelessness of that strategy.

She'd never studied self-defense. But she'd been far too familiar with a lack of safety earlier in life, and she'd been trained by those experiences.

That early training opened up from a deeper place, a place she'd suppressed. Now, her brain turned more primal, but not with fear, with predatory intent. She refused to be a victim again or let Shaun be one. She was certain at that point, sure that she could do whatever it took to protect Shaun, to ensure his safety, to get him out of danger.

It no longer mattered what happened to her, and that made her formidable, the most dangerous animal in the forest. A plan formed, then another, and finally, one took shape. Her future actions unfolded in her mind sharply and clearly.

She began making slight noises of discomfort as she stepped. She picked up her feet gingerly as though stepping on hot coals. "Ow." She leaned on him a bit, using him like a crutch. He held her right upper arm in a tight grip with his left hand, and she focused on that carefully. He shifted a bit in response to her lack of balance. He still held the gun in his right hand.

"They know we're here," she told him. "It's only a matter of time before they catch up to us. There's nowhere for you to go."

"Shut up!"

His grip tightened, and in that moment, she felt his agitation increase. She'd rattled him. She just had to be careful not to rattle him over the edge.

The mind first, then the body, the physiology. A person could deal with one or the other in a given moment, but it was exponentially more difficult to deal with both at the same time. An agitated mind, off balance with the surge of adrenaline, wasn't nearly as capable of making good decisions. If the body wasn't in control, the mind moved to solving the problem of balance, unable to focus elsewhere.

She grunted, slipped, and leaned more heavily on their captor. "I'm telling you, this won't work! You're much better off just letting us go. I think I hear them now. They're not far behind us. You still have time to get away."

"Shut up!" He whispered fiercely. "Stand up straight!" He jerked her arm, but she used that opportunity to pull even more out of balance, yelling in the process. He jerked her arm again, but he also looked behind them quickly, searching for followers.

Up ahead, Shaun stopped and turned back toward them, letting them close the distance she'd been desperately trying to create with her diversions. She had to move her plan into high gear.

"I'm barefoot, in case you didn't notice," she spat at him. "It *hurts*. You're going to have to slow down so I can find places to put my feet that aren't filled with little sharp sticks!"

He yanked her arm again mercilessly. "You won't be in pain much longer, trust me." He pointed the gun at Shaun, then her, his arm vibrating with the tension of indecision. "Move it!" He looked behind them again.

Perfect. She yelled at Shaun to run and get help while she dipped and fell, pulling him off balance.

It was one thing to control an upright person. It was another thing altogether when one hundred twenty-five pounds of person fell, the weight of the body as it yielded to gravity far stronger than the force of any hand grip. The tighter the hold on the falling person, the stronger the pull in whatever direction they went.

There was no choice. He would fall with her. Or be forced to let go.

THE EXPERT WITNESS

Her arm slipped out of his grip, and she rolled on the ground, getting as far away from him as possible. She pulled herself up into a sitting posture and backed up against a tree, breathing heavily.

Run, Shaun, she willed him in her mind, praying for his escape. She heard his rapidly thumping footsteps receding.

Steve advanced on her, pointing the gun her way. A breath of fresh air, or was it something else, swept over her, sharpening her mind. This was it. She'd helped Shaun escape, and she was ready, knowing death was imminent. *Jade*, she thought. The one person she knew without a shadow of a doubt would truly miss her.

Her hand brushed something, and a new thought emerged.

She felt a sense of clarity of mind and heart, a sense of purpose. She took a deep breath, waiting. He moved closer, and she had her one chance. She swept up the large branch she'd found on the ground and jabbed it with all the force she could, aiming for his face, while she scrambled to her feet to run. She felt the branch hit his face and heard him yowl in pain.

But before she could run, he was on her, shoving her back down. The breath promptly left her body. She struggled to get air. Her body felt powerless, as though someone had unplugged her. "You are going to pay for that, you little bitch."

She gasped as he leered at her like some maniacal specter in the woods. He raised the gun, telling her what would happen if she pulled any other stunts. But he didn't fire. He seemed determined to take her somewhere else before killing her. Or maybe not. *Maybe he'd finish her off here.*

Surely, she'd get another chance to fight him. Her mind raced with possibilities. But the gun was pointed at her, and he continued to vibrate with adrenaline and who knew what other forces. She was out of time and chances.

Suddenly it went off, and the sound emitted by a bullet

traveling at something like 1,000 miles per hour, over 1,200 feet per second, was like nothing she'd ever heard before. She jerked, knowing she'd been hit in the chest because that was exactly where the gun was pointed.

A body fell on her, and she opened her eyes to his face, his eyes staring at her. She saw blood and wondered how he had managed to shoot himself and her at the same time. Her eyes closed, and darkness descended.

CHAPTER THIRTY-SEVEN

His legs felt extraordinarily heavy. Shaun stumbled over small branches and through the dips and rises of uneven ground, his hands grasping at trees and limbs—anything to help maintain an upright position so he could continue.

Dr. Jill had told him to run and get help, and he would do that. He gasped for air, wondering if a person might experience cardiac arrest from fear alone. He'd have to read up on that later.

Katie's killer. If only he'd been able to stop him. He'd failed again, but that thought made him push harder. He had to get back to the house to the first responders who would save Dr. Jill. She'd been able to reach him when even his own parents hadn't. She'd believed him. *She'd put herself in grave danger to save him.*

That spurred him on with more speed, the energy arising from someplace in him he didn't recognize, a new place, one that gave him strength and determination.

He burst out of the trees at the end of his street. Ahead, blue-white lights pulsed, splashing the night sky and blinding him. He held up his hand to his eyes and yelled for help.

Or did he? It was so difficult to understand where his voice went at times, whether or not people heard or understood him. He tried again, now running toward his house, around the vehicles parked haphazardly.

He ignored the neighbors lined up outside their homes, pointing at him, some calling his name, aiming their cellphones, the walls of their homes awash in the emergency strobe lights they'd not seen since Katie's death.

Their street would never be the same. The communal sense of safety, the belief in their immunity to disaster, the shared identity of sane suburbia would perhaps never return. A sense of purpose arose in him, a belief that he mattered, that he could do something to allay some of the pain startlingly revealed as inherent to life. *Dr. Jill.*

At last, he reached the house but couldn't find his mom. Out of nowhere, Ellen appeared at his side. "Where's my mom? Dr. Jill...she's in trouble...help her," he managed to blurt.

"Your mom's going to be fine, Shaun," Ellen reassured him quietly, putting her hand gently on his arm, which, surprisingly, he didn't mind at all. It felt calming. "She has a couple of burns, so they're taking her to the hospital to treat them."

"Dr. Jill," he said frantically, eyes searching the area and landing on someone who might help. He stumbled over to the stocky guy in jeans and jacket, a distinct bulge showing at his waistline.

The guy turned to Shaun and rapidly closed the distance between them. "Shaun Thayer? Detective Rick Stone here. Where have you been? We've been looking—"

"You have to help her! She's out there with...he's got a gun, he's going to kill her...please, help her!" Shaun measured his words carefully, making sure all of them spilled out in the right order. He stood up straighter. "She's out there. I'll show you!"

Detective Stone's eyes shot to the end of the street. He shouted orders and motioned a uniformed officer to go with him, and as he hustled away, he told Shaun to stay there.

Shaun started to follow, but Ellen held him back. "Let the police handle it, Shaun. Right now, your mom needs you safe." He protested, but another uniformed officer made it clear he wasn't going anywhere. Finally, he gave in, slumping with Ellen's comforting hand still in place. He mumbled a prayer for Dr. Jill, something he'd never done before.

Nick Webb rolled the body off of Jill as if it were a feather, frantic to get to her. He dropped to his knees and tried desperately to assess the extent of her wounds, but it was so dark. He checked her pulse, but he couldn't be sure. Was it strong? Was it thready? His own adrenaline made his heart race, so he wasn't clear whose pulse he was feeling.

He ran his hands over her face and chest, coming away with blood. He barely contained a cry of rage as he glanced at the killer. But there wasn't much point killing someone twice.

Gently, he put his arms under her and lifted her like a child, willing to take the risk of further injury. There was no way he could leave her here to go get help. He cradled her weight and headed back the way he'd come, careful to keep branches from brushing her face.

Dips and rises in the forest floor, grabbed at his balance, threatening to send both of them flying. He concentrated hard, putting his feet carefully in the next spot, semi-crouching at times to maintain his balance. She wasn't heavy, but as time stretched in this slow march through the woods, he strained to keep her steady in his arms.

If only she'd heeded his warning, stayed away from this cursed neighborhood and the troubled people who lived here. He was trained to deal with situations like this, for God's sake. She was a *freaking shrink*, untrained, and completely unprepared for what had happened here. He'd been to a shrink in the past, one who'd taken careful notes, nodded his head a lot, and asked what Nick felt. *What a colossal waste of time.*

But Jill was different. He knew that somehow.

Still, she'd had no business doing what she'd done tonight. Even as he nursed his anger toward her, he marveled at her determination, her fierce will, and her passionate handling of the case. He had fleeting thoughts about her intense eyes and the way she listened, not only to whoever happened to be speaking, but to something else not audible, perhaps an inner voice.

Back in Trevor Cade's apartment, she'd paused as they were leaving, her eyes slightly unfocused. And then, she'd found Sophie's bag. *How had he missed it?* But she'd found it. If she hadn't, hours might have passed without Sophie's input to the case.

He heard crashing ahead, and suddenly, his partner stood in front of him, huffing for air. That guy was seriously going to have to get in better shape.

"Webb! What the hell is going on out here?" Stone gasped, bending over with his hands on his knees, his double chin wobbling. He registered the body in Nick's arms. "What the...is she...?"

"I don't know, but I have to get her to medical attention.

You'd better head back there and secure the scene. I took the guy's gun, and I think he's dead now, but I'm not certain."

Stone pulled his gun and headed back to the place Webb had just left, but not before thumbing a handheld radio and alerting paramedics, as well as summoning more officers to the scene.

Nick forged ahead, and finally, he made it to the street. Paramedics were waiting. "I've got her," he tried to tell them, irrationally possessive. "She's got a gunshot wound. We have to find it, stop the bleeding." He'd placed her on the gurney and was now pulling away her blouse, popping buttons, frantically searching for the wound.

One of the paramedics, a guy with a friendly face, placed his hands on Nick's chest and gently but firmly pushed him away, reassuring him. Nick pushed back aggressively, then realized how crazy he must look, and stopped. "Sorry, man. I'm a detective, and I'm just...is she...is she okay?" He couldn't bring himself to ask if she was dead, and his heart hammered in his chest.

They worked on Jill, offering no reassurance.

Soon, the vehicle roared away, sirens blasting, and he stood there helplessly. He made his way to Karen Thayer's house, quickly spotting Shaun in the care of a neighbor.

Shaun stood silently, tears coursing down his face. He'd clearly seen Dr. Jill on the gurney. "This is my fault. She saved me, and now..."

Ethan stared in shock at the screen over the bar. It was the case Jill had been working on. The headlines scrolled, and the newscaster babbled, but he only registered one thing.

Two people have been shot, one apparently an investigator

for the legal team set to defend the teenage boy accused of killing Katie Ramsay. Authorities have not released the names or the condition of both gunshot victims. Witnesses on the scene have indicated that at least one person is dead.

His hand shook as he knocked back the double shot he'd been sipping, his third of the night. After the burn receded, he fumbled his cell to call Jill, but it went to voice mail.

He summoned a ride. Then it occurred to him he had no clue where to go. All he knew was he had to get somewhere, get to her.

How could he have been so stupid? Ignoring her texts, her calls, *ghosting her*. Nursing his wounded feelings because she hadn't jumped at the chance to marry him. Of course, she hadn't said 'yes' that night. What girl wanted a drunken proposal like that? And no ring, either. Yes, she should pick it out since she was so choosy...*what was he doing?* Finding fault with her again.

His mind raced with the possibilities and with the surge of will—to make things right with her, to get back to the place they'd been before she took on this insane case, before she ran around playing amateur sleuth, putting herself in danger. Well, that would stop. He'd make sure of that.

He had to get to her now. At least he could get home and start the calls, figure out where she might be going, and get to her side. He could sober up and take control of this situation.

Then, the paralyzing thought struck him that it might already be too late.

CHAPTER THIRTY-EIGHT

The following afternoon

Nick Webb stood stoically in the back of the room, allowing his partner Rick Stone to run the final de-briefing of the case. Nothing had turned out the way they'd originally thought.

The cell phone of the guy he'd shot, Steve Hoyt, had provided a wealth of information. Hoyt's blatant text messages about *taking care of that girl, like you asked*, dated the day Katie was murdered, along with an actual photo of the crime scene, was enough to shift the District Attorney's focus to Councilman Willis, who they charged with multiple indictments, including conspiracy to commit murder in the death of Katie Ramsay.

Luckily for them, Steve had survived his gunshot wound, and once he got out of surgery, he'd immediately flipped on Willis in exchange for a lighter sentence. With Steve Hoyt's testimony, Willis would be going away for a very long time.

Ironically, Willis now faced a far longer stint in prison than he would have for his other crimes—taking bribes, even the teenage porn. It was one of the things that endlessly fascinated Webb. People who committed one crime, one that would net them a sentence that could be over within a few years with good behavior, but in their zeal to avoid that, they'd commit a far greater crime.

With conspiracy to commit murder, Willis had landed himself in a special club, that of the most violent offenders. And perhaps he'd have gotten there anyway, at some other point. It was who he was. Webb would never forget the ice-cold look in Willis' eyes as he'd arrested him, the way he'd displayed no fear as he read him his rights. And the arrogance with which he'd openly stared at Webb as if Willis believed he had the upper hand. *Sociopath*, Webb thought.

The best part, though, had been when he'd visited Karen Thayer in the hospital to tell her there would be no charges against her son Shaun, that the investigation had ultimately proven he'd had nothing to do with Katie's murder. He'd simply been in the wrong place at the wrong time. Karen had burst into tears of joy while Shaun had smiled shyly from his chair next to her bed.

Ironically, the neighbors that had once called for his arrest had filmed Shaun running to fetch the police for Dr. Rhodes, and in the wake of the exposure of Willis, Shaun had become the hero, the short video going viral on social media. He'd shied away from the requests for interviews, but when Webb had last seen him, he'd carried himself with a surprising strength and confidence.

And Jill Rhodes... that had been the surprise of his life.

THE EXPERT WITNESS

Earlier

Jill's vision swam as she looked up into the concerned eyes of a stranger. She wore a navy jacket, her hair pulled into a tight ponytail. Jill's eyes wandered from her to the IV-line snaking up to a bag, swaying next to the gurney on which she lay. Nearby sat a guy, also wearing an identical navy jacket, who smiled at Jill.

She tried to sit up, but the woman pushed her back down. "No getting up. How are you feeling?"

"I'm fine," she said as it all flooded back. The woods, Shaun, the killer with a gun, *the shot!* "Oh, God, am I dying?" she asked as she looked down at her blouse, buttons torn off and covered in blood. She tried to cover herself up as the guy drew a blanket over her.

"Nope, and this is your lucky day," said the guy. "Apparently, someone else got shot, and the blood sprayed on you. You've been out for a few minutes, maybe due to all the excitement. We think you got the wind knocked out or something, but you have no bullet wounds or any other obvious injuries. Still, we're going to have the E.R. guys check you out to be safe."

She lay back, her mind spinning. What had happened out there in the woods? *Shaun.* Was he okay? She pulled the sleeve of the guy, blurting out questions. "Did you see a teenage boy out there? Was he hurt? His name is Shaun, and he was with me. Please, can you call someone?" Her heart thrummed with anxiety. "Um, call Detective Nick Webb. His number is—" But she had no idea what his number was. His voice was a quick push of an icon away, just like everyone else's.

"Ma'am, we don't know anything about anyone named Shaun. You have to stay calm. You're on your way to get checked out, so you might as well take it easy and enjoy the ride." The guy smiled reassuringly.

"Are you talking about that hot cop? He sure does have a thing for you," the woman said, her sidekick grinning. "He carried you out of those woods like a Hollywood scene, didn't want to put you down, all protective like."

The two of them shared a good-natured laugh at her expense, but her mind circled around and around on Shaun as she prayed for him to be okay.

Then she thought about Nick. Was he the 'hot cop,' and had he carried her out of the woods? But she had no memory of that. Probably didn't happen that way at all.

Jill was startled awake. *How had she managed to doze off in these conditions?* More importantly, when would the doctor get here to discharge her? She'd been here for hours, submitted to blood work and EKG, and who knew what else.

Apparently, she'd been so intensely focused on the case she'd forgotten to hydrate or eat properly, and that had led to plummeting blood sugar and electrolyte levels. That, plus the added stress of the confrontation in the woods, had caused her blackout. Consequently, her short stint getting checked out had led to a longer stint of replacing fluids and various tests.

She considered pulling out the IV line and checking herself out.

A shadow fell across the doorway to her room. "Hey," said Nick Webb, giving her a slow smile.

"Hey," she answered as she fumbled for the bed controls so

she could sit up. The ER thrummed with activity, although her small, private area was quieter.

But he'd already reached her side. "Am I glad to see you're okay. I thought I'd taken out the guy without hitting you, but then, you were covered in blood. I almost didn't do it, but he had that gun trained on you, and—" he paled a bit. "Anyway, I'm sorry you wound up like that." He touched her arm and smoothed a bit of stray hair on her forehead.

Jill held her breath for a moment and allowed herself to fall into his gray-green eyes, the small lines that hinted of humor to balance the heaviness of his job, and his gentle touch. "It's okay. I'm glad you did what you did. But—Shaun—is he okay?"

"He's fine, and his mom, Karen, is recovering from some serious burns, but only on her arms."

"What about the guy who you—"

"The investigation is ongoing, and I'm not supposed to talk about it, but I figure you've earned the right to know. It looks like he's the guy who killed Katie Ramsay and Trevor Cade."

She let out a breath, grateful to hear that Karen and Shaun were okay and that Shaun would soon have his life back. *What an insane case.* Nothing had gone the way she'd thought, especially the level of darkness and danger.

"Oh," she said. "I remember something that might help. There was a lockbox in the closet where we found Sophie in Trevor's apartment. I wonder if he kept evidence of the pornography, thumb drives, and so on."

"The team we left that day found it. It was full of evidence against Willis and Hoyt. We figure he kept it as insurance, which ultimately didn't help him. But it did help our case."

The door blew open, and this time, a smiling, good-looking E.R. physician breezed in. "Looks like everything checks out,

Dr. Rhodes. You have no wounds, no concussion, just a bit of electrolyte imbalance, and replacement seems to have righted the ship. You're free to go," he ended with a flourish. "Someone will be along shortly to get you checked out." He lingered, his eyes moving to take in Webb and then focus on her again. "Can I call someone to take you home?"

"I'm taking her home," said Webb, standing straighter at her bedside.

"Are you her—"

"I'm her person, yes." He said it firmly, leaving no room for argument.

The doctor's shoulders seemed to slump a bit as he turned to leave.

Had two hot guys just sparred over her? Maybe she did have a bit of a concussion. Things like that didn't happen to her. Anyway, there were more important things to deal with. She looked around and noted her pants draped over a chair, shoes underneath. But no blouse.

"I brought you something to put on. I'm afraid your blouse didn't make it." He pulled a sweatshirt out of a bag, gray with the white outline of a longhorn. *U.T. graduate.* "Uh, it may be a bit large," he said apologetically, "but it was the best I could do on short notice." He stepped out so she could change.

Jill unlocked the door to her condo, indicating Webb was invited in, but he stalled at the door. "I really have to get going. Is there anything you need?"

He'd said it with care, but she sensed his need to escape. *So much for hot guys sparring over her.* "No, nothing. I just need to rest." But she'd stalled at the door as well.

"Well, if there's nothing else, I'm supposed to be back at the station already for a briefing."

"Of course, you are. I should have taken a ride home," she said apologetically.

"Driving you home was the least I could do. Thank you for all you did on this case," he continued. "Your help made a real difference."

He seemed to have more to say as he stood there. "Look," he cleared his throat, "you should know... These things have an aftermath, uh, emotions you may not be familiar with. We're not supposed to see things, experience things like you did today. Most people find it difficult to deal with, so if you ever want to talk about it, you can talk to me."

She nodded gratefully. Still, he lingered, gazing at her quietly. A tiny flutter in her chest was all it took. "Look, I'm exhausted," she said, giving him and herself an easy out. His eyes changed then, no longer warmly focused on her, now distant. They said goodbye with a bit of awkwardness, and then he was gone.

Jill threw her cell phone down, flopped on the sofa, pulled a throw over her legs, and passed out within minutes. Text messages flooded in, but she had no idea. The sound was turned off. She slept deeply for hours.

Jill ran through the woods, not sure how she'd gotten back there. But the sounds of relentless pursuit were unmistakable. Suddenly, he was there, right behind her, charging in her direction, even as her legs became unbelievably heavy and slow.

Panic rose as she tried desperately to escape, her pace now dragging, the ground stretching ahead, her feet unable to move her forward. His long, ropy arms reached for her, and she saw his face clearly, the maniacal grin, long teeth like a rabid dog, black holes for eyes, blood on his hands which ended in claws. She screamed, but no sound emerged. She screamed again, and now she heard her own voice. "No, no, no!" It was hoarse and low, not like her.

She jerked awake, heart racing, breathless. Her forehead felt warm and sweaty. She threw the blanket off and sat up too suddenly, causing little black dots to dance in her fading vision. "Oh, God," she whispered to herself. A wave of heat and nausea swept over her, and in it is wake, she felt an intense fear of dying, right there, in that moment.

She bent forward with her head between her knees, in her hands, and gulped in breaths, short ones at first, then gradually longer ones. Finally, after what seemed an eternity but was actually only a minute or so, her heart slowed down, and her lungs filled most of the way with air. She looked up to take in her living room. Her vision was clear, no dancing dots.

Maybe this was a one-off nightmare, the result of the day and evening she'd had, never to be repeated. But she'd never had a nightmare so intense, so real, and with the aftereffects of a panic attack like this.

Perhaps she'd take Nick up on his offer to talk, maybe meet him for coffee. They'd shared a common traumatic event, at least for her. She remembered hearing the paramedics joke about the fact that he'd carried her out of the woods, and although she'd apparently been unconscious, she could almost recall the feeling of strength and safety in his arms.

She pictured them sitting across from each other in the

lounge of a neighborhood coffee bar, she with a latte, he with black coffee—somehow, she knew it would be black.

Maybe sitting quietly, maybe with conversation, and she knew it would be okay either way. His gray-green eyes gazing steadily at her, the warmth of understanding spreading between them, calming her.

Her heart rate gradually slowed to its usual crawl, the sweat on her forehead dried, and she continued the fantasy for a few moments longer. *Fantasy—her usual escape*, one that had sustained her growing up when the reality of whatever drama being played out was too much.

You have a wonderfully active imagination. Her mentor had told her that once. She'd thought it was a diagnosis, at first, that it meant she bordered on schizophrenia. But then graduate school had been one long introjection and examination of various diagnoses, several of which might have been hers. Given her background, it was a miracle that none of them had seemed to stick.

Her eyes strayed to her phone, and she checked the screen in shock. *Jade*. She'd been texting for hours, the last signifying her desperation. *I can't believe you're not answering! I really need to talk!*

Then there was the thread from Ethan. *I'm so sorry. Please forgive me for being such a jerk. I love you. Tell me where you are so I can come see you*. Heart emojis and sad faces...

Then a pair of familiar gray-green eyes came into view, but she quickly shoved the fantasy aside.

Nick was a passing fancy and nothing more, someone she'd briefly encountered at a time of high tension and adrenaline. The phantom guy she'd seen in her vision of the coffee bar was born out of that peculiar mix of arresting chemistry. He was no more real to her, or a part of her life, than one of the sexy rom-com or action-hero guys she ogled occasionally on screen.

Jade could also wait; there was something she needed to do.

Ethan pulled open the door and immediately pulled her in, picking her up, covering her face and mouth with kisses. "Oh, God, I'm so glad to see you! Please don't be mad at me. I'm such an idiot, but I didn't mean any of it." He carried her like that, feet dangling in the air, his arms wrapped tightly around her waist, toward the bedroom.

"Wait," she said breathlessly, grinning and wriggling to get down. "Definitely going there with you, but first," she stood in front of him, clasping his hands. "Ethan, will you marry me?"

The End

TITLES BY NINA ATWOOD

The Deep End: Jill Rhodes Mystery/Thriller Book Two, is available on Amazon.

About Roxanne: A Psychological Thriller, is available on Amazon.

Free Fall: A Psychological Thriller, is available on Amazon.

Unlikely Return: A Novel, is available on Amazon.

For more of Nina's books, visit Nina's author page on Amazon here.

John Nina's email list for FREE fiction, notification of author inside stories plus upcoming titles in the series, and discounted book deals:

https://www.ninaatwoodauthor.com

Reward Special note: If you introduce me to someone in the moviemaking industry [big screen, streaming content, etc.] that results in a signed contract and paid advance on any of my books, I will pay you a reward of $10,000!

— Nina Atwood

Contact: nina@ninaatwoodauthor.com

About the Author

Nina Atwood is a licensed psychotherapist and award-winning executive coach. A published self-help author for the past 24 years, Nina now writes fiction. Her three previous books include *Unlikely Return*, *Free Fall*, and *About Roxanne*. *The Expert Witness* is Book One of an ongoing series. She lives in Dallas, Texas, with her husband and their adorable fur babies.

To my readers: I am an independent author. I don't have a huge publishing company and marketing army behind me. I publish and market my books on my own. Your review on Amazon is one of the many ways that authors like me gain traction with our books. If you enjoyed reading this book, please take a moment and write a positive review. Or simply provide a starred review. It makes a huge difference, and for that, I thank you in advance!

Nina

Made in United States
North Haven, CT
13 July 2024